LOVE BURNS

Edna Mazya

LOVE BURNS

*Translated from the Hebrew
by Dalya Bilu*

Europa
editions

Europa Editions
116 East 16th Street
12th floor
New York, N.Y. 10003
www.europaeditions.com
info@europaeditions.com

Copyright © by Edna Mazya
Worldwide Translation Copyright ©
by The Institute for The Translation of Hebrew Literature
First Publication 2006 by Europa Editions

Translation by Dalya Bilu
Original Title: *Hitpartzut X*

Library of Congress Cataloging in Publication Data is available
ISBN 1-933372-08-7

Mazya, Edna
Love Burns

Book design by Emanuele Ragnisco
www.mekkanografici.com

LOVE BURNS

One day at the end of winter I left the *Technion* two hours earlier than usual. There was a ticklish sensation in my throat and though I didn't really feel ill the thought of spending a rainy afternoon with my wife turned me on, so I coughed exaggeratedly and Davis, the relatively fatherly dean of the faculty, told me to go home and get into bed, they would have the meeting without me, and that's exactly what I did. I got into my old Volvo, ignoring a student lying in wait for me with an aggrieved expression on her face—her name escaped me, although her personality had begun to irk me recently—and a little before five o'clock I climbed the stairs to my apartment in Hannah Senesh street, confident that I would find Naomi at her desk—she illustrated children's books—opened the door, prey to that same feeling of apprehension that had been my constant companion for the past two years, and said, Naomi, are you there? But the house was dark and empty, she was obviously not there, unless she had fallen asleep in the bedroom—she liked sleeping, and being young she had a real talent for it too. I took off my coat, which was wet and heavy—the rain hadn't stopped for two days. She had to be sleeping, what would she be doing wandering around in the rain with her thin arms? I thought I'd slide into bed next to her, the idea gave me a painful thrill, and I hung up my coat and went straight into the bedroom, which was cold and empty. I wasn't worried yet, what was there to worry about, maybe she'd just gone out to do some shopping, and I got undressed and filled the bath, and lay down in the hot water, but before closing my eyes I foolishly looked in the mirror opposite at the red spots which had begun to gather on my skin, tiny burst veins, an ugly but harmless hereditary afflic- tion, and I got out of the water for a minute to switch off the light so she wouldn't come in and see me exposed like that. But as I lay in the rapidly gathering darkness a chill of anxiety began crawling through my body. I'd spoken to her on the phone at eleven o'clock that morning and she hadn't said any- thing about going out, on the contrary, she'd gone out of her way to stress that she had a lot of work to do and that she intended to work right through until I came home that evening. I suddenly lost patience and got out of the bath, dried myself quickly, and went to the kitchen in my bathrobe to make myself a cup of tea to soothe the tickle in my throat, and as I filled the kettle I scolded myself for not phoning to let her know I was coming home early, all I'd done was to waste a free afternoon on worry, but as I waited for the water to boil I couldn't avoid thinking that it was strange the heating wasn't on, if she'd only gone for a little while she would have left it on. The water boiled, I poured myself a cup of tea, squeezed in some lemon juice, and went to sit in the living room opposite the big window overlooking the stormy sea. The wind swept the balcony, I stared at the newspaper, squinting in the direc- tion of the door, and after a moment I heard footsteps on the stairs and hurried to the door with the cup in my hands. Drops of boiling tea splashed onto my fingers and exacerbated my distress, but it was only the woman opposite with her slight limp, who greeted me flatly and asked if I was ill because I looked pale. As she spoke she bore down on me so keenly that I was forced to beat a retreat all the way to the wall—she was one of those people who cling to you when they talk—Naomi liked imitating her, it became a kind of game of ours, with her limping towards me and closing in on me as she spoke, while I

waited eagerly for the moment of clinging itself, which sometimes turned into actual necking—and now, pressed to the
wall, I asked her straight out if she'd happened to see Naomi.
She looked back at me strangely, or so it seemed to me, and
said that they'd met on the stairs early in the afternoon, was
anything wrong, and I said no, nothing, it was just all this rain,
and returned to my armchair, and a few minutes later I decided to get into bed in order to pass the time. I tried to fall
asleep, but then I thought that maybe something had happened to her and I couldn't just go to sleep as if I was the only
person in the world, but what could have happened to her,
already, these worries would destroy me in the end, and so I lay
with my eyelids trembling, trying to chase gloomy thoughts
from my mind, but they kept hopping back in like fleas, until
in the end I got out of bed and returned to the living room, and
at that moment the phone rang. It was my mother, telling me
that she'd returned from Sinai, I'd forgotten that she'd gone
there at all, and she said that maybe it was the place for her, she
was sick and tired of Haifa, the tranquility and the dryness of
the desert had done her a lot of good. I was impatient and
wanted to cut the conversation short, but I also wanted her to
reassure me, and so I said casually that for some reason I hadn't
found Naomi at home when I came back early from work and I
was a little worried, but my mother scolded me and said there
were millions of possible explanations, and what would I do
when something really happened, how could I go through life
like this, I was forty-eight years old already, and it was time to
put an end to all this hysteria, how could Naomi stand me, I'd
be better off finishing the book that should have come out long
ago—the previous autumn I'd helped organize a conference in
Sicily on X-ray bursts and I'd undertaken to edit the conference proceedings, as well as writing an introduction and sum-
mary—and she added that I'd better not say anything to
Naomi when she came home, a person had to learn to cope on

his own without bothering others. But there was no need for her to say this because during the past two years I'd learned to keep my hysterias to myself and not to burden Naomi with them. I always maintained a lighthearted, casual tone, I never forced anything on her, on the contrary, I exercised the utmost tact in organizing her life around the house for her, arranging a working space for her next to a window overlooking the sea so that she would like being at home and wouldn't want to go out, and Naomi, who was quite withdrawn, or so I thought, found peace at home, and apart from three times a week when she taught drawing at a school, she hardly ever left the house. It was only to my mother, from whom I never hid anything, that I allowed myself to say I was worried, what could I do, it was my nature—I was really worried now, even if she did think I was exaggerating. Maybe she went to visit a girlfriend, my mother said impatiently, but Naomi didn't have any girlfriends in Haifa and in my heart I was glad of it, girlfriends are unsettling and subversive, there was only Noam, her gay friend, but he was abroad, and I said in a hostile tone, she never went to any girlfriend's, and my mother said, a man who worries should live alone and not with a twenty-five-year-old lollipop, and I hung up and went back to my armchair facing the sea, glancing at my watch even though I knew it was already six o'clock. The sea was vanishing into the darkness—where could she have gone with all this rain on the roads?—and I took half a yellow Valium, and after a moment I swallowed the other half too, and by half past six the Valium had dissolved in my blood and spread an alert calm through my body. At least now I could think rationally, but what was there to think about? Horrific pictures swarmed into my head, Naomi squashed flat on the road somewhere—maybe it was time to call the police—and I phoned my mother again and told her that I couldn't pull myself together. This time my mother didn't scold me, she only said that I should try to be logical, how

could Naomi know that I'd come home early, by seven she
would have called, and everything would seem reasonable, like
all the other things that seem reasonable once they've been
cleared up. But why did she take the car and why in this rain,
I asked in a voice naked of masks, and my mother said, I knew
Naomi before you did—Naomi had worked for her as a cleaning woman when she was a student, and it was there that I had
met her over two years ago—she loves the rain. Drink a glass
of brandy and relax, she added in the curt tone that always succeeded in emptying things of their complexity and leaving
them shrunken and insignificant, as if nothing was worth making a fuss about, and this time she was the one who hung up,
and I actually did pour myself a glass of brandy, but I immediately remembered that I'd taken a Valium and I wondered
whether it was advisable to drink alcohol on top of Valium,
and automatically I dialed my mother's number again, mainly
to pass the time, and with her last shred of patience, after
telling me on no account to drink brandy on top of Valium, she
said that ninety-nine percent of our worries didn't come true.
But what about the one percent I nagged, it happens to someone, so why not me? I was already convinced that something
terrible had happened, but I suddenly pulled myself together
and decided to think rationally. There was no point in continuing this conversation with my mother and so I said goodbye
and put the phone down, took three deep breaths and forced
myself to believe what she had said, there was no way Naomi
could know that I was already at home, and in the surge of
hope this thought brought in its wake I remembered that we
had discovered a leak in the carburetor of her Volkswagen, she
had simply gone to the garage to get the car fixed, how come
I'd thought of everything but not of that, Naomi never put
things off, and I was sorry I'd taken the Valium, I would glad-
ly have had a drink now and put on some music. It was already
night outside, without moon or stars, only heavy clouds hang-

ing over the roofs. Naomi was a careful driver, what was there to be hysterical about, and I calmed down completely, put the *Cesar Franck Symphony* on the CD player, and ran to the armchair to sit down and close my eyes in time for the opening, for the sake of which I had bought the disk. The truth is that I wasn't interested in music, I just liked it in an emotional kind of way, I wasn't really interested in anything apart from Naomi, even astrophysics had ceased to interest me lately, I got by on doing the bare minimum, and in any case there was nowhere for me to advance to, in the past two years I hadn't published a single article in a reputable journal, all I worked on was editing the book, and that too without any enthusiasm. If possible I would have stopped working altogether and stayed at home with her, but I knew I mustn't burden her, I managed the relationship between us with careful and calculating maturity, guarding against the moment when the halo of important professor would fade to reveal an aging semi-intellectual with a tendency to morbid introspection, and the effort was draining my strength, the only person I could relax with, drop my masks a little, was my mother, and she listened to me with little more than bored concern. I had no real friends, except for Anton, and I hadn't had a heart-to-heart with him for ages either, and even now, as the music played, I wasn't really listening but planning how I would position myself for Naomi's entrance, as if I had been utterly swept away by the music and hadn't spared a thought for her whereabouts, as if I had a whole private world of my own, just so she wouldn't get a fright and think everything depended on her. The opening chords shattered the silence, somber and solemn, and I dropped my head against the back of the chair and for a moment I actually did disappear into a place free of thought, or at least relatively so, proving that there was a possibility of rest, for when I listened to music with Naomi I didn't rest for a single second, I was busy all the time trying to snoop after her thoughts, perhaps she was escaping to inner worlds illuminated by the music, her face was with me but her eyes were sometimes blank, how could I possibly know where she was wandering, and I would grow tense and worried, but I would never ask her anything because anyone who asks another, "What are you thinking about" deceives himself in advance, and so now, for instance, I was training myself to sink into a state of musing about nothing, like some gentle current coming into being of its own accord—in the midst of this insane love, I was trying to get used to the moment when she would leave me and I would be alone, so that I could fall back on myself and find something there. When I told my mother I was going to marry Naomi she said, bless you my boy, there are very few people capable of seeing reality clearly, and consequently of somehow mastering it, and you, darling, aren't one of them. But I had managed to live before Naomi, and presumably I would go on living after she left me, if only I trained myself for it, like now, for example, when I was alone and I had nothing to do except to wait for her, and why think that she would leave me anyway, we'd had two good years together, true I'd invested a lot of work, but I was plucking the fruits every day, and she needed me, she didn't have anyone but me, her mother died when she was a girl and her father had disappeared even before that, she never told me the details, and here too I didn't put any pressure on her, all I know is that she drifted from one temporary home to another, until I made this home for her, and she was happy, for some people happiness is peace and not necessarily lots of laughs, Naomi isn't a starry-eyed type, or a type that laughs her head off either, or so I thought, even though my mother says there's no such thing as a type that doesn't laugh, it just depends on who's in charge of making them laugh, bless you my boy. You couldn't say she didn't like Naomi, and she was certainly glad to see me having a bit of a life, but like all mothers she saw not only the beginning but also the end—Naomi was twenty-five, gorgeous, wise with the maturity of a veteran orphan, and since she, at the age of seventy-four, did have the gift of seeing reality clearly, what could she say but, bless you, my boy. My father, she had never loved him for a single day, she was a confused young refugee from Berlin and she fell right into his arms, he had a sunburned face and an American passport, nothing like the pale Berliners who tied her to a tree and made her stand for five hours with her hands in the air—she of all people, who had wanted so desperately to join the Hitler Youth and wasn't accepted simply because she was a Jewess and, she might add, through no fault of her own—and in my father she found an acceptable, if not thrilling, antithesis. Love didn't come into it, love was a privilege of peacetime, and so, two weeks after she met him she married him and saw herself flying off to America, and to hell with the rest of the world, but my father, who was horribly naive and didn't understand the first thing about her, announced proudly a few days after the wedding that he had renounced his American citizenship because he had decided to be an active Zionist, and it was clear to her then that she, the heartthrob of all the boys, was going to be stuck with this over-enthusiastic man, that it wouldn't pay her to leave him, with her healthy instincts she understood that he was a very good deal with a home and an income, while she was nothing but a refugee with a pretty face, and so she stayed with him and she only hoped that he would die before her. She told me all this a few years ago, before I met Naomi, apparently in order to encourage me to grow up and not be so fastidious and cautious in my search for a wife, because life was whorish by nature, and there was no need to get into a panic about it, and in the meantime the disk comes to an end and I change it for Tom Waits—Naomi would like that, she bought me *The Black Rider* and asked me to learn to love its cracked and distorted lament, in her opinion I was urgently in need of a musical shake-up, because anyone who listened only to clas-

sical music was in danger of becoming fossilized—and I sit
down again and try to concentrate on the words, "Take off
your skin and dance around in your bones . . . ," and I lose
interest and all I want is for her to come home already, the
Valium has calmed me down completely, I feel limp, even
pleasantly groggy, partly because of the hunger, maybe I'll take
her out to eat and afterwards to a movie, I have to check and
see what's on at the Cinematheque. I myself don't like taking
her there, I suspect the youngsters in their slippers might turn
her on, but she likes going there more than anywhere else
because of the old movies, sometimes she goes with Noam,
who in the right doses amuses me too, and suddenly a new
thought jumps into my head—what garage, the garage closes at
four, and with jittery fingers I dial the number, mainly in order
to do something concrete, and of course there's no reply. In a
second my hunger becomes nausea, something real and terrible has happened, I have to do something—not phone my
mother, that won't do any good, maybe Anton. Anton works in
the Criminal Investigations Department, he'll know what to
do, and I call his office—he works at all hours, and when I hear
his authoritative, "Yes," I force myself to ask him how he is
first, but Anton knows all my forty-eight years, we used to play
in the fabulous swamp next to Wadi Nis-Nas, every winter,
together we would conquer the little island rising out of it.
Anton is a year older than me, short and sturdy, with the
patience of a Bedouin, and I was always infected by his practi-
cality, and together, working efficiently and almost without
speaking, we would construct a path to the island with stones
and planks, and plant a yellow flag on it, because he refused to
plant the Israeli flag, and now, hearing the anxiety behind my
would-be casual tone, he asks, what's up, and I say, I'm worried, Naomi's disappeared, and he asks, since when, and at
once I feel like an idiot and I calm down and say, I was only
joking, how are things, we have to meet, and we make a date

to have lunch in the bistro next to the courthouse the next day, and I hang up and start worrying again, and at five to seven Naomi opens the door, wet and serious, and finds me absorbed in Tom Waits, but she seems to have her mind on something else, because she stops dead in her tracks with a startled expression on her face. What are you doing at home so early? she says, with a note of disguised complaint in her voice, and I stand up, smile brightly and say in a genial tone, look how wet you are, this rain is really something, and she seems suddenly confused and asks, are you ill, and she takes off her coat and shakes her short blonde hair, which is wet and wild, and I still don't look at her properly, and she comes up and kisses me, she doesn't look at me properly either, and she asks again, are you ill, and I say, not really, my throat's just a little sore, and I don't ask her where she's been, there's a slight feeling of tension in the air and in order to relieve it I bring up the rain again, telling her that I too got wet on my way home from the *Technion*, and I suggest that she take a hot bath, hoping that she'll ask me to join her—in the first months we used to take baths together by candlelight and look warmly into each other's eyes—but she only says that a bath is a good idea, and when she goes into the bedroom she says that it's a pity I didn't call to say I would be back early, in which case she would have stayed at home. From where I'm standing I can see her walking around the room, she doesn't look at me and so I can examine her as she quickly removes her clothes, and I feel drawn to her rounded shoulders and slender arms, which for some reason I find particularly arousing, and when she walks out of the door in uninhibited and self-satisfied nudity she sees me watching her, and I smile at her and ask if she wants to go out to a movie or a restaurant, I speak in a matter-of-fact tone, as if she isn't standing in front of me with her stunning body and she makes a vague movement with her head and goes into the bathroom, I can hear the water splashing on her body. The need to go in after her fogs my thoughts and after a moment I can't control myself and I go into the bathroom, and without looking at her I open my cupboard and tell her that I'm looking for an aspirin—I saw to it that we each had a separate medicine cupboard, even though Naomi never snoops in my closets, she isn't a snoop by nature, unlike me, but I don't need her to know about the dialogue I conduct with tranquilizers, and especially not about the parcel in the plastic bag hidden at the back of the cupboard. A few years ago I asked for three packets of aspirin at the pharmacy and by mistake I was given three packets of Hypnodorm instead, I didn't know exactly what it was, but I understood that it was some kind of tranquilizer, and I instinctively refrained from pointing out the pharmacist's mistake, thanked him and walked out with the pills, which Anton later told me were exceptionally strong sedatives given to junkies with withdrawal symptoms, and ever since then they've been waiting in their hidingplace at the back of the cupboard, you can never know when they might be needed, and now I search energetically for the aspirin, squinting at her reflection in the mirror, her eyes are closed, tiny droplets of sweat are glittering on her upper lip which is stretched into a faint, enigmatic smile, and my distress returns, her cheeks are flushed—from the hot water, I say to myself, but I discern a kind of gratification on her face which has nothing to do with me and I slam the door of the cupboard, she opens her eyes and hurries back to me, the smile disappears, and another smile, familiar and related to me, takes its place. So should we go out to eat or take in a movie, I ask, and she says, fine, and I realize that she's miles away, and I search for something to say that will lighten the obscure uneasiness between us, the obsessive need to know everything has not yet taken possession of me, I only hope that we won't be going out anywhere, and she gets out of the bath and asks for a towel, and for a moment I don't remember where the towels are, and she says, never mind, and goes to the cupboard under the basin herself, her body wet and gleaming, and because of my anxiety I can't take the sight, sometimes I feel that there are sights so loaded with emotion that I have to avert my eyes, and she says, in this weather perhaps we should stay at home. Since emerging from the bath she has come back to me completely, and with her sweet bossiness she tells me to get into bed and she'll take care of me and my mild case of flu, her cheeks are still pink, there is a kind of gaiety about her which she for some reason is at pains to conceal, and my uneasiness grows, and so I really do get into bed, and while I wait for the tea she is making for me I listen attentively to the sounds coming from the kitchen, I think she's singing to herself but I'm not sure—the storm outside swallows the voice—and for some reason I have to know now if she's singing to herself, I've never heard her singing to herself before, and I get out of bed and steal into the kitchen. She's standing at the window and looking into the black maw gaping outside, her hand straying over her wet hair which now looks dark and not actually blonde, singing Tom Waits to herself, "I'll shoot the moon right out of the sky for you, baby," and my heart contracts inside me, not because she's singing to herself but because of her dreamy pose, which has nothing to do with me, and when the phone rings I run back to bed and pick up the receiver, it's my mother, asking if the missing person has been found, but just then Naomi comes into the room with the tea and so I say that everything's fine, and she says, you don't sound fine to me, what have you found out? Nothing, I say and hang up, in her tone I detected that faint mockery which always succeeds in getting to my most exposed places, and I tell Naomi that it was my mother, and I wish she'd stayed in Sinai. What did she want to know, Naomi asks, and I say, nothing, in a voice which comes out shrill and resentful, and she looks at me with a surprised expression, and I notice, not for the first time, faint traces of impatience in her, and a

sulky childhood sensation wells up in me—on winter nights, in
my resentment against my mother, I would throw off my blan-
kets and remain exposed, only she didn't know, and so I would
lie shivering with cold and anger, with the wild sounds coming
from her bedroom ringing in my ears—and I draw the blanket
up to my chin, and Naomi, who thinks that the flu has made
me drowsy, puts the tea down next to me and leaves the room
in relief, or so it seems to me, a suffering person always seems
like a creditor demanding his debt, even though I myself celebrate when she's sick, those are my finest hours, once she had
a tooth extracted and her cheek swelled up and her face was all
out of shape, and I couldn't stop looking at her, communing
joyfully with her defectiveness, and the memory elicits an
uncontrolled groan which brings her back to the room. What's
the matter, Ilan? she asks in concern, and I can't discern any
traces of phoniness in her concern so I wake up and make a
place for her next to me, I have to make love to her now, and
I pull her to me gently, praying that she won't evade me but
preparing myself for precisely this eventuality, if I feel even the
faintest whiff of reluctance I'll leave her alone, which is what
I've been doing for the past two years, but in the meantime she
shows no reluctance, on the contrary, she throws her head
back, her eyes go blank with a strange, unfamiliar intoxication,
a different kind of music is playing here, her movements are
long and slow, heavy with pleasure, and she whispers something I can't understand even though I want to understand it
very much, but this is no time for nagging, what did you say, so
I keep quiet and after a few minutes I don't care what she said,
because she abandons herself in my arms with a kind of reck-
lessness, and my head empties out. She lies on her back with
her arms outspread, her eyes closed, an enigmatic smile like the
one I saw in the bathroom on her face, and I obliterate myself
inside her until the storm subsides, only the wind and the rain
continue beating at the window, and I embrace her, she cud-

dles up to me, her forehead buried in my cheek, and since I have no doubts about the warmth flowing towards me now I permit myself to tell her frankly and simply about the happiness she gives me, and when I ask her if all this burdens her I realize that she is sound asleep, and I immediately banish the insult and content myself with the gain, at least I haven't exposed myself in the weakness of my love. She mumbles something in her sleep and I look at her and give myself up to the fresh new memory, there was love here, no doubt of that, I reconstruct the last few minutes, from the minute she sat down next to me on the bed, isolating every detail, and as I do so I get excited again and masturbate quietly and alertly, watching to see that she doesn't wake up, and gradually the concrete memory grows vague, there are no more details, only a vivid mélange of abstract images, and I come, but into the relaxation spreading through me a jarring note penetrates, and the wind increases, a renewed torrent of rain lashes the window and flings it open, I get up to close it, raindrops spray me, Naomi moves in her sleep, now she's lying on her back, her mouth parted slightly as if in surprise, and the jarring note grows sharper in my mind, I stand next to the bed and look at her attentively for a while, and then I ask myself who really caused the storm in which I participated like an accidental audience, for now I have no doubt that I was enjoying the leftovers of a banquet served somewhere else, and I go back to bed, force myself to lie down and count, a technique for emptying the mind of thoughts, and gradually my body surrenders to weariness and my head empties and at some point I fall asleep.

2

When I arrive at the bistro next to the courthouse in Hasan Shoukri Street, Anton is already waiting. I am not enthusiastic about the meeting, the buzzing from yesterday has not yet stopped and I find it difficult to get out of myself and into somebody else, and so as I sit down I decide to order a brandy in spite of the early hour. What mountain fell on you, he asks, but just then the unpleasant waitress turns up, allowing me to ignore the question and to wonder aloud whether to order chicken or lamb in the hope that in the meantime he'll change the subject, it's clear to me that I have no intention of confiding in him, mainly because I don't yet want to put anything into words, which can sometimes create a reality that might never have taken form had it not been stated, but also because even before Anton, who knows me as well as it's possible to know anybody, I prefer not to expose myself in my weakness. I'm well acquainted with the mechanism—what at first gains sympathy gradually turns to an inferiority that leads to revulsion, however well disguised. Ilan, they're waiting for you to order, he says, and I wake up to the impatient waitress who in any case feels that she's too good for the little bistro and decide to order stuffed vine leaves and brandy, Anton orders lamb chops and beer and in the meantime he lights a cigarette, which makes me long for one too, but there's no way I'll go back to smoking cigarettes, it's completely out of the question, and I take out my pipe, which is an unsatisfactory substitute, and as I clean it I'm conscious of his heavy calm, which depresses me. When we were children and I started a fight and hurled insults at him, he would never let himself be dragged in, but would turn around and go home unbeaten, leaving me unsatisfied, and now too I feel anger rising in me, for no reason, why should I envy him, and he sits in silence, unembarrassed, and when the waitress finishes slamming the plates down in front of us I ask him about the girl he's going out with, her name escapes me, Mary, he says, and his long lashes rise and he looks at me, her name's Mary, and we broke up, I'm seeing someone else now. What's her name, I ask, and he says, it makes no difference, let's eat, and I understand that she's Jewish and this immediately arouses my sympathy, not because he's seeing a Jewish girl but because of the agonizing conflict and the cracks breaching the wall of his fortress whenever he goes out with a Jewess, and the calm and indifference and enviable confidence give way to a vulnerability which leaves room for me and lets me in, and I send him a real smile, but he makes haste to disavow my empathy, knowing very well what gave rise to it and having no wish to gain my sympathy by exposing his weakness, since he knows the damage caused by exposure as well as I do, once we still used to talk about things like this—and as I cram the last vine leaf into my mouth I see Naomi's very noticeable yellow Beetle passing in front of my eyes and disappearing at the bottom of Hasan Shoukri Street. At once a red light in my mind begins blinking, a few days ago I found a speeding ticket she got in Hasan Shoukri Street and when I asked her what she was doing in Hasan Shoukri she mumbled something indistinct, and since it's impossible to investigate all the details in order to get to the bottom of things, this one too got swallowed up and forgotten in the daily round, and now she's here again, in Hasan Shoukri, and I know that this morning she was at school teaching, and after work she was supposed to go home, what the hell is she doing here, and the vine leaf gets stuck in my throat, I wash it down with the brandy left in my glass and with an urgency which Anton immediately latches onto—there's a limit to the amount of self-control I can muster—I say that I have to run, and he doesn't ask any questions, just probes a little with his dark gaze, and I hurry out to the Volvo parked across the street, make a forbidden U-turn and race off in the direction where she disappeared, and when I reach the junction and look right, I see the Beetle parked next to steps leading up to the abandoned houses of Wadi Salib. I park my car and look around, the area is abandoned and deserted, there's no sign of Naomi anywhere except in my feverish brain, I begin to climb the crumbling stairs leading to a ghost quarter strewn with hypodermic needles, condoms, cigarette stubs, the sordid residue of a nocturnal hell, and there's still no sign of Naomi or anyone else, for a moment I hesitate, lost, but suddenly a pile of garbage next to me begins to stir and a living creature who was once a human being, ageless and dressed in rags, emerges from it, stares at me with blank, lifeless eyes and in a dull voice asks me for a cigarette. I don't smoke, I say, taking a few coins out of my pocket, he holds out a limp hand and takes them, and I ask him if he's seen a young girl in a red sweater, but he's lost me already and returned to the wasteland of his thoughts, and I go back down the steps and stand next to the yellow Beetle, staring aimlessly into space, unable to imagine what she could be doing in this ghost quarter, and I force myself to look at my watch, my class begins in fifteen minutes and I'm stuck here in this hell, there has to be a logical explanation, people don't just disappear into abandoned neighborhoods, but I have to leave right now, and I get into the Volvo and drive away, the lateness of the hour deepening my anxiety a little. I can't be late, but since Naomi came into my life I've been neglecting my work, last week Davis invited me to a friendly but humorless lunch and explained to me in his warm tone that brilliant people like me, who succeed early in life and become professors prematurely, tend to dry up early too, and I should pull myself together and find a new subject to ignite me, and I realized that I couldn't take his affection for granted, and that in fact I had disappointed him, and all this saddened me but I said nothing to Naomi, only to my mother, of course—I can always dump everything I spare others on her, which is her only good point as far as I'm concerned—and she said that Davis was right, there was no doubt about it, and I lost my temper because I'd expected to get some sympathy, and now I look at my watch again, and five minutes before my class is due to begin I drive into the physics department parking lot, and at exactly a quarter past two I spread my papers on the table and my mouth, which at this moment is an independent entity, starts lecturing on instabilities and collapse, and out of the corner of my eye I see that student with the aggrieved face looking at me, maybe she's in love with me, but the thought gives me no pleasure and does nothing to dispel my feeling of oppression and dread.

3

When I get home in the evening I find Naomi sitting at her desk. She tenses and jumps quickly to her feet, and I see that the drawing paper in front of her is full of the kind of absentminded scribbles people make during a long telephone conversation. She seems jumpy, I can't get her to meet my eyes, she immediately offers to make me supper and I say that I've already eaten at the *Technion*. She asks with a glassy look, what do you want to eat, I say again, more slowly, I've already eaten, Naomi, and she asks, should I defrost a steak for you? I stand there and wait for her to come back to me, and after moving restlessly to and fro she pulls herself together, faces me without looking at me, and asks, is anything wrong, and I repeat in the same tone, is anything wrong, and now she almost looks at me and asks in a different tone, is anything wrong, and I say, nothing's wrong, why should anything be wrong, I'm simply trying to explain to you that I've already eaten, and now that I've finally caught her attention she understands, and she kisses me lightly and says that in that case she'll carry on working, and she sits down distractedly in front of her scribbles again, and I sit down in the armchair opposite the big window and look at the street, there's a whole world out there, with lawyers and shop assistants and greengrocers and homeless people and sick people and well people and people getting married and they're all leading their separate lives, and they've only got one thing in common, there's no Naomi in their lives, they're all busy leading their lives, happy or sad, but they've got no Naomi to worry about. This thought bores me, I can't see any point in it, just like all the thoughts sailing aimlessly through my head, I still can't bring myself to admit what's happening here, I'm still shrouded in the dense fog which envelops every event in the minutes before it is revealed by the full light of day, and out of the corner of my eye I see her stretching slowly like a cat, but not a cat that belongs in this house, and abruptly I dive into the vortex, the horror of the realization tightens my stomach, I sit dumbly in the armchair and stare with paralyzed eyes at the curve of her back with its milky skin, and in a grim inner voice I say to myself, Naomi has a lover.

4

In the morning I can't wake up, fragments of a dream cling to me and I haven't got the strength to tear myself away, all I took was one Valium and one Numbon, but Naomi's voice drags me to the surface, she's standing above me, stroking my forehead and telling me that it's late, that I have to get up, and now she gives me a look free of subterfuge, sits down next to me, holds my heavy head and asks, what did you take, and I say, I must have taken a sleeping pill instead of an aspirin, and she kisses my neck warmly, and she's not anywhere else except right here with me, and I hug her and what seemed clear and unequivocal yesterday is now, in the soft light of the winter morning, far from clear. Why did I jump immediately to a lover, perhaps the whole thing grew out of my rotting brain cells, everyone has an obscure inner life which may lead him to disappear for instance in some abandoned neighborhood and the explanation is usually as trivial as most explanations, maybe she sits and draws there, just like her not to tell me that she sits in some romantically sordid place and draws disintegrating landscapes—she doesn't like artists to talk about their creative processes, she finds it boastful and self-important—that's probably what happened, what else could it be? and why did I jump straight to a lover? she's so pure and innocent, she wouldn't be capable of leading a double life, but why has she been disappearing into herself so often lately? And now she takes my head in her hands and says, sometimes I think there's no connection between you and you, as if you're two different people, and I love them both, and she lifts herself up and sits on top of me, parting her legs and wrapping them around me, and I feel her flimsy panties, so what if she disappears into herself, she really is herself, and where do I get off trying to push myself into her every passing mood, there are things about her that have nothing to do with me, the fact that I myself have no passing moods that she doesn't give rise to doesn't mean that the same thing is true for her, each of us is a separate being, and I lift my hand and slip it into her blouse, caressing her warm, smooth skin, and it's really late now, I have to get up right this minute, and I pick her up and move her gently aside, killing two birds with one stone—I'll make it to work on time and have the added bonus of showing her I'm not a slave to my passion—and she asks me when I'll be home, and to my bitter regret I remember I have a meeting with some guests from Finland this evening, and I won't be home before eleven o'clock. What a pity, she says, slightly breathlessly, in that case we'll meet at eleven at home, and I immediately begin calculating how many hours I'll have to wait, and I get dressed and as I leave the phone rings. She blows me a kiss and runs to the phone in the bedroom even though there's one closer, and I hear her responding with a tense hello, and then I can't hear anything, only muffled whispers, and the sour note I succeeded in silencing this morning comes back to my ear, I slam the door so she'll think I've gone and open it again softly, tiptoe to the bedroom and hide behind the door, she's so absorbed in her conversation that she wouldn't feel it even if I touched her, and I hear her say in a pampered tone, Ilan's busy till eleven so I'll be with you at a quarter past eight, and my feet move quietly of their own accord to the door, and my hands open and shut it, and I have no idea how I get to the *Technion* but I get there on time, and once again a whole world runs parallel to me, I'm only a visitor there, and I lecture, see students, go over two papers, listen to Davis tell me a joke and laugh, and explain glibly that I won't be able to entertain the Finns this evening because I have to go to a wedding, and his expression clouds but in the face of my unembarrassed determination he gives in immediately, and only says I owe him one in the future—what future?—and a little before eight I reach the junction of Hasan Shoukri and Bialik Streets, silence the engine and wait for her yellow Beetle to arrive.

I'm dying for a smoke. My health, which is usually a subject of exhausting concern to me, doesn't bother me now, only I've left my pipe in the office and now I desperately need a cigarette, but in this moment I have no chance of getting hold of one, I can't leave the junction, it's already after eight and she should be arriving at any minute, the need for a cigarette dulls my suspense and becomes a burning issue, a very fat man walks past on the pavement and I ask him for a cigarette in a desperate voice that makes him stop, I offer to pay him for the packet which is sticking out of the back pocket of his jeans, he thinks about it and gives me one cigarette, I light it and inhale with a savage enjoyment, it's been ages since I smoked a cigarette, on reflection I leave half for emergencies, in the bistro next to the courthouse I see Anton sitting by himself and drinking beer, who could have thought when we were children that things would come to this, who thought then at all? Two aging idiots sitting in Hasan Shoukri street, we haven't had a real conversation in years, not just because of the tendency to withdrawal, but mainly because of the futility of talking, which grows more acute with the years—apart from the need for professional boasting here and there, which is also fading, chess has become a substitute for speech, before Naomi came on the scene we would sit for hours opposite the board, each with his own sack full of different baggage. It's already eight-fifteen, and what if she took a different route, via Independence Street, for example, and I remember the material I was supposed to read by tomorrow that I forgot in the office, I'll have to go past the *Technion* on my way back, but back from where, and where's Naomi? and what did I expect when I fell in love with her, when I saw her for the first time with her cropped hair wringing out a floor rag in my mother's house and thought she was a boy? and that first picture, of the boy turning round to face me and turning into a girl with exquisite lips looking into my existence with a generosity rare in women of unequivocal beauty, springs up before my eyes. She came up to me, wiped her wet hand on her tee-shirt and held it out to me, and an enchanting smile lit up her frank face, and I thought how nice it was of such a beautiful girl to smile at me so generously, for twenty years I'd been negotiating with young and sometimes beautiful female students, accepting their flattering admiration, which in recent years seemed to me to be faintly tinged with contempt, leading me to put a stop, even before Naomi, to the discreet affairs I used to have with them, today I'm the same age as their parents, and even though I'm in good shape, age is age, never mind how you try to deny it, and I learned to treat their complicated attitude to my age with prudence, and to wear a mask which protected me from harm while leaving an opening for dialogue, and the familiar chugging of the Beetle wakes me up, she appears suddenly behind me, hugging the wheel intently, not seeing anything, and after she passes me and turns right I start the engine and drive behind her to the bottom of Hasan Shoukri, at the junction she turns into Wadi Salib, parks in the same place as yesterday, and gets out with a flashlight. I park at a safe distance and wait, and when she starts climbing the stairs I get out of the Volvo, for a minute I hide behind the wall, the need for concentration precludes all other thoughts and I stand and watch her hurrying up the steps with her youthful lungs, the beam of light from her flashlight dancing in front of her, her pale coat shining in the heavy darkness of the moonless, starless night, and I climb after her in a tense silence, swallowing my heavy breaths, and at the top of the steps I stop for a moment, lean on the wall and look around me—there's no sign of her or her flashlight, she's disappeared again, only this time I'm not going back, she's here, somewhere in this dark reality, and I'm not leaving until I've discovered its secret.

For half an hour I wander around, entering gaping, abandoned houses, the cold creeps into my coat, heavy drops of rain splatter on me, lightning shatters the darkness followed by thunder and sheets of rain, falling heavier and heavier, threatening to drown me here and now in this ghost town, and still there is no trace of Naomi. I sit down on a stone, abandoning myself to cold, wet oblivion, self-pity wells up in me but I immediately dampen it, I'm forty-eight years old, a professor of astrophysics at the *Technion*, in good health and with a good salary, and there is a slight possibility, for now, no more than theoretical, of life after Naomi. Suddenly I hear a kind of slow moan through the rain, I look intently into the darkness, and at an imprecise distance I see a faint, flickering light, and I begin walking over the rubble, careful not to blink an eye in case I lose sight of the light, I'm concentrating so hard I don't feel the rain, and I advance towards the light, the only thing visible through the rain and dark, I stumble, collide with objects which scratch and bruise me, the light grows clearer and clearer, it's the light of a candle flickering in one of the houses, and slowly the moan becomes the voice of a singer, unfamiliar to me, mournfully singing the blues, and in the poor light I make out an abandoned house, patched up and relatively intact, its windows boarded up with planks, its doorway covered with a sheet of red plastic through which the light is visible, a sudden gust of wind wreaks havoc with the plastic curtain, the light dances wildly, muffled laughter is swallowed up in the wind, there's a party going on inside, and I go up to one of the windows and without preparing myself in any way stick my eyes into a crack between the planks and see Naomi sitting astride a strange man, dressed only in a cut-off white tee-shirt of mine, in her sculpted nakedness she sits on him, dances on him, struggles with him, gives in to him, nothing exists for her, only the strange man in his dark sweater, whose face I can't see from where I'm standing but who definitely isn't young, despite his mane of yellow hair. I could go up to the red plastic curtain now and tear it down and say this and that, but I go on standing there, wet as a floor rag before it's wrung, and before my eyes is spread the very banquet whose leftovers I had enjoyed the night before last, and Naomi throws her head back, the tee-shirt becomes taut on her body, he thrusts big hands into the gap and pushes her down without coming out of her, and now he's sitting on her and I can see him clearly, his face is broad, masculine, he looks like the movie star Nick Nolte, but I don't feel anything, only a strange blankness, as if I'm not really standing here, not really looking at Naomi, this isn't the Naomi who sleeps in my bed, the woman in my house is a saint untouched by dirty hands, and I go on standing stony and blank until the rain washes away my paralysis, and I succeed in tearing myself from the scene and I point myself in the direction of the car, but it isn't easy to find the way in the darkness and the confusion and especially the hopelessness which assails me, I drag myself through the ruins which become an exhausting labyrinth, and only when I feel a sharp and unexpected pain in my ankle I realize that I've stumbled on the steps, and the pain brings me back to myself, and I wake up and hurry down, get into my car and drive away.

7

The rains stopped and I drive up Hasan Shoukri, the heating on at full blast, I've changed my coat for the dry one I luckily got back from the dry-cleaner's yesterday, but inside my wet socks my feet are freezing. At the traffic lights I stop, there's nothing behind me and I let the lights change again and again, I have to focus somehow, my instincts tell me to hide my discovery from Naomi, in any case the betrayal has happened, the harm's been done, if I confront her like the wounded, and therefore inferior, party, insisting and proclaiming this and that, she'll do one of two things—either she'll promise, and maybe she'll mean it, to put an end to the affair, and I can imagine only too well how she'll brood about it afterwards—an affair broken off at its peak through no wish of her own—or else she'll seize the opportunity to leave me. She'll leave me, the thought pierces my chest, the thing rises before me, both probable and impossible, and with the lucidity that sometimes descends on me I know now that I have no choice but to keep quiet and carry on, I'll swallow her lover like a wise Jew, perhaps it's even less terrible than it seems, I once read a sentence by Beckett that impressed me, and now I'm going to put it to practical use. Habit is the great deadener, he wrote, and now I succeed in penetrating to the heart of this sentence and I understand that extreme situations do not allow, in the heat of the discovery, for the mobilization of one's reasoning powers, and therefore decisions are taken which when the storm subsides seem primitive and shameful. What happened to reason, how did it permit itself to collapse so supinely in the face of the insult which dictated vital decisions—decisions which lead in the end to self-hate and certain failure? And I light the second half of the cigarette and come to the conclusion that my battle for Naomi will be conducted with patience and restraint, with the satisfaction gained by restraint, I'll live on the fruits of her feelings of guilt, because that's all I can manage, a living hell is preferable to the emotional desert I inhabited until two years ago, vacillating between boredom and anxiety. My mother said I was a cripple, well, at least people feel sorry for cripples. Most of the women I went out with embarrassed me in their atavistic eagerness to get married, especially since on the face of things I was an excellent catch, except that the model I brought with me from home didn't put marriage at the top of my agenda, and so I would find myself sitting opposite women who on our first dates seemed glamorous and independent and sometimes even really promising, but very soon disappointment would distort their faces, and the sex was no compensation, because it was almost always steeped in guilt on my part and submission on theirs. Perhaps only two or three times in my life I succeeded in experiencing something you could call ripples of being in love, but only with Naomi did the thing itself appear in its full oceanic force, stunning me with the power of its inner energy, shaking me to the core and opening up before me a world whose limits receded further and further into infinity, so that I would look at people and ask myself if it was possible that others too experienced such intense emotion. And so I know that I have no intention of giving up the person who woke me from my lifelong sleep, anyone who lacks the talent for living and is doomed to be an eternal observer doesn't give up someone like Naomi so easily, and even now, in spite of the wild scene that I keep seeing in my mind's eye, I have no hate or anger in my heart but only sorrow, which I'm used to anyway, there's every reason to assume that I can go on living

with her in the same house, especially since the affair might be
no more than a passing infatuation. This idea cheers me up a little, but then I am suddenly confronted by the thought that
maybe she'll leave me, perhaps at this very moment the two of
them are considering this very possibility, and I begin to imagine the conversation between them, until I'm exhausted by the
grinding of my inner mills and I force myself to see things from
a perspective which is easier to digest: Naomi won't leave me
for an aging hippie who lives in a dead hovel, the romance will
quickly fade, logic will prevail, I'm a generous provider, in addi-
tion to my job at the *Technion*, I'm much in demand as an occasional lecturer to laymen on astrophysics—space apparently
stirs people's curiosity, its threat seems to give them a thrill.
Naomi sometimes comes with me to these lectures, giving me
an opportunity to impress her, which I exploit with restraint,
and she fixes me with the eyes of an admiring student, as if
someone who lectures about the cosmos can solve its mysteries
too, and after the lecture we go to eat fish in Atlith, and she
looks at me, aroused, and these moments fill the following days
too, until, that is, my raiment of brilliant lecturer dissolves into
the gray routine of daily life.

Anton is still sitting in the bistro, I park on the pavement outside, he isn't completely surprised to see me, and he doesn't look too pleased either. There are four empty beer bottles on the table and he is sunk in profound reflection, or the lack of it, but I don't care, I have nearly two hours to kill and I plan to spend them here, waiting for the yellow Beetle to appear. I'll let her get home before me, and spare her the squirming and excuses and myself the humiliation of listening to them. Anton pulls up a chair for me from the next table and asks me a general, "What's up," without going into specifics such as where have you been, questions like that aren't his style. He ignores my wet hair and muddy shoes, I order a brandy, the old guy who owns the place brings us the chess set, an hour and a half passes, and I am about to lose the third game too when his cell phone rings. He rouses himself from the beer bottles, says a businesslike, "Yes," listens with calm concentration for about five minutes, while I try to learn how he does it, simply listening without the need to demonstrate listening, says, I'm coming, and switches off the phone. A man's murdered his invalid wife, he says, pushed her down a flight of stairs, and he finishes his beer, wondering aloud why people have to murder their wives at night and not during normal office hours. At precisely that moment the yellow Beetle drives past and Anton says, wasn't that Naomi? Naomi's at home in bed with a sore throat, I say decisively, and he looks again in the direction of the yellow car, which disappears into Prophets

Street and ceases to interest him, he's got a murder to worry about, he yawns and says goodbye, and I wait for a few listless minutes then drive home.

The house is dark and cold and Naomi pretends to be asleep. Her clothes are strewn around the bed, I stand next to her in my coat, looking at her closed eyes, and she exhibits rhythmic breathing, her eyelids flutter, she can feel me standing there, it's a nervous flutter, now she tries a faint snore, designed to give the effect of deep sleep. I take off my coat and she suddenly opens her eyes, her body twitches as if she's been sucked out of the deepest levels of sleep and I feel sorrow at this expert cunning of hers, and my sorrow is tinged with a new admiration for a versatility that I never knew she possessed, and which is capable of challenging even my long-practiced skill in reading reality. She sits up in bed and asks in a tone of rebuke what time it is, as if I am the sinner here, coming home late after roaming the town at night. Go to sleep, I say with a tenderness which moves even me, and she gratefully snuggles up into her own private space, from which, I imagine, she heads straight for that desolate, ghostly quarter of town where the aging man with tresses of yellow hair waits for her, she wraps herself in memories of him, and actual experience, as I know, improves in the act of recollection, and I decide to make myself a cup of tea, change my mind, decide to have a bath, but I don't move, all I want is for this night to be over somehow, and I drag myself to the bathroom, take a quick shower and get into bed, straight to her warmth imprisoned under the blanket. Her contact with my wet body feels like an electric current, tomorrow is a new day, tomorrow I'll think, now I have to go to sleep, and I get up and take an entire Numbon, sleep will come in half an hour, and in the meantime every minute passes round and separate, illuminating then darkening detail after detail, and I remember that I didn't pass by the *Technion* to get the article, how am I going to teach tomorrow without reading it, and the first drop of sleep rolls into my brain, I can always identify the beginning of the process, it spreads like a delicate cloud growing fuller and fuller until it envelops my whole body in its heaviness, tomorrow I don't start teaching until twelve, if the pill provides me with eight hours of sleep I'll be able to think properly tomorrow, tomorrow a whole new story will begin.

The mask I've chosen fits snugly on my face and Naomi doesn't sense anything or suspect anything. The gap between me and myself grows, but the house goes about its familiar routine, in the evenings I come home and she's waiting for me with supper, we eat together and I wait in suspense for the next tortuous pretext which will get her out of the house, and in the end it comes. Kabbalah lessons every Tuesday afternoon. Perhaps you'd like to come too, she suggests in a barely audible mutter, and immediately changes the subject. On Tuesday afternoons I teach, I say, as if she doesn't know, and she says, oh, right, acting badly. I feel a little cheered to see that she hasn't really mastered the art of sinning yet, and on Tuesday I come home to find a note saying that she's gone to a Kabbalah lesson, there's food in the oven, love, Naomi. I chew the chicken with rosemary, and from every page of the newspaper the scene leaps out at me accompanied by their wild laughter, maybe they're laughing at me too, in illicit affairs, alongside suffering, the sense of sin gives birth to malice and spite, the complicity in wrongdoing gives rise to a dark kind of intimacy. Two are power, two are an army, they're pitying me there with savage glee, Naomi says to him, stop it, it isn't nice, poor Ilan, he doesn't deserve it, and another peal of laughter bursts out. Why did she choose an aging man? how many fathers does she need? but that was no father I saw there, I can't console myself with that, and again, like probing an aching tooth, I abandon myself to panic which grows so acute that I can't breathe and I go out to the balcony. The sea lies there calmly, what does it care, I search for Wadi Salib and when I find it I suddenly remember the idiotic telescope my mother gave me when I got my first degree, as if astrophysicists stand on their balconies and look for stars. On an impulse which I know is ruinous I go back inside, take the cobweb-covered telescope down from the storage space under the ceiling, and without even cleaning it, so as not to waste the daylight, I focus it and begin to search. Less than one kilometer as the crow flies, I need concentration and a steady hand, slowly I swivel the telescope, looking for the red plastic curtain, find the steps, climb them carefully, and suddenly a ray of light pierces the clouds and illuminates the ruins as if someone had switched on the light for me. For the second time this week I feel that I'm being watched, and I find the plastic sheet, the patched-up house is sharp and clear, but I can only guess at what's happening inside, and I sweep the broken paving stones around the walls, a patch of turquoise catches my eye but I don't linger on it, I try to penetrate the boarded-up openings, to get inside, my other, closed eye twitches but I take no notice, intent on my task, as if I'm watching the enemy from an observation post on the border. But nothing happens, they're lying there in each other's arms inside the house, why should they come out, and I leave off and sit down on the wicker chair that's still wet from the rain. Ever since she started her affair she's stopped bringing in the chairs when it rains, what does she care about the chairs we once bought with such a sense of importance, it was a whole project—buying furniture for the balcony, and I sit there for a moment longer, not knowing what to do with myself, and again the sun breaks through the clouds and illuminates the sky with a bright blue, reminding me of the patch of turquoise which I passed over before and which now for some reason pricks at my brain. I return to the telescope and find the patch, lying in a puddle next to a broken stone bench not far from the red plastic curtain, and it occurs to me that they may be Naomi's turquoise panties, except that I can't understand what they're doing outside. Maybe she left after they'd finished their frolics, and he suddenly felt like more, the fresh memory aroused him all over again, and he went out after her, taking her by surprise from behind, lifting her up in the air and putting her down on the stone bench, pulling up her skirt and tearing off the turquoise panties which fell into the puddle, and with an urgent movement he unzips his pants and thrusts himself into her, and she opens her strong thighs for him, writhes underneath him, moans into his ear, driving him crazy, his big hands move roughly over her body— this man is living my fantasies, the fantasies of a refined professor—and they are swallowed up in a big bubble, the laws of this world no longer apply to them, they're a law unto themselves, completely autonomous, and my eyes are blinded and I fall back into the wicker chair. But the images refuse to dissolve, the torture of my imagination is even worse than the sight itself, and all of sudden I feel tired of myself, I fold up the telescope and return it to its place, and decide to sit down and relax with Verdi's *Agnus Dei*, which usually succeeds in cheering me up, and before I put on the disk I open my briefcase to take out my pipe, but it turns out that I've forgotten it at the office. For lack of an alternative I decide to use the pipe Naomi bought me when I gave up cigarettes, an expensive but unsuccessful Savinelli which I only smoked in her presence, because I preferred the plain pipe I bought for myself, and when Naomi discovered this she was disappointed and hurt, especially because I hid the truth from her, so she said, and why was it so hard for me to say I didn't like the pipe, why be so devious, what did I think, that she was a little girl whose feelings would be hurt because her present wasn't a success? But that's exactly what hurt her, I know that tendency to disguise the truth by putting on an act of offended self-righteousness, and I said, you're right, Naomi, because what else could I say? And now I'm going to smoke precisely this pipe, and she'll come in and look surprised, and I'll say affectionately that I suddenly missed her and consoled myself with her gift, at least I'll profit by her guilt—a very modest profit compared to *his* spectacular gains. But in the meantime I can't find the pipe and I give up, only without smoking I don't feel like listening to the music either, and I give that up too, and lie down on the couch instead, maybe I'll succeed in dozing off. But her turquoise panties jump into my head again, and now I have to know if those really are her panties lying there in the puddle, and I get up and go to her chest of drawers and rummage in the heap of underwear. I find one pair but I know that there were two, and I grow more and more obsessed by the need to find those panties in the house, and I hurry to the laundry hamper, but just as I lift the lid I hear the door opening and her guilt-saturated voice saying, Ilan, are you at home? I quickly drop the lid, taking in what seems to me to be a patch of turquoise as I do so, but I can't be sure, and the first thing I do when I go out to meet her is stare hard at her mini-skirt, trying to see if she's wearing panties. She comes up to me with a smile and kisses me lightly, and I try to slip my hand casually under her skirt, but she evades me and asks if I've eaten, and before I can answer her she begins to yawn, so there won't be any misunderstandings about tonight, and I look at her skirt and there's no doubt in my mind that she's naked underneath it. I'm going to take a shower, she says, and gives me a smile as a consolation prize, and while she's showering I pull myself together and decide to deny the whole business of the panties, or at least to banish it from my mind, and when she emerges from the bathroom I tell her the joke Davis told me, and she laughs in an exaggerated fashion, no doubt seeking an outlet for her inner arousal, and goes to get dressed, ruffling my graying hair as she walks past me. I was perfectly satisfied with my hair until I saw his, but now see myself as a cliché of a middle-aged man with graying temples, and we sit and watch the news and afterwards we see a movie, which I can't get into, and at a certain stage I see that she's fallen asleep, her beautiful face saddens me and I wake her up gently and suggest that she goes to bed. She gets up with her eyes half-closed, to prevent her sleep escaping, and goes to the bedroom, and I switch to the shopping channel, which reminds me of a play we saw together in London, *Shopping and Fucking*. The name succeeds in amusing me slightly, and I stare at the kitchen knives which the presenter describes in detail, as if we can't see them for ourselves, and for a moment I even consider buying the set, which makes an excellent impression, and the presenter goes on to the next product, which she recommends in the same enthusiastic, detailed tone, this time it's a piece of exercise equipment for home use which depresses me, and I turn off the television and sit without moving.

11

For a number of days now she's hardly left the house. I know this because I keep tabs on her constantly. From time to time I phone the house from the *Technion* and hang up when she answers, or find some reasonable excuse and ask her something, the main thing is to keep in constant touch and know what's happening, I don't argue with my obsessive need to know. The rest of the time we spend together at home, she asked me long ago to give her Bible lessons, and these dead days are a good time for it, I have to do something to relieve the tension a little, even if I've decided to live with it, and here I even have an opportunity to impress her. If I want to win I have to be at my best, the natural tendency to sink into depression won't do me any good, and so I look up original interpretations of the story of Jacob and Esau in the library, and in the evening she reads the chapter and I interpret it for her. She looks at me with an expression of concentration, perhaps admiration, I choose my manner of speech carefully, animation without hysteria or ranting or hand waving, the lecture itself doesn't bother me, I'm an experienced, stylish lecturer, in the popularity polls I always come out high on the list, and as I explain the story of the birthright to her I note that she's definitely with me now, only me, she won't leave me, what's so bad about living with a professor, intelligent, generous, sensitive, quite handsome, gentle, damn it, *gentle*, the revolting thought of my gentleness fills me with an aggression which I take out on Esau, on the brute attraction of the primitive, who lives in abandoned places, scorns society and at the same time exploits it. What's the connection, she asks, taken aback by my tone, and a shadow darkens her eyes. Unworthy people take for themselves the freedom to survive, I say, and she asks again, what's the connection, and I wave my hand in a gesture of dismissal that belittles her and elevates me, and she's immediately convinced that she didn't understand, because she's only little Naomi who doesn't know anything and I'm the big professor who compared to her knows everything, I couldn't possibly say something silly, and I smile at her in despair disguised as impatience, say I'm worn out, and go to the bedroom. She follows me and asks what's wrong, and I smile at her and say, I'm exhausted, I had a hard day. If she had any suspicions they evaporate, and she comes up to me and puts her arms around me. You're so clever, she says in a coy tone that maddens me and fills me with a savage lust, and she tries to evade my eyes but I pull her to me roughly, push her panties aside, open my trousers and penetrate her, and all the time I look at her with violent concentration but I feel nothing except for a desperate need to hurt her, and she lies under me like a submissive, apathetic rag doll, until I get off her and go to the bathroom to wash, and when I come back I find her lying open-eyed staring at the ceiling, and I say, I'm sorry, Naomi, and she says, it's all right, it's all right.

12

The next day, while I'm standing in front of the door and turning the key in the lock, I hear the phone ring and I go quickly inside. I see her silhouette through the opaque glass door of the bedroom reaching for the phone and picking it up, and I pick up the phone in the living room. I know immediately by the way she spreads herself out on the bed that it's him, and I cover the mouthpiece with my hand and hold my breath. Oded, hello sweetheart, she says, and he answers in a matter-of-fact tone, his voice is deep and husky, I'm going down to eat at the fish restaurant on the jetty in Bat-Galim, come if you can, and she says, I can't, Ilan will be home at any minute, and he says, O.K., another time—there's no preoccupation with hurt feelings here, he seems quite casual about the whole thing—and she says that she misses him and she'll try to come tomorrow night, she'll try to come this evening too, but she can't promise anything, it depends on the way things work out. I hang up when she does, hurry to the front door and go outside, where I walk around a bit and stop at the kindergarten on the corner to watch the children, the wonder of whose being has begun to interest me during the last year or so, before which I saw them mainly as a naturally occurring nuisance. They're standing pressed to the fence, waiting for their mothers to come and fetch them, worn out and helpless at the end of a day of exhausting survival, and my eyes fall immediately on a skinny ginger boy standing in the sandbox with his nose running, while another little boy with a thin pigtail at the back of his head pours sand over him from the spout of a watering can, and the sand sticks to the snot on his lip and the tears stream from his eyes leaving tracks on his dirty cheeks, but he doesn't move, he stands buried in the sand, submitting humbly to his humiliation, and the children look at him and see nothing, they simply accept what's happening as the way of the world. Except for one little girl with an Alice-band, who turns to the little boy with the pigtail and says, Yoavi, that's not nice, and he answers tonelessly, yes it is nice, and she says without interest, no, it's not, and returns to the fence to wait, and I say in a gentle but authoritative voice, stop that, Yoavi, you're making him cry, and the good-looking Yoavi says, okay, and goes to the fence and the redhead collapses onto the sand and lies there defeated, and I go inside and say to him, come along, I'll help you wash your face, and he says, I don't want to, and the little girl with the Alice-band says, he's just a cry-baby, and I leave them and go home, preparing myself for a new round. Naomi greets me warmly and while she makes coffee I wait in suspense for her to come up with something about this evening, the thought that he's waiting for her at the restaurant is wreaking havoc with both of us, and here it comes, she asks, what are the plans, she doesn't ask what my plans are, she asks what the plans are in general, and I say that I was thinking of working on the book, and she says nothing for a minute in order to give the subject a rest before renewing her attack, and I wait for her to continue, but when she begins to say that she was thinking of dropping in to a movie with Noam who's back from Amsterdam—"dropping in" always sounds more casual—I suggest that we go out to eat, but I immediately apologize and ask, what did you say, as if I interrupted her without meaning to and didn't hear what she said, and she says it doesn't matter, let's go out to eat, but I insist, you wanted to do something else, and she squirms, no, no, it doesn't matter, I just thought I might drop in to see a movie with Noam, and I say immediately, fine, no problem, we'll go out to eat tomorrow. I say this with a benevolent beam, and she looks at me—for a moment our eyes meet with disconcerting suddenness—but my generosity softens her and she says, no, I'd rather go out to eat. I ask her if she's sure and she nods exaggeratedly, and I say, okay, whatever you like, and go to get my coat, but then she says, just a minute, maybe you'd prefer to stay home and work, I don't want you to say afterwards that you didn't finish the book because of me—as if I ever say things like that to her—and in a patronizing tone I manage to produce from some dormant cell, I add, my dear Naomi, just decide what you want, it's up to you, and she says okay then, let's go, where do you want to go? Wherever you want, I say, and she says, Atlith, and I say, great, and we go out into a fine, crisp evening, the city has been washed clean by the rain, in the last hours of daylight it looks really beautiful, life is full of potential, no doubt about it, and when we approach the central bus station junction I say in the most casual tone I'm capable of producing, as if the thought has just this minute popped into my head, why don't we go to the fish restaurant on the quay, Anton says the trout in horseradish sauce is really fantastic. The intensity of her surprise embarrasses me, she looks as stunned as if a beam just fell on her head, and since it would be unreasonable to ignore her exaggerated reaction I pretend to attribute it to something else, and I say, don't exaggerate, it's not as bad as all that, last time we made a mistake by not listening to the proprietor's recommendation, and she recovers and says, but at Atlith the appetizers are better, and I say fine, we'll go to Atlith, it's just that Bat Galim is closer and Atlith is at the other end of the world. I sneak a look at her and I see that the idea of going to the restaurant on the quay excites her in some perverse way, because now she says, if you're so keen to go to Bat Galim then let's go there, I've heard of the trout in horseradish too, and I say, then we'll go there, and at the traffic lights I don't turn left but drive straight ahead to Bat Galim. Her tension fills the car, the anxiety of the risk outweighs the excitement, I suppose she's afraid her lover won't realize she's not alone and will throw himself at her, even though that doesn't seem to be his style, and perhaps this isn't what's bothering her, but something is definitely bothering her, because at the entrance to Bat Galim she suddenly panics and says, maybe we should go to Atlith after all, but I say, Naomileh you're driving me crazy, and she retracts and apologizes, and I feel that the power is in my hands, because knowledge gives you some power at least, and we arrive at the restaurant and go inside. I see him immediately, he's sitting at the last table, facing the entrance, she pushes past me in order to go in before me, but I manage to pick up the signal she sends him anyway, and he smiles sardonically and goes back to his Oriental salads. She sits down at a front table with her face to him, but I point out that she's sitting directly under the heating and proceed to a table nearer him, where I sit down facing in his direction, leaving her no option but to sit down opposite me, with her back to him. He looks at me, not too hard, but he definitely looks, and when the waiter comes we order the trout with horseradish sauce and Oriental salads and I try to think of a subject to talk about. Nothing comes to mind, the only thing I can think about is her burning back, the salads arrive, we both make an effort to swallow them, and he beckons the waiter with a self-confident gesture and while he's busy ordering I take the opportunity to examine him discreetly: just as I thought, impressive, sure of himself in a cool, matter-of-fact way. Aren't you hungry, I ask her before she can ask me, and she says that she had a sandwich before I came home, and I say, you should have said, what's the point of going out to eat if you're not hungry? You eat them, she says, I reluctantly begin to tackle the array of salads, which stick in my throat. Suddenly she stands up and says she's going to the toilet, and as she passes him she gives him a look which I can't see but I can feel, and a moment later he too gets up and follows her out. I deserve it, what was I thinking of coming here, I can't believe I wanted to torture myself, all I wanted was to be near them, to feel some perverted sense of control, and I ask the waiter to remove the first course which is making me sick, where I'm going to put the trout he now brings I have no idea. I look at the clock on the wall, keeping a close watch on the second hand, which advances at its usual pace, two minutes, three minutes, four minutes and twenty seconds—and here she comes with a pink face and falls ravenously on her fish while I sit opposite her and battle with mine, and now he comes back to his table and lights a cigarette. A cigarette, that's what I need now, that's what will save me. Have you got a cigarette, I ask Naomi, who occasionally smokes, but she says, what do you want a cigarette for, I thought you'd given them up. By now my need for a cigarette is overpowering and I call the waiter, but he's busy and he doesn't smoke anyway, and Naomi says, forget about it, but I'm already on my feet and on my way to her lover. She whips round as if her chair's on fire, and in a genial but neutral tone I ask him if he could please let me have a cigarette, pardon my cheek, and he, with amused generosity, offers me the pack, saying, take two, keep one for afterwards, and I say thank you very much, one's enough, and he lights it for me. I'm very close to him now, my hair's almost touching his, and for a second our eyes meet, no more than a second, and I immediately return to Naomi, who in order to dispel the embarrassment begins to tell me that my mother is angry with me and Anton for not taking the trouble to attend the funeral of Henzi Bauer, the old neighbor who used to be our kindergarten teacher. You didn't even tell me she was dead, we should have gone to the funeral, she says in a self-righteous tone. Why should I have told you, I say and drops of hostility begin to spray from my mouth, what's it got to do with you, an old kindergarten teacher you didn't even know, why on earth should you have gone to her funeral, not to mention the fact that the whole thing happened two weeks ago, why drag it up now—I say this with a tooth-pick stuck in my mouth, trying to make my attack seem normal and everyday, but again she is bewildered by my reaction, and I see how for a split second her eyes flicker from me to him, she's trying to read the situation, but I yawn as if there's noth-ing on my mind but a general impatience, and immediately her eyes stop darting and she smiles and says, I just remembered, we never had a chance to talk about it before. What's there to talk about, it's not important, I say, and she asks, rather resent-fully, what is important to talk about, and all of a sudden I can't go on sitting there, and I ask for the bill, and when we get up to leave I turn my back to them, I haven't got the strength to see their eyes ignite, and when we're outside she hugs me, she's cold and she disappears into my coat, intoxicating me with her clean smell, and I lift up her chin and kiss her full lips and say to myself that I've lost this round too.

The house is dark and cold, a dead fish is stuck in my throat and I feel helpless in the face of the depression sucking me in. I tell Naomi that I want to work and she kisses me and goes to stare at the TV screen and, presumably, to think about her lover, while I switch on the computer, open the file "X-ray bursts," and to my own surprise succeed in working for three concentrated hours and finishing the introduction. I spend another half hour going over it, tidying up, cleaning up clumsy sentences, but nevertheless leaving more than usual for the style editor to do. Perhaps I should ask Givon to go over the article, this negligence isn't going to do my career prospects any good, a thought which sends me to the Internet to check for recent articles and make sure that I haven't ignored any fresh information. In the meantime Naomi's gone to bed, after giving me a cheerful kiss, and when I switch off the computer the distress comes back to fill the place vacated by work, and I go to sit in the armchair opposite the window. If only I had a cigarette everything would be different, I decide that tomorrow I'm going to start smoking again, a decision which both cheers me up and depresses me, and I take a pink Xanax and gradually abandon myself to its effects.

In the morning I'm woken up by a phone call from Ra'ed, Anton's little brother, who announces in his laughing voice, mazaltov, I got married. It takes me a moment or two to focus, as he blathers: we got back yesterday from Cyprus, we decided on the spur of the moment. In the background I can hear his wife's laughter, her name escapes me, and he goes on talking but I'm not listening any more, because the need to remember her name takes up all my attention, and only at the end of the conversation I gather that he's inviting me to a party at his mother's house on Saturday night. I open up to him and his happiness, and congratulate him with a warmth that warms me up a little too, it isn't difficult to be happy for Anton's little brother with his frizzy curls and his round face, which is almost always illuminated by a mischievous smile. Michal Rinot, I finally remember his wife's name, and the small relief brings a small happiness, a girl from a farm in the Emek, with the same basic smiling expression as Ra'ed. The first time I met her I thought to myself that she was the natural flow of life, she lived in it and therefore it lived in her too, and the two of them looked as if their lives were a constant round of wild laughter. Ra'ed was like that from the minute he was born, with a comic view of life, for one of my birthdays he bought me a copy of Emil Habibi's play *The Optimist* with a dedication that read: "That's the way things are, what can you do." And that's exactly how he lived, without confronting reality, without giving a damn, and this talent of his enabled him to ignore the difficul-

ties which life constantly placed in his way, and to go out with
a Jewish girl, for example, as if it was the most natural thing in
the world. In the days when we still had heart-to-hearts Anton
would accuse his brother of being selfish and cynical, until he
realized that Ra'ed was simply blessed with a genuine ability to
see things from a distance which cut them down to size and rid
them of their poison. Anton, too, appeared to see things in a
similar perspective, but he lacked Ra'ed's integration between
outside and inside, and therefore he lacked the gift for happiness too, with the result that he, in fact, inhabited the same
mental zone as me. When I'm on the point of leaving the house
Ra'ed phones again to say that he forgot to tell me that at midnight, after the party, a small, exclusively male group of guests
are going down to the docks to get drunk with the fishermen,
and that I should leave my beautiful wife for a while and go
with them, and on Saturday night, when we're getting dressed
to go to the party, Naomi says, with the special casualness she's
developed lately concerning her movements: so I'll come home
alone in the car and you'll take a taxi later, you really shouldn't
drive with all the boozing you guys are going to do down there.
I understand that she's putting out feelers to see if she'll be free
after midnight—I threw her the information about the stag
party at the end of our conversation about the wedding—and I
say, I don't know yet, mainly because I really don't know yet,
I'm busy taking into account the calculation that if I let her go
to him after the party she'll compensate me for it when she
comes home, I have no problem with the humiliation any
more—"That's the way things are, what can you do"—and I'm
about to tell her that I've decided to go with them after the
party, but when I see her in her black dress, with her long legs
and shining eyes, my middle-aged pose deserts me, an ageless
pain pierces me, and consolation prizes no longer console me.
Actually it sounds to me like a lot of fun, going to get drunk
with the fishermen at midnight, she says, and I try to smile, a

lump of jealousy is stuck in my throat, and I say, we'll see later, and a drop of venom sticks to the words and produces a jarring note which makes her turn towards me in surprise. I immediately fall back upon the middle-aged professor and say, my dear, the price of a night of drinking is too high for someone my age, and she hides her disappointment and says with her sweet smile, you don't have to decide now, and her partial readiness to forgo her lover partially melts the lump of jealousy, and now I'm the one who feels the need to compensate her with a little hope and I say, maybe I will go, we'll see how things turn out, and she says, fine. We drive down Arlozorov street, she's animated and full of energy, and in the same casual tone of hers she says that the Cinematheque is having a midnight show of some Nigerian movie tonight and maybe she'll drop in to see it, she knows I can't stand ethnic movies and so she told Noam to call her at the party later to find out if she was free—you don't mind, do you, she asks vaguely, and I say, not at all, and throw her a warm smile. When Anton's mother opens the door and kisses me I immediately recognize her compassionate smile— when my mother told her I was going to marry Naomi she said, I hope God can spare the time to help them, and by "them" she meant anyone who went too far by conventional standards— and I put my arm round Naomi, mainly to please Anton's mother, and Naomi immediately makes herself at home, getting into girl talk with Michal and Anton's cousin, the judge, whose name I can't remember either, and the arak flows, and the evening advances to the uninhibited laughter of Ra'ed and Michal. How did you meet, Naomi asks them, and Michal says, let me tell her, I want to tell her, and she sits on his lap and hugs him like a happy bear and says, we met at the funeral of a neighbor of ours, up to then we only met on the stairs, and we're standing there at the funeral, sad and all that, and suddenly the Hungarian woman from the ground floor's skirt falls down, I swear, and everybody pretends not to notice, and she stands there in long winter underpants, and I try to ignore it too, and then my eyes meet Ra'ed's, and I can see that he's trying to control himself too, and I feel that I can't stand it any longer, so I begin walking slowly backwards, out of the circle, and I see him moving back too, and we find ourselves behind a big tombstone, and there we just collapse, we laugh ourselves sick, and that's it, from then on we've been together, and Ra'ed plants a ringing kiss on her neck, and his mother averts her eyes from them, and Naomi asks Michal archly, have the men left you out of their party with the fishermen too? From the beginning of the evening I've been wondering how she plans to bring up the subject in light of the passing time and the telephone call she's expecting any minute—and now I've got my answer, and Michal says, I wouldn't dream of intruding, I'll get him later, merry and horny, and she bursts out laughing again. You have to go with them, Ilan, she says decisively, and I think that before, during the girl talk, Naomi may have asked her to encourage me to join the stag party, and now everybody looks at me, or so it seems to me, and I'm trapped and I say, sure I'll go, and my reward is a caressing look from Naomi, who immediately enters into animated conversation with Anton, and the telephone rings and Anton's mother says, Naomi, it's for you, and Naomi excuses herself brightly and goes to the phone, and I see her face immediately soften, but then she turns to face the wall, shutting us all out, and I hoist myself out of the armchair and make for the toilet and the phone in the hall. I pick up the receiver and put my hand over it, their voices are swallowed up in the wild beating of my heart, my fear of being caught eavesdropping torments me more than the conversation itself, and at first I can't take anything in. I stand there with my back to the wall and my face to the danger, their voices stroke each other like pet animals, and in between the mutual stroking and murmuring they arrange to meet after midnight at a pub on the south side of town called the Windy Inn, Naomi gives him directions how to get there and I hang up and return to the armchair and the merriment in the room. A dry coldness encloses me in myself, and after a couple of minutes Naomi comes back with her face burning and sits down on the arm of my chair, glancing out of the corner of her eye at her watch. Most of her is already with him in the Windy Inn, only her tracks are left, she wraps her thin arm round my neck, her fingers rumple my hair, maybe she's comparing it to his mane, and all the time Anton's mother's dark look sears my face, perhaps she saw me listening to Naomi's conversation, but now I don't care, I'm sunk in apathy, as if everything's already over and it isn't all that important anyway. But Naomi, her senses sharpened by guilt, reads my mood and she brings her face up close to mine and asks if I'm feeling unwell, I smile a resigned smile, a shadow darkens her eyes and she asks, do you want to go home? I'm tempted to say yes, but I feel as if I can't take her disappointment, and so I say, no, of course not. The shadow lightens, she says, then I'd better make a move, otherwise I'll be late and I don't want to keep Noam waiting, and she stands up and says goodbye brightly to everyone and prances light-footedly from the room. Now I know that I can't carry on like this anymore, but nothing solid takes shape in my head, my thoughts are shaky and distracted, and at midnight I follow them outside like a lump of jelly, and when we sit down in Anton's Escort on the way to the fishermen he asks me, where's your head at? In bed, I'm dead tired, I answer, preparing the ground for an early departure. In the old hut the fishermen are waiting with vodka and *ikra*, they throw Ra'ed in the air, open a bottle of champagne and spray him with it, and break into a stiff-backed, stamping dance, a kind of *debka*, and Anton too allows himself to be dragged into the circle, abandoning himself to the herd. They look to me like an illuminated fortress, and I'm outside, in the dark, not knowing what to do with myself, unable to go home to an empty house, or to go and see Naomi with her lover in the pub either, that's an experience I have no desire to repeat. In the distance I can see the red lights of the whores' bar at the entrance to the harbor, and I decide to go and have something to drink there, they're used to depressed people. I part the bead curtains and enter a small room illuminated by a bright red light, two women are sitting at one of the tables conducting a weary conversation with a man and a very large woman who are sitting at the bar, his hand indifferently kneading the flesh exposed by her plunging neckline. May I have a brandy please, I ask politely, and one of the two women sitting at the table gets up from her chair and comes over to the bar, and at the same time the big woman sitting at the bar pushes the man's hand away and turns to me. Sit down, why are you standing, she says, and I say thank you, and sit down at the furthest table. There's something friendly about the place. Maybe you want something extra, the big woman says with a sexiness that's all used up and puts the brandy down on my table. No, really, thank you, I was here at a party with the fishermen and I just came in for a brandy, I'm leaving right away, I say apologetically, so they won't think I'm a snob. Whatever you like, honey, she says and smiles at me with closed lips which presumably hide poor dental work, and I begin to relax and I ask myself why this dark place gives me a feeling of being protected, as if it's okay that nothing's okay, and in the meantime the woman at the table who took my order sighs and gets up and says, I'm going, and her friend says, what are you cooking, and she says, *cholent*, it's the easiest, you think I've got the strength to fiddle around with stuffing vegetables? I leave an exaggerated tip and get up to go. Thanks honey, have a good life, the big woman says, and I go out into the night and discover that in spite of all the drink I've consumed tonight I haven't succeeded in getting drunk. At the kiosk on the corner I buy a bottle of beer and sip it as I walk along Independence Street, I want to stop a taxi but can't bring myself to raise my hand, there's something pleasant about walking in the dark in this dead street, I'll go up Ben Gurion and stop a taxi there, but I go on walking straight ahead, knowing that I'm going to land up at the Windy Inn in spite of myself, the beer has put the finishing touch to the disintegration of my will. Suddenly music breaks the silence, and I see a sign saying "The Windy Inn," and I know that I won't go in, even though now, standing hidden next to the entrance, I can see myself doing it, telling them in a polite, embarrassed tone that we have to talk, and after a few minutes, when I've grown accustomed to the place, I go inside, hiding behind the back of a tall man, and I see them at once, sitting at the bar with their backs to me. The tall man joins a group at one of the tables, leaving me exposed in the entrance, if they turn around now they'll see me getting in the way of the people going in and out who push me to the left and then the right of the door. Naomi twists her leg around his, they're absorbed in each other, there isn't a chance of them turning round and seeing me, and I walk out of the pub. My only hope now is the exhaustion which drops me into the first taxi that passes.

15

The next morning I wake shrouded in a feeling of dry despair. The alarm clock went off long ago, but I haven't got the strength to get out of bed. Naomi is sleeping by my side, I have no idea when she got home, I look at her but no meaning emerges from her face. I get up to make coffee and go to sit in the armchair, but nothing emerges out of the view through the window either. I feel completely limp, my jaw sags, soon I'll begin to drool, I tell myself sternly to stop it and try to work out what the worst thing about the whole situation is. Everything about it is terrible, but the worst thing is the possibility that Naomi will leave me, and not because of the insult, that's just an added extra: without Naomi I'm not me, she blocks the anxiety and the emptiness, anyone who doesn't have this cross to bear doesn't need Naomi either—and therefore I'll go on waiting with the patience of a tribal elder until the stormy wave breaks and turns into routine. I know what the euphoria of beginnings is like, when boredom doesn't even hint at its existence, but at some point the symmetry is spoilt and one of the sides begins to slow down, spurring the other on to excessive zeal, which soon becomes a nuisance and if it's Naomi who becomes the nuisance, she'll need me to pick up the pieces, and if she's the one who leaves him, she'll come back to me stable and grateful. In both scenarios I'm in a relatively good position, maybe things aren't as bad as they seem, and on my way to the *Technion* I add my satisfaction at having written the introduction to the wave of optimism which overwhelms me. When I read it over quickly this morning it looked like a solid, up-to-date piece of work, Davis will be pleased, and I decide that this evening I won't stop her from going out, on the contrary, I'll give her every chance to exhaust the possibilities of the affair as quickly as possible, I'll tell her that I have to work and that she should go out and enjoy herself, thus getting the credit for nobility and pushing the affair closer to its inevitable end at the same time. When I drive into the parking lot I remember my decision to start smoking again, a decision I have no intention of going back on, on the contrary, I think with pleasure of the cigarette awaiting me, on the way home I'll buy a packet of Marlboros, and in the evening, while Naomi is exhausting the possibilities of her love life, I'll sit in the armchair with brandy and a cigarette and the new Richard Strauss CD I haven't opened yet, and I won't give a damn, or so I'll tell myself, and thank God I won't have to tell anyone else, since my dialogue with my fellow men has recently come to a halt. I go into the library, exchange a few wisecracks with three students, take out a few books in order to prepare my course on close binary systems, go up to the office, go over a few test papers and give them higher grades than they deserve—let the young be happy, they're not the enemy at the moment. At lunch time I drop into the faculty office and spend a few minutes sucking up to Shoshi, the secretary who's too senior and too tired to do more than the minimum required to keep the whole structure from collapsing—for instance, the pests who call excitedly to announce that they've found a scientific proof of the existence of God she passes on automatically to me, in my role as the most polite and tactful professor in the department. I leave the book with her and ask her to give it to Givon, who's not teaching today—avoiding Givon takes a good couple of hours, at least—and meanwhile the day passes, and on my way out I bump into Davis, who tells me that Givon is driving him crazy about his appointment, and I pretend to be interested, and after we've exhausted the subject he asks with feeble mockery, how's your lovely little girl—I can imagine the way they make mince-meat of me in the department—and I say, fine, thank you, and take my leave. On the way home I buy a packet of Marlboros and decide to smoke three cigarettes a day, or six halves, as I choose, and make an inner bargain with myself: if I smoke more than my daily ration Naomi will leave me, Naomi will leave me, and at once the relative clarity I have won for myself disinte-grates, and the bitterness and anxiety return. I make a U-turn on a white line, and without giving myself an account of my actions I drive down to Wadi Salib. I have no plan, I'll let things take their course from one moment to the next, and I park at the bottom of the steps and get out of the car. Something fran-tic and uncontrollable has taken hold of me, I hurry up the steps, my head empty of decisions, except for the action of get-ting there, like a horse smelling the stable, and when I reach the red plastic curtain with the words Oded Safra written on it in black letters I realize that I've arrived. I stop, not because I have any doubts about going in, but only because of the embarrass-ing question of how to make my entry. There's nothing to knock on, shouting "hello" would make me feel a fool, walking in without knocking is out of the question, I'm not in a movie here, and I pull myself together and say, excuse me, but my voice is barely audible, and I wonder if he's there at all, and I say again, excuse me. This time I sound like a pizza delivery, and I hear his voice deep and clear saying, yes, and I ask if I can come in, and he says, come in, come in, who is it, and I move the plastic curtain and go inside, but since he apparently stood up and moved towards me at the same time, we bump into each other. At first he doesn't recognize me, he just grips my shoul-ders, he's about the same height as me, perhaps a little taller, and only after I lower my eyes he does a double take, wipes all expression from his face, and says, so it's you, she told you!— and I say, no, she didn't tell me, I found out myself, she doesn't know I'm here. Sit down, he says and I sit down. He asks if I want something to drink and I say, alcohol if you have any. I do, he says and goes to fetch it. The place is tidy, functionally furnished, a huge mattress, a lot of books, a few African carpets on the stone floor, two "Fireside" oil stoves burning, here and there a few more African souvenirs. I still have no idea why I came or what I'm going to say, nor am I emotionally free to decide, I am completely caught up in the moment, in the overpowering reality of his house. A cigarette, I remember in relief, and I take the packet out of my pocket, open it as naturally as if I never stopped smoking, take out a cigarette and light it. I feel a little dizzy, and wonder whether to smoke only half, so I'll still have another five halves left, or to smoke a whole one now and the other two at home according to plan. The first two puffs are wasted on these vacillations, and when he comes back with the arak and sits down opposite me I decide to smoke it to the end. He refuses the cigarette I offer him, and simply sits there, unembarrassed, looking me straight in the eye without any specific expression on his face, apart from one of pure attention, like Anton, and waits for me to begin, not concerning himself with the how until he knows the what. His self-confidence undermines me even further, not a single word comes out of my mouth, my eyes flee from his, and then he says, I'm listening, and I say apologetically, I just came, I wasn't completely in control of myself, and his lips twist into a half-smile. She'll leave me for him, he has an impressive presence, the prince of the ghost quarter, and in the meantime he waits patiently, my embarrassment doesn't break him, and I say again, so I just came, Naomi has no idea I'm here, and he asks, are you going to tell her? I don't know, I really don't know, I say, and I don't know what else to say either, so I keep quiet and wait in case he says something, and in fact he stands up and says, good, so if there's nothing urgent I think I'll go and hang up the washing, I have to take advantage of the last bit of sun, you can come with me if you like, and he picks up the tub of washing and walks out. I don't know what I'm supposed to do now so I accept his invitation and follow him outside, sit down on the stone bench and watch him take one item after the other and hang them up with efficient movements, and he says, I hope there's no more rain today, I can't get the damn washing dry in this weather, and I say, why don't you spread it out in front of the oil stoves? Because I can't stand putting my underpants on display all over the house, he says and goes on hanging up the washing, and suddenly I see the turquoise panties which he has fished out of the tub and is now holding in his hand and hanging on the line as if they are his own. There's no fetishism in his attitude to Naomi's panties, and I immediately envy him his ability to relate to objects as objects and not as the signs under whose weight I myself collapse. I envy the talent I have never possessed to experience reality in its natural flow instead of being preoccupied with myself experiencing it, admiring myself admiring a flower, as Baudelaire wrote. His long hair falls over his eyes and he pushes it out of the way with his big hand, incredible how much hair he's got on his head, like a broom, and after he's finished he says, let's go inside, and I follow him like a robot. He sits down on the armchair with the arak, full of magnificent disdain for the world and its ways, the essence of freedom, and in the silence I suddenly ask him, surprising myself with the question, which sounds as if it came straight out of a movie, do you love her? What's not to love, he replies, and silence falls again. The silence weighs heavily on me, and so I ask him, just for the sake of saying something, what he does for a living, and he tells me as naturally as if we've just met on a train journey, that he's a cinematographer of nature movies, he sometimes goes abroad for a few weeks, mainly to Africa and Australia, and shoots movies for the zoological departments of universities all over the world. He lives here because he lost his apartment in a bad business deal he got into out of stupidity, and this way he doesn't have to pay rent, the conditions don't bother him, the neighborhood is fine, and anyway, he has no alternative, he doesn't like debts, he has a father with Alzheimer's in a nursing home on the French Carmel, the place is called something ridiculous like "Golden Miracle," and he has to pay to keep him there—and that's it, no apologies, a straightforward, matter-of-fact report. Silence falls again, and this time he breaks it by asking what the book Naomi told him I'm writing is about. The thought that they talk about me soft-ens me and I say, I'm not exactly writing it, it's the book of a conference about a phenomenon called X-ray bursts that I'm editing. What phenomenon is that, he asks, and I wonder vaguely if he's asking because he's interested in the subject or because he's interested in anything to do with Naomi—once I met a high-school teacher of hers, a pest of a woman who seemed fascinating to me only because she had known Naomi—and he asks again, what exactly is the phenomenon? Are you really interested, I ask. Why else would I ask, he replies, and this time I recognize a definite note of mockery in his voice, if I thought that he was unconscious of the situation I was mistaken. Many stars live in pairs, I begin—because of my lectures to laymen I'm used to presenting scientific information by means of human analogies—after they're created they revolve around each other, but each of them has to pass through the stages of the evolution of a star, from birth to death, separately. The problem is they each have a different mass, and therefore there's no harmony between them. The mass determines the star's rate of evolution, the higher the mass the more rapid the evolution, but if they're too close to each other, the evolution of one will influence that of the other—I pause in order to light another cigarette, he goes on sitting at his ease, waiting for the lecture to continue, and I go on: Naturally, the one that evolves quickly also burns quickly, and when it explodes a very dense star core remains, what's called a neutron star. At the same time its partner burns itself up at a much slower rate, and when it runs out of fuel it begins to expand with the intention of dying quietly as a white dwarf. But when its outermost part reaches the range of influence of the neutron star it's trapped, and then a series of bursts begins to take place, and since the quiet star emits X-rays, the phenomenon is called an X-ray burst. The interesting thing is, I add, that little by little the neutron star, which is actually a dead star already, absorbs more and more of the material of the live star, until it oversteps the limits of what it can bear, it simply can't wake up to that extent, and it collapses onto itself and is destroyed, and at the same time it apparently destroys the live star too. I fall silent and look at him. If it's dead how can it be active, he asks and I reply, actually it's only relatively dead, you could say that it was living without energy, I can't understand what made me say anything so nonsensical, once more we both fall silent and I feel like an idiot. So how can I help you, he says with a half smile, and I say, I don't know, and with a sharpening of the mockery in his tone he asks, do you want me to promise not to see Naomi again? Would it do any good if I asked, I say, in spite of his mocking tone, and he replies, if you're ready to believe me I'm ready to promise. Why promise if I'm prepared to believe you anyway, I ask and he says, people like promises, it gives them a feeling of security—he says this slowly and with an enigmatic smile and I don't understand what he's getting at, his whole existence is a riddle to me, all I'm certain of is his control of the situation and my own inferiority. It's not so unreasonable for me to sit here opposite you and ask you to leave my wife alone, I say and feel like a scout master. Professor Ben Nathan, he says, drawing out the "professor," I suggest you pay the price of marrying a beautiful young girl and wait patiently for the affair to die, if it does die, in the meantime you'd better accept the situation, but if you want me to promise I have no problem with promising. Now he's smiling broadly, and I sit there exposed in all my inadequacy, which is beginning to arouse his sadistic instincts. I take out a third cigarette and play with it. More arak? he inquires and I say, why not, and when he goes to the kitchen I stand up and walk around in circles, he comes back with the arak and sits down, but I go on standing, smoking and drinking the arak, and then, with that smile plastered on his face, he puts his hand in his pocket and pulls out a pipe, and I immediately recognize my pipe, the one I looked for on the day I saw her turquoise panties through the telescope, the one with the words "with love" engraved on it, no name, just "with love"—a love now intended for him. In the meantime he takes a tobacco pouch out of his pocket, opens it, inserts his finger and thumb, rolls a bit of tobacco between them—I notice that his fingers are long and slender—and pushes the tobacco into the pipe. That was my pipe, I say, unable to control the childishness of my tone, she bought it for me when I stopped smoking. This pipe, he asks with a broad smile. Yes, precisely that pipe, I never used it, I say and a bitter anger begins to burn me up, not because of the lousy pipe but because of my helpless defeat in the face of the fortified wall opposite me, which nothing I can say or request will breach. Then I think we should both be proud of our clever little girl, now he's really beginning to enjoy himself, instead of throwing money away she recycled an unwanted gift, you should be pleased, it's your money after all, and he puts his hand in his pocket to rummage for his lighter. The anger blinds me and robs me of breath, everything swells in front of me, I try to control myself, I wasn't expecting empathy here after all, I have to pick up my heels and get out of here right away, simply turn around and walk away, but the heavy anger seeking an outlet fixes me to the floor, there's no way I'm going to leave without getting rid of this load, and with the remnants of logic left to me I tell myself that anger always subsides, if I can only drag myself out of here the situation will return to its proper proportions, but from the depths of my being a kind of buzzing vibration begins to rise and it has nothing to do with logic and it keeps me standing where I am. Have you got a light, I hear him ask, his voice sounds as if it's coming from somewhere else in the room. What, I say and try to silence the buzzing which is now like the concentrated whine of a blowtorch, and I hear him say, I asked if you had a light, and I put my hand in my pocket and take out my lighter, and at that moment the last rays of the sun break out of the clouds and illuminate the gloom like on the day I looked for the house through the telescope. The plastic curtain glows fiery red and needle-sharp rays of light penetrate the cracks in the boards on the windows and ignite his hair. He leans back slightly, now his eyes are shining, and sticks the pipe in his mouth, waiting for a light, I approach him with heavy steps, as if my body has doubled its weight, enter the field of light, and bend over him. He wants to take the lighter from me but I light it myself, very close to him, I can smell the shampoo on his hair, I'm so close that my eyes squint and I see him blurred and double, two overlapping men are sitting opposite me with a twisted smile, and I am launched into another existence, the light blinds me, for a second I meet his surprised eyes, and suddenly, before he has time to raise himself from his relaxed pose, my right hand, which lit his tobacco for him, pushes the pipe hard and forces it deep into his mouth. The suddenness of my movement causes the stem of the pipe to penetrate the windpipe instead of the gullet, strangled noises come from his mouth, but I go on pushing until the thick mouthpiece shuts him up, and then I take his hands, which are gripping mine with violent force, and press them to the arms of the chair. The fire in his throat drains his body of strength, his neck strains for air, his throat swells, his eyes open wide in monstrous fear, and his body convulses. Threads of blood film his eyes, he begins to turn blue, and I go on pressing his hands to the arms of the chair, until I feel them gradually giving up the struggle and I let go, mainly in order to block his mouth and nostrils, but it isn't over yet because his hands rise again, in a kind of spasm, but then they immediately fall to his sides, and his whole body seems to drop, the irises disappear from his eyes, leaving only a white field behind them. I lie on top of him, empty of sensation, my hands still gagging his mouth and nose, a warm liquid trickles from his mouth onto my hand, but still I don't let go, or breathe or move, my hand is burning, and at last I get up and stand stiffly in front of his limp, silent body. Suddenly the air imprisoned in his lungs is released in a kind of deep sigh, the pipe falls out of his mouth, and I fling it in horror to the floor and collapse.

16

I may have fainted, because I wake up suddenly with no idea of how much time has passed. But I know immediately that the man sprawling on the armchair and looking as if he's asleep is dead, and that I killed him. I try to scream, more the idea of a scream, since I certainly don't intend actually to scream out loud, but my mouth is dead. I didn't kill him, I murdered him, that's precisely what happened here—at this moment I am granted the privilege of seeing reality crystal clear, not of controlling it, that's out of the question, but I see it clear, and I look at it and feel as if I'm in another dimension containing things that can't be contained in normal life. As if my body has a secret safe containing reserves of strength that opens like a reserve parachute, which is apparently what picks me up now, and I sway for a moment but immediately steady myself. My eyes unintentionally meet his, which are sharply focused, as if his whole dead being is staring at me, and in one crowded moment I narrow down the possibilities available to me: he's dead, that's the situation and no remorse will change it, no one knows that I know him and no one knows that I'm here, I'll get rid of the body and if there's no body there's no crime either. All I have to do is act like an ant, which has no sorrow and no pity and no doubts, but only a lot of hard work to do. I'll have to wait till dark, which is rapidly approaching. It's already dusk, I'll have to hurry to take care of everything in the last of the light still penetrating the room, but first I have to clean myself up. I go into the bathroom and wash my hands obsessively, digging my nails into the soap. As a matter of habit I look into the mirror and suddenly there are two of us, me and the face opposite me, which I know is mine in spite of its strangeness, and I dry my hands on the toilet paper lying on the floor next to the lavatory and lead myself into the kitchen, where I wash the arak glasses and another two cups of coffee in the sink. I dry them on the toilet paper I brought with me from the bathroom, in the meantime the plan takes shape in my head, and once I've made sure that there's nothing else to wash I put on my gloves and get to work, coldly, efficiently, suppressing any emotional distraction. I insert a sheet of paper into the baby Hermes standing on the desk, take it over to the body, pick up his finger and begin to type: Darling, I got an urgent call to go to New Zealand, I don't know when I'll be back, yours. Then I return the typewriter to the desk, make sure that the paper's sticking up, take the big army blanket folded on the bed, spread it out close to the body until it's touching his shoes, and pull his legs. He's heavy, his head bangs on the floor, I lie him down on the blanket and drag him to one side so I can begin to roll, I close his open eyes, now he looks as if he's resting, he's still warm and soft, and I roll him up in the blanket. I don't have the time to look for a rope so I tie him up with three dark shirts I take out of the closet, and as I tighten the knots I tell myself that I have to leave the place looking as if he's gone for an unknown period of time. I cram all his personal effects, of which there aren't many, only the bare minimum, into a rucksack I find in the closet. The light is fading quickly, I remember the turquoise panties on the line and run outside to fetch them and cram them too into the rucksack, I put out the oil stoves, fold the bedclothes, throw out the cigarette stubs, and I still don't know where I'm going to bury him. I sit and wait for darkness to fall, and in this state of inactivity I remember the first thing that always comes into my mind, Naomi, I have to let her know that I'll be late. I come back to life at once, and in the few minutes before it gets dark I hurry to the nearest public phone and when I hear her voice I put on my most well-worn mask and say, Hi Naomileh, but before I can go on she interrupts me. Where are you? In the library, I say, I forgot myself in the work on the book. When will you be back, she asks. Late at night, I say, I have to entertain guests from Scandinavia. How late? Very late, I may have to drive them to Jerusalem. It's going to pour, she says, drive carefully, and I say, don't worry, and she says that she is worried—she's worried about me, I've just murdered her lover and she's worried about me. The thought of her worry chokes me, and I say goodbye quickly and hang up. The weather's changing fast, the light's disappeared, heavy clouds are hanging over the sea, there's no doubt about it, it's going to pour, which isn't going to make my job any easier. I go back to the house, and when I sit down to wait for it to get dark I begin to think about where to bury him. I'll have to find an abandoned field, there's one in the place where the swamp with the island used to be, not far from the house of the Greek gangsters who were shunned by everybody except my mother, who liked them and didn't take any notice of the rumors, today it's a neglected stretch of land which can be reached by car. Suddenly a suppressed memory surfaces: I was about eight, and the symptoms from which I had begun to suffer after my father's sudden death, like shortness of breath and eczema, had undermined my status with my peers, until one frosty day I jumped into the swamp and swam among the tadpoles to the island, but this act, which seemed to me both daring and amusing, gave rise to cruel laughter among the girls who found the whole thing revolting, and therefore I refused to come out of the water, where I remained floating like a dead fish until the eldest son of the Greeks, who ran errands for my mother, fished me out and dragged me crying home. I get up and go outside to check the darkness, and I stand there for a long time with my head empty. There's no light in the immediate vicinity, the clouds have swallowed the stars, the heavy rain hasn't begun yet, only big drops announce its coming, and suddenly, in the middle of the oppressive silence, I hear a muffled noise which gradually becomes recognizable as the chugging of Naomi's Beetle. From where I'm standing I can see the paths of light the headlights cut through the darkness, my blood freezes, but I immediately recover—this is the way it's going to be from now on, every minute I'll have to reorient myself and hope that habit will help me to behave naturally in the danger zones, like a secret agent or an ordinary criminal with eyes in the back of his head—and I hurry inside and drag him to the triangular space behind the closet standing in the corner at an angle between the two walls. It isn't easy, first I have to move the closet, which turns out to be heavy, and then I have to squeeze both of us into the space, me standing and him folded over with his head on my legs, and when we're more or less in place, I pull the closet back behind us, leaving a narrow crack to see through. After a minute, the plastic curtain moves, the beam of a flashlight jumps in and Naomi enters and says questioningly, Oded, and then again, in a disappointed voice, Oded? She stands there for a minute, her silhouette sharply drawn behind the flashlight, turns the beam onto the bed, from there to the kitchen, and apparently she begins to take something in, presumably the emptiness and the tidiness, and she begins to walk round the room, prying into corners with the flashlight. She comes close to the closet, I can smell her special soap, which last year was the reason for three days in Paris, and I stifle a theoretical urge to fall at her feet and weep brokenly. She opens the empty closet and I can sense her tension, her bewilderment and apprehension, I understand her so well, for two years she's been the only project I've invested in, and suddenly she shines the flashlight straight into the crack, giving me such a fright that I jerk my head and bang it on the back of the closet with a small but audible thud. We both freeze, and she says, Oded, not sure of where the sound came from, I stop breathing and she moves away and comes back again with a chair which she stands next to the closet. She climbs onto it and shines the flashlight, the beam sweeps over my head, luckily for me, or not, the chair's too low and she gives up and climbs down and moves away. I manage to slow my heart down and peep through the crack. She moves round the room, the beam of light dances about in front of her and stops on the typewriter, she goes up to it, pulls out the letter and reads it, I can't see her expression, I can only sense it—surprise and disappointment and insult and anger, which in the course of time will be joined by longing and sorrow. She crumples up the letter, which falls to the ground, stands still for a moment with her head bowed, and then goes up to the armchair and drops into it. The flashlight on her lap shines onto her face, which seems to be looking straight at me, she takes out a cigarette and smokes it without moving and without thinking until it burns her fingers and a childish cry of pain breaks the silence. Suddenly she gets up and walks out, leaving me alone with her dead lover.

17

I go on standing behind the closet with him curled round my feet in a fetal position for several minutes more, and then I give the closet a shove and emerge from my hiding place. The horror, which is yet to reveal its deeper layers, is still not completely real. I feel an icy numbness crawling inside my face, and I fall into the armchair in a kind of floating detachment, as if I don't belong to myself and am therefore not responsible for myself either, everything seems unreal, all that exists is an almost imperceptible flow of disjointed fragments—until a flash of lightning illuminates the house for a second in a cold light, followed by a clap of thunder, and reality returns to bark at me. I have to hang onto it, I have to mobilize all the alertness I can dredge up from the bottom of my doubtful existence, and I go outside to make sure that the alley is deserted, and after I take the knapsack with his belongings down to the car I come back for him. I harden myself and approach him, determined to be practical. I have to find the right way to carry him to the car. I dismiss the thought of dragging him by his feet immediately, I won't be able to stand hearing his head bump on every step, I'll have to carry him like a wounded soldier. I practiced this for three years in the army, but now I'm pushing fifty, and I decide to put him on the low stone wall outside. I drag him there, pull his legs onto the wall and hoist the rest of him into the air, and then I push my head under his stomach, heave him onto my shoulders like a weight-lifter, and begin to descend the steps. The temptation to throw him down and run away increases with every step, I can't go on, he's too heavy, I feel sick, the parcel begins to come undone, his right hand pokes out and dangles in front of my eyes, I thrust it away with my head and push on, squeezing the last drop out of my emergency reserves. Another twenty steps to go, I negotiate them like a machine, without feelings or wishes, step after step, praying nobody walks past, the blanket is peeling off him, a flash of lightning illuminates the sky again followed by a roll of thunder, and the rain begins pouring down. The blanket comes off together with the three shirts I used to tie it up, and he gapes out. Now the blanket is half draped round me, half trailing on the steps, and there is nothing to mediate my contact with him, I can feel his cold head on my neck, his long hair whips my face, my shoulders are full of a dull, heavy pain and I have no strength left. I go on descending, five steps, four, three, the end of the blanket is tangled in my feet, I can't go on any more, and at the bottom of the steps we both collapse into a puddle, for a moment the relief is stronger than the disgust and we lie twined together in the water, my head rests on him and I abandon myself to the physical relief. But then I tell myself to stop sinking, I have to get up this minute and go to the car, reverse it to the puddle and put him in the trunk, only I can't manage to stand up, so I crawl on my hands and knees to the car. The rain's coming down harder all the time, and when I start the car I see someone approaching from the opposite direction with a kind of dancing step, which turns out to be a drunken reel. He walks past the puddle, stops, lurches back, bends over the dead body, shakes it, and begins searching through the pockets, who knows what papers he may find there, but I realize immediately that all he wants is money, other people's troubles are the last thing on his mind, and he pockets whatever cash he can find and disappears into the alley leading to El Pasha. The little rest has given me a chance to recharge my batteries, and I go back into action, fixing all my thoughts on it, I reverse to the puddle,

open the trunk, and in an act of supreme concentration I succeed in lifting the water-logged body and heaving its upper half
into the back of the car, after which I pick up the dangling legs
and fold them on top of it in a position which no living body
could endure. His head is now facing me, imprisoned between
his legs like a contortionist in a circus, the jolts have opened his
eyes and he looks at me with the eyes of a dead shark. I cover
him with the wet blanket, and quickly shut the trunk, unable to
bear the sight a moment longer, but it won't close because of his
posture, the legs pop out, I push them back in and with all my
strength I slam the trunk; it closes with a sickening crunch. I
don't want to think about what's going on inside there, and
before I get into the car I look up into the unknown and indifferent space from whose investigation I, ironically enough, earn
my living.

18

The rain keeps pouring down on the dead roads and I drive to the abandoned field, but as soon as I am near Beth-Dagon, beginning to plan the burial, I realize that I haven't got a spade. How am I supposed to dig, why didn't I think of it before, what else didn't I think of, and suddenly I feel tired and lost and not cut out for jobs like this, as if anyone's cut out for getting rid of corpses. All I want now is to give up and go to Anton, I'll deliver this package to him, I'll simply say to him that this is the situation, this is what happened, all I want is for him to let me have a hot bath and take me in, because I don't really believe I'll get out of this, and I approach the green light and say to myself that if I make it in time I'll drive to Anton, and if it turns red I won't, and I make the green light in time but I don't drive to Anton, and I didn't really mean to anyway, I don't intend turning myself in, I'll punish myself on my own, like an autodidact, from now on I'll be an autonomous entity, and I wake up and begin racking my brains in search of a place to bury a corpse that doesn't need a spade, I tour the environs of Haifa in my mind and remember Nahal Siah, there are ancient burial caves there, I'll put him in one of the caves and cover him with stones. One Saturday Naomi and I went for a walk there, I showed her the ruined Carmelite monastery and the orchard in the wadi, with the fruit trees, and the oleanders, the springs, it was one of our good days, and I drive south, and at the Carmel Beach gas station I turn left and climb the rutted dirt road, pass through an inner courtyard between two dark

Arab houses on what might be either a private or a public road, leaving it behind me I see a very tall, thin little girl leaning against a chalky rock and looking like a long lizard. In her hand she's holding an umbrella, my headlights shine for a moment on her tortured face, I don't understand why she's sitting there, and I go on climbing, turn and twist with the dirt road until the end, stop and get out of the car with a flashlight, looking for the right cave, it's hard to see anything in this darkness, I grope among the stones, on the right I find the only wall of the ruined monastery still standing, in the middle of the wall is a little half-open door, it's impossible to move it because of the pile of stones blocking the entrance, the wall has apparently collapsed inwards. If I succeed in getting him through the door I can cover him with the stones and there's no chance he'll be found, nobody could have any reason for going through this door except to get rid of a corpse, but the thought of dragging him all the way here defeats me anew, the rain has stopped in the meantime, a heavy, ominous silence hangs over me, I'll have to drag him for about twenty meters, and as I go back to the car I see in the distance a silhouette moving towards me. It's the long skinny girl, she's gliding over the path, she's coming close to me with the umbrella in her hand, that's all I need now. She stops next to me, fixes me with big, slightly slanting eyes, her look is expressionless, I say hello just to dilute the silence a bit, but she seems to be mute because broken sounds break out of her mouth like little animal cries, I won't be able to bury him here now, she brings her face up close to me and bares big teeth, maybe she wants to bite me, nothing frightens me any more and I smile at her with a kind of grimace. My smile alarms her, her eyes are glassy and pitiful, and she begins moving away without turning around, walking backwards with her face to me, look-ing at me all the time with that mystery which is sometimes found in human defectiveness. She recedes into the distance but there's no way of telling if she's going to fetch help, and so

I get back into the car, it's very hard to turn around, there's no space to maneuver, the wadi gapes below me and I feel a faint temptation to slide down into it just as I am, together with my dead, but instead I drive forwards and backwards carefully and attentively. Why should I try so hard to save myself, my mother decided to leave my father after she saw him rushing to the shelter during the Sinai Campaign, why are you so frightened for yourself, you've lived enough, she said to him, she herself didn't go down to the shelter in any of the wars—in the Gulf War she didn't put on a gas mask either because then she wouldn't have been able to smoke—and now, here, in this darkness, I want to save myself like my father, and I begin driving back, the tall girl has disappeared, and once more I pass through the inner courtyard between the two houses, and suddenly she jumps out between the wheels, I brake with a screech and get out of the car, it's not possible that I'm going to be landed with another corpse, but she straightens up to her full height and smiles at me with her big teeth. Her craziness freezes my blood and brings me back to my own horror, the nausea rises in my throat, I escape from her eyes and hurry back to the car, but she runs after me, grabs my collar, her huge hands clutch me, I try to free myself but she's all over me, and then a light goes on in one of the houses and a broad Arab woman comes running out and pulls her off me. She's not right, not right, she says, tapping her finger on her forehead in illustration, and the girl surrenders immediately and fawns on her mother, sending me a last haunted, defeated look, and I drive away. Once again I'm on the road, not a single idea occurs to me, surely in all of Haifa there must be somewhere to get rid of a corpse—the word already slips quite naturally into my head—it's incredible how quickly the human animal gets used to the troubles he brings on himself—at the Carmel Beach traffic lights I look at my watch, sure that it's already very late, but it's only ten o'clock, the lights change but there's no one behind me and I go on sitting there, trying to exert my dying brain cells and think of a place, and it comes to me in flash, the municipal rubbish tip, you don't need a spade there, you can dig with your hands in the fresh garbage and bury him beneath it, the smell will be submerged in the general stench, and in the heat of the decision I drive into the intersection on a red light. I don't know where the municipal rubbish tip is exactly, only that it's somewhere on the road to the satellite towns to the north of the city, I'll have to ask someone, and I immediately feel pressured and embarrassed at the thought of asking such a question at an hour like this on a night like this, and again I want to give up already but I go on driving in the general direction, at the check post I turn left in the direction of the satellite towns, and at the shwarma stand on the corner I stop, open the window and shout to the vendor in a firm and complex-free tone, excuse me, where's the tip here, and he directs me in an indifferent voice, without any curiosity, straight ahead, left, left, and right, you'll see a sign, and I ask him to repeat the directions so I won't have to ask someone else, and he repeats the same words in the same indifferent tone, his eyes stray wearily through me and past me, all he wants to do is sleep, and I leave him and begin to drive, concentrating on his directions, and after a few minutes I reach a sign, but it says, "To the shipyard." That's what he heard, "ship," this night's going to go on forever, the place is completely deserted, not a living soul, I'll have to go back to the Kiryat Ata junction and ask there at one of the fast-food joints, and again the impossible question, excuse me, sir, where's the rubbish tip here, this time clear and in full, so there'll be no room for mistakes, and the *bureka* vendor gives me a queer look, the rubbish tip, he repeats, what do you want in the rubbish tip at this hour of night? I need something there, I say in a practical tone of voice, but he keeps on at me, what do you need there at an hour like this? I arranged to meet someone there, I say. You arranged to meet someone at the rubbish tip,

haven't you got anywhere else to meet? Now his tone is posi-
tively reproachful, this whole thing with me and the rubbish tip
annoys him, and one of the customers, with a hard-boiled egg
stuffed in his mouth, asks, what, what does he want? He's looking for the rubbish tip, the vendor says in an aggrieved tone.
The rubbish tip, the customer repeats, at this hour of night, he
seems put out too, and I drive away without knowing where the
cursed rubbish tip is, there's a soldier in air-force uniform
standing at the bus station, I stop next to him and ask him
where the rubbish tip is, I've said it so often it comes out easily
now, and he doesn't seem surprised by the question, mainly
because he's not interested, he's too preoccupied by his own
problems, his face is big and tortured, he asks me in a trembling
voice to take him to his base not far from the rubbish tip, I tell
him it's impossible, but he opens the door and squeezes in.
Drive, drive, he says, please drive, and I begin to drive, I ran
away from the base, he tells me, I went to my girlfriend and
found her in bed with my brother-in-law, and here he breaks
down and starts crying and talking feverishly, I can't stop the
stream of words rushing out of his mouth, where to, I ask, and
he shows me with his hands and keeps on talking and crying
and gasping and telling me how he bought her flowers and
scent and pantyhose, and how he went inside with all the presents, and found his brother-in-law in her bed, and now they
were going to throw him in prison for running away from the
base too, it was for her he ran away, and she's fucking his brother-in-law. He sits next to me and wails, I'm going crazy, and I
don't know what I'm going to do with him, and when we reach
the base he shuts up abruptly and gets out of the car, where's
the rubbish tip, I implore him, but he's lost me already, like a
sick hippopotamus he lurches to the gate, and I'm alone again,
and there's no rubbish tip or anything else, except for the
corpse in the boot which I'm already beginning to get used to,
and I go on driving, cross the Kishon river, and suddenly before

my eyes looms a sign, "To the municipal rubbish tip," how easy it sometimes is to be happy, in less than a minute I reach the gate, a long iron pole bars my entrance, they've locked the god-damn rubbish tip, what do they want to go and lock a rubbish tip for, and I get out of the car, beyond despair and acting by force of inertia, the gate opens with a push, I drive in, the stench of vestiges of life rotting in the rain assails me, I drive up the path, I'll bury him under this mountain of garbage and he'll rot with it to the end of time, and I go on driving intently, look-ing for the fresh rubbish that's easy to dig into, but it's hard to see in the dark and so I stop the car, put the headlights on high, and approach the foot of the mound of garbage. In the yellow light the rubbish looks like an art students' exhibition, and I look for my gloves in the pocket of my coat but remember that I threw them into the rucksack and I decide to go ahead with-out them and begin digging with my bare hands, the garbage is fresh and wet, cottage cheese, vegetable peels, eggs, tin cans, and I go on digging in plastic bags and papers and clothes and unidentified objects, throwing in the lighter, which up to now had been burning a hole in my pocket, and when the grave is almost ready, and the first chapter of the nightmare seems to be almost over, I hear voices, unintelligible murmurs, and in the distance I see the pale lights of dancing flashlights. I freeze, someone's playing games with me, it's all up with me, I've been followed, the soldier sent the army after me, I'm afraid to turn round and I stand there for a minute without moving, let them take me and let's get it over with, but it's not the army, only two men and a woman rummaging in the garbage. For a moment it seems to me that they've all come to this graveyard in disguise to bury their dead, but they only nod their heads at me, my presence there seems to them natural, I don't understand what's going on here. Shalom, one of the men says to me in a Russian accent, he smiles at me and his gold teeth glitter in the pale light of the flashlight, the other two take no notice of me, they go on poking in the garbage with long sticks, they have work gloves on their hands, they're not burying any corpses here, what's happening to my head, they're looking for loot, poor immigrants pouncing on the leftovers dropping from the Carmel. With a shriek of glee the woman finds a satchel, examines it with the flashlight and throws it onto the pile of loot, now she turns to look at me, with a hostile expression, for her I'm a rival trespassing on her territory, and I stand there confused, this grave too has apparently gone down the drain. There is no good, says the man with the gold teeth, there is no good, here is good, and the woman turns to him and says something I don't understand to him in Russian, definitely not in my favor, her tone is angry and bitter, and I say, it's all right, I have to go, but there's no need to apologize because they're not interested in me, and I begin walking to the car. Pardon mister, one of them calls after me, and I turn to face them. Perhaps possible you take us out, he says, and I understand that these people are going to dump themselves in my car, I'm sorry, I say, I'm in a hurry. Please mister, he says in an aggressively pleading voice, like the soldier from the air force, the night people in this region are definitely desperate, no doubt about it. I can't find the words to refuse and so I say OK, and they quickly load their loot into the big plastic bags they brought with them, the woman sends me a look charged with trampled pride, I recognize the category, they fill two bags, each of the men takes one, the woman lingers a moment longer, vacillating over a frying pan, the owner of the gold teeth urges her to hurry up, he's thinking of me, and the three of them approach the Volvo, the third man limps but seems strong and muscular, he carries the full bag on his broad back, and then, to my horror, I see him going up to the boot with the intention of opening it and stowing the bags in it. I can't breathe, terror plants my feet in the ground, his hands are already on the lock, a strangled animal sound escapes my lips, an unintelligible cry, which appears to alarm him, because he lets go of the lock at once, as if it's just given him an electric shock, and looks at me fearfully. Sorry, I say in a normal voice, not there, it's full, the owner of the gold teeth translates for his friends, it seems logical to them and they turn away from the boot, I open the car, the woman sits next to me and the two men in the back. They sit and hug their garbage, I switch on the ignition and begin to drive, the stink embarrasses me, how much can it all be worth, the woman shows me the way out, she hardly looks at me but she's very aware of my presence, there's something tough and impressive about her, she must be about thirty, we drive out of the gate and they point to the caravans not far from there. Please you come to us, drink some little vodka, says the man with the gold teeth, no thank you, I say in alarm, the woman gives me a penetrating look as if she can see something in my face, I begin to sweat, she doesn't take her eyes off me, without meaning to I turn to look at her, our eyes meet for a second of embarrassing intimacy, I try to calm myself, she can't possibly know anything, but she doesn't take my presence at the rubbish tip in the middle of the night for granted, like her companions, and I stop next to the caravans and they get out and thank me in a babble of Hebrew and Russian words and disappear with their precious garbage, and I stand there for a minute, knowing that the woman will turn around, and she does turn around, in the darkness I can't see her look, I can only feel it, and I drive away, and again I have the sense of existing in another dimension, parallel to the usual one, as if I have been sucked into an orbit of a different order of reality, all the elements are familiar but contained in a new awareness, while I am living a kind of hallucination, and again I find myself next to the *bureka* stand at the Kiryat Ata junction. I have to think logically of the right place to bury him, I can't go on like this all night long, and a dark wave of loneliness engulfs me and draws me towards my mother—my mother, that's what I'll do, I'll go to my mother, I'll dump this load on her, I'm too exhausted to cope with it alone. The decision gives me a bit of strength and I drive towards the German Colony, I'll wake her up and dump it all on her, give her the bottom line, like she did to me throughout my childhood, the news that she was divorcing my father she threw at me on my eighth birthday—not that she remembered it was my birthday, it was just a coincidence—she woke me up, and before I knew where I was she told me in a dry, matter-of-fact tone, you father and I are getting a divorce, and I burst into frightened tears, and she said, there's no point in crying, but the crying turned into a howling that brought my father running to the room, and then, when she told him in more or less the same tone, Avigdor, we're getting a divorce, and his face changed color, I understood that he didn't know anything either. What are you saying to me, he mumbled, that we're getting a divorce and that's final, she replied in a scalding tone, and he went down on his knees in front of her, I lay in bed wailing, and while he knelt in the middle of the room she explained to him in a matter-of-fact tone that she had never loved him, and since there was no second life, and he was still healthy, there was no reason why she should go on submitting to the nuisance of cooking and washing and putting up with his petty preoccupation with details, and he, who had loved her all these years with the dumb loyalty of a dog, and therefore had never demanded any reciprocity, couldn't take it in and clung to her skirt, and she said, your crying won't help you, and neither will the boy's, we're getting a divorce, but owing to bureaucratic difficulties she didn't take the trouble to get divorced from him officially, and therefore he never succeeded in understanding that relations between them were actually over. She rented an apartment for him, but he continued coming almost every day, sitting in the kitchen and looking at her with leaking eyes which were in such sharp contrast to his solid appearance and sunburned face, and when at a certain stage she asked him to cut down on his visits, he disappeared for a few days, but returned with the excuse that he had someone suitable for her to meet. We would sit in the kitchen and eat her usual carrot quiche—without thinking he would also eat the greaseproof paper underneath it—and I didn't really exist as far as he was concerned, but I accepted this as self-evident, it was from him apparently that I learnt to treat children as theoretical creatures. I hardly even intervened in their conversations, mainly because whenever I spoke he would look right through me and wait for the interference to pass, and I would sit and chew the revolting quiche and listen to him praising someone he had met and who he was sure she would like, once it was an engineer and once a farmer and once a theater director, all excellent fellows to whom he was prepared to introduce her. I haven't got a real picture in my head, the memories were confused long ago with her stories about him, which she began to tell me intensively after he fell down and died one day of cardiac arrest, just when she was telling him that it was enough already, she wanted him to leave her alone, what did a man have in the end but his self-respect, and how could he humble himself like that in front of her? Ever since Naomi appeared in my life I've thought a lot about his exaggerated love, I'm thinking about myself of course, about those loves that burst the heart, because of a love like that I'm sitting here now with a corpse in the boot of the car, and when I drive down Independence Road it occurs to me that I could bury him under the oak tree in her yard, yes, that's what I'll do, I'll bury him there. This solution relaxes the tension in my shoulders a little, and it begins to drizzle again, and I turn into Ben-Gurion Boulevard, and from there into the winding little street that leads to her house. I park in the empty parking space and ring the door bell, a light goes on, a voice says, who's there, I say, it's me, open the door, and she opens it and looks at me in shock with her sunken eyes, I forgot that I'm stinking of garbage. *Mein Gott*, what happened to you? she says in a voice husky with cigarettes, where have you been, and so we stand in the doorway facing each other, and I know immediately that I won't find any consolation here, but it's not consolation I'm looking for, I have work to do, and at least I'm not alone. You're ill, she says immediately and moves out of the doorway, and I go in after her, her look follows me, I'm not ill, I'll tell you in a minute, bring me some alcohol, and she brings out her lousy brandy, I drink a few gulps straight from the bottle and my distress pervades the room in all its suffocating heaviness, and therefore she doesn't say, take a glass, but only sits down and waits, the brandy makes me giddy, and I sit down opposite her and begin to tell her about the lover, and when I reach the bit about the visit to Wadi Salib an expression of horror crosses her face, but I go on and bring the story to its climax, I speak in a monotone, only the outlines, giddy but sober, and all the time I make an effort to keep my eyes on her face. Help me, I whisper in ostentatious helplessness, she has to take pity on me now, I need her pity, and it's not easy to get it, all her life she's detested sentimentality, she even regards the expression of feelings as sentimentality, arguing that people prefer to embrace this hollow and portentous pathos simply because they lack the courage to face up to the really difficult gray area where things happen as they happen. We never celebrated birthdays, presents she regarded as obsequious and wasteful gestures, even the ritual of kissing seemed to her embarrassing and superfluous, and it's hard to say that I missed it, when something doesn't exist you don't feel the need for it, and still she's silent, and I don't know how much time passes. I'm in her hands, let her turn me in if she likes, I'm exhausted, as far as I'm concerned we can go on sitting here forever, but she stands up and comes over to me, in her eyes is an unfamiliar and gentle expression, she puts out her hand and pushes my wet, sticky hair out of my eyes, her tender gesture floods me with self pity, and I begin to sob without restraint or dignity, the whole impossible night drains into these tears which well from the depths of my being, there's no past and no future and only this moment between me and her, and I let myself go and the helplessness fells me to the floor at her feet, and she bends down and embraces my stink-ing head, and I nestle up to her as I've never done in my life, her body is strange to me, and time passes and I calm down, I feel very cold now, and she pulls me to my feet with her meager strength—I don't remember her ever being so thin—and all of a sudden her face clouds over and she returns to herself. Enough of this, Ilan, she says, stand on your feet, we have work to do, she rebukes, as if she asked me to wash the dishes and I'm too lazy to do it, and we go out into the garden, the street is dark and deserted, and she brings me a spade and a flashlight, and I begin to dig under the oak tree, but I didn't take into account the height of the rock and the shallowness of the soil. It's impossible to dig there, try somewhere else, she says, and I begin poking in the soil all over the garden and the feeling of helplessness overwhelms me again, all night long I've been try-ing to bury someone without success, even at home I can't do it, and my mother stands over me and says, get up, Ilan, get up, and again I attack the soil, but it's hard and impenetrable, and I go to the southern corner with the remnants of the roses and try there too, but nowhere is the soil deep enough, and sud-denly the light goes in the house next door, and our gentle neighbor sticks his head out and asks if anything's wrong and if he can help. His warm heart is unsuspicious, people are digging up their gardens in the middle of the night and all he wants is to help, it would have been a different story with his late wife, and my mother says, it's all right, Yosef, we're just looking for something here, I'm sorry if we woke you, and he insists on helping anyway, but her commanding tone keeps him at bay, and again I want to cry but I don't dare, and I lean on the spade and say in a matter-of-fact tone, it's useless, I've been trying to bury him the whole night without success, maybe it's a sign that

I should give up, and I want to give up too, after all, I don't really believe that I can live with it even if I'm not caught. The
thought of getting it all over and done with galvanizes me for a
moment, and I tell her that I'm going to call Anton and even
start walking in the direction of the house, but her skinny hand
stops me with a strength I would never have believed she possessed. You're not going anywhere, don't be an idiot, you're not
going to rot in jail for the rest of your life, you made a mistake
and you'll pay for in your own way, she's speaking in a whisper
but every word is sharp and clear, and I stop in my tracks. So
what do you want me to do? I ask, yielding myself completely,
and she says, I can tell you what Anton's mother would do if
Anton brought her a corpse, Anton's mother would eat it,
because that would be the only way she could be sure that it
would never be found, that's what Anton's mother would do for
him. Stop it, I shriek, and she says, calm down, I'm not going to
do it, I'm only telling you what Anton's mother would do,
because it's the most final solution, and I say to her, do me a
favor, I feel bad enough already, and she says, let's go inside and
think quietly, but I can't produce a single thought, all I can do
is wait for her to come up with something, and after walking
around for a bit she says, I have an idea. What idea, I ask, a
good idea, she says, I'm going to get dressed and don't sit on the
armchair with all that dirt, it's enough that you've already dirt-
ied the carpet, and she disappears into her bedroom, leaving me
alone in the living room, and once again conflicting thoughts
begin to battle in my mind, my head is bursting, I have to empty
it and I fix my eyes on the bar of the electric heater, unblinking,
riveted by the red bar, but the light takes me back to the
"Fireside" oil stove, and from there to his face and his yellow
hair, and the surprise in his eyes when I approached him with
the lighter. What's the time, I shout to distract myself, I'm coming, she shouts back, there are meatballs in the fridge, Anton's
mother brought them yesterday—she really thinks I'm capable

of putting anything in my mouth now, and I only take another sip of brandy, which seeps enjoyably though my body, and after a couple of minutes she appears in a purple track suit which is a few sizes too big for her, and a child's red woolly hat, and clumsy running shoes. Where are we going? I ask her, let's go, she says, I'll explain to you on the way, I have an excellent plan, and I stop asking, and from the cupboard in the hall she takes out a folded luggage trolley, maybe we're going abroad, and I take the trolley without asking any questions and without caring either, and she locks the door and when we go to the car she says, show him to me. Who, I ask, the corpse, she says, I want to see the size, and I open the boot and look up so as not to see, and she pushes her head in and looks as if I've brought her produce from the market. He's big, she says, go and get the spade from the shed. What for, I ask, and she loses patience, just go and get it, she says, and I go and get it, and put it next to his head and close the lid, she's already waiting for me inside the car with a closed face, not a hint of the previous loving kindness remains, judging from her present expression it's hard to believe that it ever existed. Where to, I ask as if I'm only the driver here, to the Sde Yehoshua cemetery, she says, that's next to Nahal Siah, I say, I've already been there tonight. So what if you have, just do what I tell you, she says and withdraws into herself, giving off the sense of alienation that used to frighten me as a child. There were periods when she was silent for whole days at a time, at night I would lie in my bed in the silence and wait for her to sneeze or clear her throat, and the memory revives the fear, but I'm not about to return to my infantile fear of my mother at the age of forty-eight, and as I drive south again to the Carmel Beach intersection I begin counting backwards from a hundred to one, and thus I succeed in reaching the area of the cemetery without any thoughts in my head. She signals me with her hand to turn left, in the direction of the south bank of the Siah riverbed, and we pass a sign saying, "To the Sde

Yehoshua cemetery," her plan is becoming clear to me but I don't go into it, she remains hard and withdrawn, the mutual hostility between us is palpable. Stop, she barks, and a moment before we get out of the car she turns to me, her sunken eyes pushing themselves into mine, her look cold and hostile, and she says, pronouncing each word distinctly, so what, Ilan, are you going to start killing off all her lovers now, and then she gets out of the car. Put him on the trolley, she says as she opens the boot, he's very cold and stiff, and I search for a convenient way of getting him out, but her looks confuse me. Well, what are you waiting for, take him under the armpits, she says, as if it's not a human being lying there but only a job to be done, and I succeed in concentrating enough to remove him from the boot. She pulls him by the shirt, which slides up and exposes his smooth stomach, and he collapses into the trolley, she folds his legs up and ties them to the trolley with a rope which she takes out of her bag, one leg to the right side and one leg to the left. Stop dreaming, she snaps, and bring the spade, and I bring her the spade and the blanket and the three shirts and the ruck-sack, not thinking, just carrying out orders, and when I've finished I stand there empty and lost, and for a moment she looks at me attentively and says quietly and without anger, pull your-self together, Ilan, I have nothing better to say to you now, and I wake up, cover him with the blanket, put the other things on top of him, make sure that he's tied on tight, and when he's ready we enter the cemetery. Follow me, she commands, and I obey, pushing the trolley after her like a delivery boy from the supermarket, she totters in front of me, in her tracksuit and red woolly hat and sports shoes, and with the spade in her hand, she looks like a character in a cartoon movie, and soon she stops in front of three fresh mounds of earth. This is your kindergarten teacher's grave, whose funeral you and Anton did-n't take the trouble to attend, she says and points to the middle grave. OK, so I'm here now, I say, but she has no patience for provocations. Start digging, she says and pushes the spade into my hand. In Henzi Bauer's grave, I ask in a meek voice, where else, she replies and where will we put Henzi, I ask, and her patience finally snaps. Wake up, Ilan, she says crossly, we're not going to put Henzi anywhere, we're just bringing her a guest, at long last a man will lie on top of Fraulein Bauer, let's look at it that way. Her reading of reality, which always annoys me, makes me particularly indignant now, but she's already pushing my hand and saying, start digging, there's no time to waste, you never know what lunatics might be wandering around cemeteries at night, and I remove the upper mound and begin to dig, the absurd swallows up reality and with it the shame and I feel as if I'm floating, I dig carefully so as not to injure my old kindergarten teacher. You don't need to be so careful, you won't hurt her, there are cinder blocks on top of her, she says with her impatient mockery, and this calms me a little, and I proceed to intensive digging, the earth is soft and I reach the cinder blocks in a jiffy, the fact that I won't have to see the decomposing body brings me significant relief, but before I have time to climb out in order to fetch the corpse she tells me to take off the blocks. What for, I ask and immediately understand for myself. You can't put him on top of the blocks, they'll find him when they lay the gravestone, lie him on top of her, and put the blocks on both of them, she says and approaches the verge of the pit with the flashlight, which she shines into it, and I begin to take out the blocks, preparing myself for the sight and stink of the end, the ultimate bottom line, but no preparation will do. Don't daydream, she says, get out now and take him, and I immediately go into action again, untie the ropes from his legs, drag him to the edge of the pit, and without looking, roll him in. His body crashes onto hers with a thud, the noise paralyses me, and she says, go on, Ilan, straighten him out, otherwise you won't be able to put the blocks back, and I descend into the pit and straighten him out so that he'll lie completely on top of her, but because she's shrunk, her head, or what's left of it, is crushed between his legs—it's impossible not to notice. *Bon appetit*, Henzi, says my mother, and now the absurd fades and the shame begins to weigh on me, a great heaviness is lurking under the ridiculousness, and again I sink, and I feel like joining in this orgy of the dead, let the earth cover us all, the husband, the lover and the kindergarten teacher, and I cover them with the blanket my mother throws at my head to warm me up, tucking the ends in under him, trying to make it feel like a shroud. Something primordial penetrates the skin of my callousness, I sense the terminal helplessness of the dead, lying deep in just repose, and giddiness forces me to sit on the edge of the pit, but my mother stands over me like a soldier, get up Ilan, don't let it get to you, she says, and there's a smidgen of empathy in her tone, and I get up and pick up the spade, cover them with the cinder blocks and fill the pit, working with practical movements like a peasant until the mound of earth is back in place, and my mother sticks the little sign with the name and date of death into it and says, come on, let's go, but I can't part and I say in a certain panic, wait a minute, I want to say *Kaddish*. What *Kaddish*! she says, *Du bist verruckt*, but I don't dare defy the inexplicable urge, and I say, I have to say *Kaddish*, wait for me in the car, and she rightly judges the metaphysical confusion she sees in me as something against which logic has no chance, she gives in and says only, do it quickly, and goes to the car and I run to the gate, take a prayer book from the stone shelf, run back, light the cigarette lighter, and by the light of the little fire which burns my fingers I look for the prayer, the pain sharpens my senses, *Yitgadal vayitkadash shmei raba, be'alma di brakha ure'utei, veyamlikh malkhutei, behayeikhon uvey-omeikhon ubehaiyei dekhol beth Yisrael, be'agala ubizeman kariv, ve'imru amen,* and I say amen, and the Aramaic words, which so many funerals have turned into an obscure cliché, make me feel at home with their recognizable sound, as if I am in a shadowy but protected zone, and I go back to the car, the mission is accomplished, if there's no corpse there's no murder either, and she says, drive. On the way back we don't talk either, we've exhausted each other's possibilities and we withdraw into our shells, I take her home, return the spade to the shed and go back to the car, she's already gone inside, she too wants to conclude this harrowing night, and I drive off, my head aches, it's hours since I had anything to drink but for the brandy, I light a cigarette, take a long drag, it's stopped raining, the clouds have lightened, there's a kind of clarity suffusing the city, and I tiptoe into the house, lift the door so it won't creak, take off my shoes and coat in the hall and go into the bedroom. Naomi is sleeping on her side, a ray of silver illuminates her face, she looks like a photograph, and I go into the bathroom, peel off my clothes, shove them into the washing machine, and stand under the jet of hot water, scrubbing myself violently, but since I still don't feel completely clean I fill the tub too, the thought of sinking into the hot water attracts me, and I switch off the light and sink into the water, resting my head on the rim of the bath, close my eyes and let the vapors open my face, to avoid thinking I concentrate on the monotonous chugging of the washing machine, and little by little I absorb the sounds which repeat themselves like a stuck record, and my head begins to empty, and I sink myself into the water, shoulders, neck, chin, a pleasant warmth seeps through my body, I sink down deeper, without opening my eyes which are being covered with water I sink, concentrating on the warmth, I stop breathing, tempted to slide down deeper and deeper, to become nothing, to want nothing, to love nothing, to be nothing, but my wretched survival instinct jerks me to the surface, the giddiness is beating inside my head, and I know that I'm doomed to live the life waiting for me outside the bathtub, but nevertheless I slide down into the water again, not to die, just to sink into a warm temporary oblivion, and all at once I wake from my swoon

because the door opens and Naomi is standing in the doorway—about her, for a change, I haven't been thinking for the
last few minutes—Ilan, she says, what's the matter with you,
why have you got the washing machine on in the middle of the
night, and I stick my head out of the water and look at her like
a washed dog. She's angry and impatient, I can see at once, and
I say, the car got stuck on the way out of Jerusalem, something
to do with the carburetor, but she hasn't got the patience to listen or inquire, my nocturnal adventures don't exactly interest
her at this minute, she's got something else on her mind, her
lover's done a vanishing trick, and she turns round and goes
out, and again I try to sink into the water but the pleasure's
gone out of it, reality has woken me up and I get out of the tub,
dry myself and go into the bedroom. She's lying with her back
to me, not sleeping, she too has woken up to her own reality
which she can't share with me, and I get into bed and lie on my
back, letting the exhaustion take over, now I can feel it in all its
weight, it knocks me out, my eyes close, scraps of thoughts fly
out and leave my mind hollow, but now too, as on almost every
other night, I take note of the second between waking and
sleeping, and now too I say to myself that this moment is the
most final and also the freshest of my life.

19

In the morning I wake up heavy and stiff. My head is burning, I feel cold, and I lie shivering until I realize that I'm not covered and I grope for the duvet, drag it round me, and the shivering abates somewhat. I go on lying with my eyes closed and gradually slide into a kind of trance, radiant objects dance in my eyes, and at the receding margins of my consciousness I hear someone calling my name. I try to open my eyes, but the temptation to sink into oblivion sucks me in and I give way to it. Something sharp and cold concentrates in the center of my head and I put my hand up and find Naomi standing over me with a block of ice. What's wrong, I ask, and she slides the ice over my numb forehead and says, you have a high fever, I called the doctor, he'll be here soon. I wake up completely and at once the events of the night come alive in my mind and disintegrate in a series of sharp explosions, everything is vividly present and I can't contain the intensity of the moment, all I want to do is sink, but the freezing touch of the ice prevents me from drifting off. I try to get rid of it but her hand is firm, and she says, one more minute, I have to get your fever down, that's what the doctor told me to do in the meantime, it was over forty, and I lie there frozen and empty and wait for the torture to end, and when she takes the ice away and goes out of the room I try to swoon again but I can't manage it. She comes back with a cup of tea, raises my head and puts the tea to my lips and says, drink it, it'll do you good, and I lie there like a baby from whom nothing is expected but to open his mouth, and the tea immediately relieves the dryness, and she says, take these aspirins now too, you wouldn't wake up earlier, and I swallow the pills and lie down again and close my eyes. You said a lot of strange things last night, she says just as I begin to sink, and I suddenly sit up with a jerk, almost spilling the tea, and ask in a nervous voice, too ill to put on a mask, what did I say? You said weird things, I couldn't understand. My senses immediately sharpen, I have to be very careful now, and I ask again, this time in a neutral voice, what did I say, Naomi? I don't remember, why is it so important, she says. It's important, I say and look at her tenderly. You talked about your father, you said that . . . and she falls silent. What, Naomi, I say and I relax a little—if all I did was complain about my father I have nothing to worry about. Forget about it, what does it matter now, you're ill, you were out in the rain last night and you've got the flu if not pneumonia, you were delirious, it's really not important now. Her evasiveness makes me nervous again, and in an impatient voice that reminds me of my mother I say, come on Naomi, spit it out, I can take it. She averts her face slightly and says, you said that you murdered your father and you couldn't bury him. Is that all, I ask. Isn't it enough, she says and I close my eyes and ask myself what kind of things are going to leak out of my mouth in the nights to come—from now on I'll never be able to get any rest, even sleep won't provide me with a refuge now, during the day my consciousness will torment me and at night what lies beneath it. What's the matter with you, Ilan, she asks, I can feel her look prying into my closed eyes and I open them, smile weakly and say, I've got the flu, that's all, and I ask her to cancel the doctor's visit because I feel better already. But she protests with the bossy tone she adopts whenever she decides to play the mistress of the house, and at that moment the doorbell rings and she ushers in the doctor, a short, fat, jolly old extrovert who reminds me of someone, but I can't remember who. So what have we here, he asks cheerfully and divests himself of his coat and hat with an air of getting down to business. I'm fine, it's only the flu, I say. So we're a doctor too, are we, he says jovially, and adds immediately, without giving me a chance to prepare myself, if your daughter will leave us alone for a few minutes we'll be able to confirm the diagnosis. Naomi quickly drops her eyes, embarrassed for my sake, comments of this nature always defeat me, and neither of us correct the little doctor's mistake, as if nothing has been said, and she leaves the room in obvious relief while he sits down next to me, takes a wheezy breath, and begins to examine me. For as long as I can remember I have always been tense in the presence of doctors, keeping a close watch on their reactions, but now I feel nothing, I sit opposite him apathetically, let him find what he will, after yesterday nothing about myself can shock me. He pokes and prods me, taking his time about it, and in the end he says, we have a bit of pneumonia here, you'll have to take antibiotics, stay in bed and drink a lot, your daughter will take care of you, it's always wiser to put your trust in members of your family than in doctors, believe me, because I have a surprise for you, Professor Ben Nathan, we doctors hardly know anything, people come to us to save them, and we pretend to know but we know nothing, neither about the body nor the soul, the soul's a locked safe, believe me. He says all this in one long, dismissive sigh, and looks at me with sad eyes, all the joviality has dropped away from him. But you have a bit of pneumonia, that I do know, he adds, and suddenly I think that something fishy is going on here, as if he's been sent here for a purpose, and I try to read him but am unable to detect anything personal, and in the meantime Naomi comes in, and he packs up his instruments and says, what a beautiful daughter you have, I once read in Tolstoy that love is what happens whenever a man sees a beautiful woman. I bury myself in the duvet again and remind myself that from today on it's a whole new ballgame, nothing will ever be the way it was before, I'll see signs everywhere, even in this harmless little doctor, and he puts on his hat and coat and sends me a childish smile which lights up his face. When Naomi sees him to the door I close my eyes and ask myself if from this moment on I'm supposed to concentrate on decoding signs sent to me, not necessarily by a personal God, nature is involved here too, it's inconceivable that the disruption of the natural order will pass quietly, I've dried up nature's flow and it will rise up to defend itself, I can't really see myself as an autonomous entity operating in an accidental world, and therefore I'll have to be attentive, alert and concentrated. I remind myself that the border between deciphering signs, an exhausting mental process of self-confrontation, and paranoia is a fine and not always perceptible one, and I have to be careful not to get into a panic. For example, in what the doctor said to me I now find only the empty mannerism of a monologue in the theater, and I turn over onto my other side, and the whole subject of the signs fades and dissolves, and when Naomi comes into the room with a cup of tea I pretend to be asleep. She puts the tea down next to me and leaves the room, and my closed eyes induce sleepiness, and again I want only to sink, and for some reason a memory surfaces in my mind: when I was a child of nine or ten I was in hospital after an operation on my coccyx, in the next room there was a young Arab woman, heavily sedated after a hopeless operation, and every few hours, when she woke up from the morphine into the pain, she would begin to mumble, injection, injection, on and on without stopping, it was the signature tune of the ward, and the nurse would say not now, she had to wait a little longer, and only when the time came she would get the injection that saved her and the rest of the ward, and I would stand in the doorway and look at her tortured face ironing out the minute she absorbed the morphine, and this transition, from ugly, haggard suffering to gentle peacefulness mesmerized and excited me, and one night I called the nurse and claimed that I was in severe pain and I needed an injection, but she only patted me on the stomach in a way that insulted me deeply and said, you'll survive, sweetheart, and the next day the young Arab woman slid from morphine into death, I realized this because a few hours passed after her last injection without her pleading for the next—in my boredom and fear I was listening for them—and I went to see what was happening. She was lying with her mouth agape and her eyes open and I knew that it was death I was seeing there, it didn't look like anything special, but it was obvious that it was something special, and I called the nurse and told her that the woman was dead, and at once there was a commotion, nurses ran in and out, I was taken from the room, and in a few seconds it was all over, the Arab woman disappeared and a new patient took her place, and in Amsterdam years later, at the beginning of the seventies, I decided to investigate the option of a hallucinatory life, and I smoked opium in a water pipe. I still remember the slow pleasurable dive into the extinction of the self, but the depression awaiting me the next day was too heavy a price to pay and put an end to my experiments with drugs, except for the occasional joint that Naomi gets from Noam, and I open my eyes and find Naomi standing next to me, and as she plumps up my pillows to make me more comfortable I think that perhaps I'll be able to achieve a certain blurring of reality with the right pills—the only privilege I've gained from the events of yesterday is that I now have nothing to lose, I'm not going to start worrying about my health after what happened, after what I did, there's no point in beating around the bush, and I get up to pee, take two yellow Valiums—a distant relative of opium, but without the depression—and go back to bed enveloped in the relaxing expectation of extinction.

20

I'm sick for seven days. The coincidence is no accident, of course, I felt better after five days, but I stretched it out for another two days to make a round seven and coincide with the traditional mourning period for the dead. I mourn him discreetly, without sorrow but with self-reproach, which is also a form of mourning, because the weeping and wailing at funerals too is usually not the sound of sorrow but the sound of guilt. In the meantime the days go by, each of us withdrawn into himself, although both of us are preoccupied by the same subject. Naomi sits over her papers, I can see her from my bed, she draws a little but most of the time she stares gloomily into space, consoling herself or not with her wild memories, and I sit and watch my beloved wife, my raison d'être, longing for her lover who vanished so suddenly from her life. Now I try to stop thinking about myself and to get inside her head, perhaps for the first time I look at her as an independent being with an existence outside my awareness of her, I try to see her not as a reflection of myself but in herself, to wonder what her inner life consists of, what her level of self-awareness is. The truth is that I haven't really got a clue about her, for two years my main concern has been with the thrill of this astonishing discovery of being in love, which is presumably as shallow as it is exciting. Suddenly the phone rings and we both start and pick up the receiver at once, she at her desk and me in the bedroom, a voice says, Professor Ben Nathan? This is the police. All the blood drains out of me and the voice continues, Inspector Anton Karam wants to speak to you, and immediately Anton's heavy voice fills my ear, Naomi doesn't hang up, I can see her holding the receiver next to her ear, and he says, I wanted to know if everything's all right. Yes, why, I say too quickly and too sharply, but then I remember that I forgot to cancel our chess game and I relax, he must have waited for me and I didn't show up, that's all, I feel so relieved that I apologize in detail, boring Naomi who hangs up and returns to her thoughts. How's your mother, I heard that she fainted in the grocery store, he asks. A faint alarm bell goes off in my mind and I say, I didn't know, when did it happen? I don't know, my mother told me, you should get it looked into, people don't faint for nothing, there's no judgment in his voice, but hostility begins welling up in me nevertheless—I could never compete with his devotion to his family, but I can do without his patronage at this moment in time. I was there a few days ago and she was fine, I say, but I immediately remember her strange thinness, which was pushed aside because of more urgent matters, and he senses my hostility and brings the conversation to a close. I hang up with a feeling of emptiness and hostility—that's what I've got to look forward to, despair, hostility, guilt, fear, nausea—and with this thought I dial my mother's number. Her "hello" is as grim as usual, I say hello mother in a neutral tone, we haven't spoken since that night, she says, yes, Ilan, in a distant or indifferent tone, and I say, Anton told me you fainted in the grocery store, why didn't you let us know, but she interrupts me impatiently. Really, what is this nonsense, his mother is worse than those Polish women, running to tell everybody that I fainted, I had a sudden drop in blood pressure, that's all. Are you sure, I say, not wanting to hear anything bad, my cup is already full, and she says, I'm sure, I don't have the time to talk now, the maid's here. She slams the phone down and I push her out of my mind and towards the end of the seven days I receive a phone call from Givon announcing that he's coming to pay a sick call, he's read the introduction to the conference book and he has a few reservations, the term irritates me and I haven't got the patience for him, but I can't find the words to tell him not to come, and he arrives with his soft paunch and his yellow skin and his eyes that are always popping out as if he's in a state of perpetual surprise, and Naomi emerges from herself and holds out her long slender arm, embarrassing him with her beauty—his self-image is so low that any hint of glamour throws him into a turmoil. All she does is ask him how he likes his coffee, but her look makes his cheeks burn, his eyes dart round the room in confusion, all his intellectual brilliance evaporates, and I can see how Naomi is turned on by her own power, or maybe I'm only imagining things. When his eyes have nowhere left to flee, he looks back at her and trembles before her steady regard, which she deliberately allows to linger on him, and only when she leaves the room his turmoil subsides and he is able to begin talking to me. For a moment I seem to myself to be just like him, even though on the face of it there is no resemblance between us, neither externally nor in the originality of his thought and the use to which he is able to put his immense knowledge, intellectually speaking he is original without being eccentric—the resemblance between us is hidden and profound. He tells me that he has read the introduction and if he may he would like to suggest that I anchor it in a philosophical context. The article is sufficiently scientific to allow it to absorb a little metaphysical spice, he says, we won't be less scientific if we broaden our perspectives, right? After all, we chose astrophysics because of philosophical pretensions, didn't we? I smile at him, and he thaws even more and praises the article with flattering but also reasoned enthusiasm, and I feel that we've talked enough about me, politeness requires that we go on to talk about him. I ask him how his wife is—his symbiotic relations with his wife are a subject of discussion in the department, Davis and I sometimes chew it over—she works at the *Technion* and turns up at the faculty office after almost every lecture he gives, a tall woman with broad shoulders and beefy legs but a surprisingly small face, which seems to belong to another body, she's a few years older than he is, Givon is about forty or a little younger, they have no children and are therefore their own babies and parents too, they treat each other with an ostentatious devotion which embarrasses those around them but fortifies them in their relationship—a symbiotic couple can be as strong as an entire army. Aviva is very happy, she's begun to take piano lessons, he says, and starts telling me about her interpretation of an étude by Czerny, and at first I'm sure he's trying to be funny, what kind of an interpretation can anyone give an étude by Czerny? But he gets quite carried away, the subject is elevated above itself, it's not the étude, it's Aviva, who has brought the depths of her personality to bear on a tragic understanding of an ostensibly simple work, and from then on his praises for his meteoric wife know no bounds—she wants to have a face lift, she wants to get rid of her wrinkles, so I said to her, Aviva, your wrinkles are the deepest thing on your face, I won't allow you to smooth them out! Without any warning the dead man's staring eyes appear before me, and the horror is real and present and it sticks in my throat. I begin to tremble uncontrollably, and Givon checks his flow of words and asks if I'm shivering with fever, and I say, I suppose so. All I want is for him to go, but then Naomi comes in with the coffee and smiles at him, and since talking about his wife has apparently inspired him with confidence he dares to look at her and even to flatter her with a clumsy flirtatiousness, and she bursts into wild and rather whorish laughter—I'm beginning to realize that there are whole corners of her which are hidden from me—and Givon, encouraged by her reaction, becomes even more liberated. He looks right at her, red as a tomato, and because of my unfortunate tendency to listen to the tone rather than concentrating on the words, I realize too late that the subject has turned to the reasons for my illness, and now I hear Naomi say, the *Technion* is to blame for this pneumonia, Ilan had to entertain guests of yours and his car got stuck in the rain in the middle of the night, and that's what made him sick. Givon asks sourly, what guests, and she says, guests from Finland, I think it was Finland, and she turns to me, it was Finland wasn't it, Ilan? Even before I can answer Givon is already entrenched in his resentment—there were guests from Finland and he wasn't told, we're ashamed of him, he isn't presentable enough—and he turns to me and asks in a thin voice, were there guests from Finland, and Naomi says, didn't you know there were guests from Finland? I realize that I have to do something and I send him a quick look loaded with meaning, and for a second the light of understanding dawns in his eyes—the guests from Finland are only my cover story—and he immediately calms down and says, yes, of course, the guests from Finland, I never met them, Davis kept them hidden from me, Ilan is the professor they show to guests, not me. Naomi looks from me to him and says nothing, but something thickens the air, and when she gets up to collect the cups and takes them to the kitchen he stares at me with his eyes popping out of his head in admiration and astonishment. The fact that he is now my accomplice in a secret sin thrills him and puts him in a state of disarray, I can feel his excitement, he's as eager as a child, all I want is for him to go, and he asks in a conspiratorial whisper, is it someone from the faculty? You don't know her, I say firmly, standing up to emphasize that the conversation is over. He jumps to his feet immediately and says aggressively that he has to go, as if it was his idea in the first place, and I accompany him to the door, inwardly squirming at the humiliation I subjected myself to in front of him. Be well, Ilan, that's the important thing, he says, cautiously, as one does with people prone to unpredictable moodiness, and is about to go into the kitchen to say goodbye to Naomi, but by now I have shed the last vestiges of my mask and I push him almost violently out of the door. When he's safely outside the apartment I say in a conciliatory tone, forgive me for my rudeness, I just don't feel well, and his face melts and he says, of course, of course, and I go into the kitchen where I find Naomi cleaning the fridge. I don't know what to say and I stand there looking at the back of her neck exposed by her short hair cut, and she turns to me and says, what's going on, Ilan? I smile at her with all the innocence I can muster and say, nothing, why do you ask, and she says nothing and gives me a probing look, which I evade with another innocent smile. I begin washing the vegetable trays and as I do so I ask myself if the oppressive atmosphere in the kitchen is due to jealousy induced by my bullshit story about the guests from Finland. I can hardly imagine her being jealous of me, and I say, this cucumber is dying of a ripe old age, and smile at her. She lowers her eyes, I feel a moderate sense of power which encourages me to go up to her and embrace her very gently, and she closes her eyes. Where her thoughts are roaming at this moment I have no idea, but she herself is here with me, and my sense of power grows stronger, and we stand close together and yet far apart, there's a kind of shame between us, and suddenly, without warning, a flood of tears burst out of her eyes and she collapses in a fit of weeping the likes of which I have never seen in her before. For a moment I feel nothing, as if I can't take it in, and only when she raises her brimming blue eyes to me like a pair of overflowing lakes, and gives me a look of quintessential helplessness, do I dare to think that these tears may really be prompted by agonies of jealousy, and I clasp her to me and feel her sobs tearing out of her mouth into my neck. I tell myself that her distress may have nothing to do with me, but it no longer matters, I revel in her despairing neediness, and gradually she empties out, the storm subsides into the whimpering of a baby, and I feel like picking her up and carrying her to the sofa in the living room, wiping her face, and telling her with the magnanimity of a temporary victor not to worry because everything will be all right. But I'm afraid I won't be able to pick her up with the requisite smoothness, the last thing I want is to crash to the floor with her, and immediately a nasty thought pricks at my brain—I managed very well to lift her dead lover and he weighed twice as much as she does. I pick her up with a controlled movement and she clinches her arms round my neck and presses her forehead to mine, the lakes in her eyes have dried up and now they are clear and pure, washed clean by her tears, she curls up on me like a big baby and I take her to the living room and deposit her on the sofa. She asks me for a tissue and with light steps—a superfluous demonstration of my physical fitness which is presumably not her main concern at the moment—I go to the bedroom, sit down on the bed for a minute to rest, I've just carried nearly fifty kilos after all, and return to the living room with the tissues. I wipe her face and she says that all of a sudden she was overwhelmed by sadness and a wave of self-pity, for some reason she remembered her brother who was killed in a training accident in the army, and how on the day of his funeral she and her mother and father left the house to go to the cemetery, and her mother stopped outside the door because she couldn't find the key and she made everyone go back inside to look for it, and she, nine years old at the time, couldn't understand what was so urgent about locking the house precisely now when her brother was dead and they had to go to the funeral, but her mother refused to leave the house and she lay down on the floor flinging her arms to the sides and said that she wasn't going without locking up, until people came and dragged her out. Naomi told me the story of her life one night in Paris, a few days before we got married, how her mother's personality had changed the day her brother was killed, how she had become increasingly obsessed with all kinds of details, for example with changing the rubber sealer on the fridge door every few days because she claimed that warm air was getting in from outside and causing a catastrophe, and the details became more and more marginal, and at first it was hard to tell that she was going mad because of the realism of the details and mainly because of the understandable intensity of her grief. It was forbidden to mention the dead son, they moved from Haifa to Tel Aviv and there they led a life of surrealistic routine, until one day her father took off with a Swiss tourist, leaving a note for Naomi in which he explained that he found life at home very depressing, and since this was the only life he would ever have he owed it to himself to get what he could out of it, and he said he was sorry as if he had trodden on her foot, so she said, and she stayed with her mother, who declined rapidly after her husband left her, pulling herself together only in order to pounce on some insignificant trifle or other, and Naomi, who accepted reality at face value, like most children, didn't realize that her mother was mad, and she didn't say anything to anybody, until an old aunt on her father's side of the family took her in and hospitalized her mother, who died in the end of natural causes. A year later her aunt died too, and the neighbors who had given Naomi her meals when the aunt got sick tried to locate her father in Switzerland, but it turned out that he had left the tourist too, and disappeared without leaving an address. To this day Naomi doesn't know where he is, and now she lies beside me on the sofa with her eyes closed and my heart goes out to her, but when I stroke her gently on her milky face the shadow of a thought darkens my mind, and I realize that it's not for her family that she's crying here. I know that nothing in nature has only one cause, but there's always a queen cause, the one that swallows up all the lesser ones, and my dear Naomi has dragged in her tragic family history here in order to disguise the reason of reasons for this outbreak of sorrow. She is simply experiencing a wave of acute longings, it is his desertion, which presumably recalls her father's desertion, that is causing her all this grief, and there's nothing I can do to help her, especially since she herself is sure that she's crying for her family—when I came home after swimming in the swamp, beside myself with misery and shame,

I told my mother that I was crying for my grandmother, whom I'd never known or spared a thought for, and when I said it I remember that I actually succeeded in thinking sad, consoling thoughts about this grandmother, who died in the Holocaust— and now the longings and the insult squeeze a new wave of weeping out of Naomi, and since I believe that the correct identification of emotional states can bring relief, I mobilize myself to deal with the situation in the right way. All that's needed is quiet, passive empathy. I embrace her and gradually this wave too, and I keep still so as not to spoil things, the silence between us now is tender and not oppressive, but suddenly I feel a cramp coming on in my neck and I straighten up, swallow the sharp pain that pierces me for a moment, and smile at her. She smiles back weakly and asks me if I feel like going out for a bit later for a breath of fresh air, since I haven't been out of the house for a week. At this stage I allow myself to settle into a more relaxed frame of mind, followed by the onset of a practical phase, and I tell myself that if life has decided to return to normal, then instead of driving myself crazy with useless thoughts I would do better to sit down and work on the introduction, and to Naomi I say that I'll work for two or three hours and then we can go out to eat, if that's okay with her, of course. She gives me a kiss on the nape of my neck which takes me by surprise and runs through me like an electric current, and I switch on the computer and load the file "X-ray bursts." For a while I sit and stare at the screen, and little by little the letters disintegrate and the face of the dead man appears. He smiles a crooked smile and apparently a muffled cry escapes my lips, because Naomi says, what's wrong, and I say, nothing. What did I think, that he wouldn't come back to haunt me? This is clearly only the first appearance of many, and I'd better get used to them. I force myself to concentrate on the article, the cigarettes I am now smoking without any feeling of guilt help, and I succeed in working with relative concentration. I go over the introduction twice, all I want is to finish it and send it off, I'll have to do without Givon's metaphysical spice. Out of the corner of my eye I can see Naomi sitting opposite the window, not even bothering to open the book lying on her lap. This is what my love has brought her—sorrow and hurt. I switch off the computer and as I shower I confront myself in the mirror and meet my eyes in a short, bad meeting, that's the situation, and when I come out I find her sitting stooped on the wooden bench in the hall, ready to go out with her coat and bag, staring dully at her shoes. I suddenly remember that for a number of days now I haven't opened my diary, I'm supposed to give a lecture to the Friends of the *Technion* society sometime, and when I look quickly at the last pages of the diary I see that the lecture is on the sixteenth of the month, in other words, today. It should have begun a few minutes ago, I understand immediately that it's too late to phone and make my excuses, too many people are sitting and waiting for me, I've done myself enough damage lately, and I say to Naomi, I have to fly to Denya, I have a lecture that's already started, and she says, I'll come with you, we'll eat afterwards, in any case I'm not hungry yet. As we run down the steps I promise her gratefully that I'll talk about a subject she hasn't had the opportunity to hear me talk about yet, and when we reach the luxurious house in Denya we find about thirty people standing around engaged in animated conversation, apparently not in the least put out by my lateness. We politely decline an offer of coffee and cake, and the hostess, a friendly and enthusiastic woman who I notice has one finger missing, asks everyone to be quiet and sit down. But it seems that the basic pattern of teacher and pupils holds true even for those who have reached a friends-of-the-*Technion* age, because hardly anyone wants the lesson to begin, and the hostess, whose sensitivity may be sharpened by her physical defect, apologizes to me and assures me that they are all very keen to hear the lecture, it's just that they haven't met for a long time and so it's hard to get them to stop talking. I say it doesn't matter at all, let them take their time, and in the meantime Naomi goes to sit on the side, and when the hubbub dies down the hostess announces in a festive tone that she is delighted to introduce Professor Ben Nathan, who as they all know is one of the senior members of the department of astrophysics at the *Technion*, and the subject of his lecture tonight will be the "big bang." I thank her and say that since I have no doubt that people of their stature are already more or less familiar with the theory of the big bang, I have decided to speak about one particular aspect of the broader subject. They immediately cheer up at the compliment and demonstrate attention, and I open by saying that one of the trends in modern astrophysics is the analysis of new observational results which will make it possible to conclude whether the universe is open or closed, in other words, whether it will go on expanding and cooling until it becomes diffuse and dead, or if at a certain stage it will begin to contract into itself again until a new big bang occurs. It all depends on how much of the universe's mass is dark, and therefore one of the unsolved problems of astrophysics is how much dark matter the universe contains and what the dark matter is made of. The trouble is, I continue, that in the nature of things it's impossible to know anything about the dark property of mass, and as a result it's impossible to decide the question of the expansion or contraction of the universe, only to theoretically predict the two options, and I glance at Naomi and realize immediately that she's somewhere else, and in the meantime a very dressed-up woman sitting opposite me asks, what do you mean by dark matter, and I say that it's unknown and therefore unavailable for analysis and definition, it may consist of exotic particles whose properties we can't even imagine, and I continue with my lecture, but the distracted expression on Naomi's face dries up my inspiration and I speak with practiced professional glibness, and an hour later I conclude my lecture, as usual, by quoting from Kant's *Critique of Judgment* and saying that the structure and composition of the galaxies will always be hidden from man. I add that presumably the same thing applies to the structure and composition of the mind, and after the thanks and the smiles and the check, which is always handed over with an apologetic air, we go out into a clear, fine evening, with a full moon hanging over the Carmel. Are you hungry, I ask, and she says, yes, definitely, trying to animate her dull voice. Where should we go, I ask, and she says, wherever you like, and strokes my cheek to make up for the despondency that she can't shake off. Would you like to go to Jacko's, I ask, and she says yes, and I begin driving down to the lower town, and when we enter Hasan Shoukri I don't look at her, but I can feel the way she freezes and turns to stone in her seat, and the silence between us is so deafening as we pass Wadi Salib that I turn on the radio to drown it out. Sixty seconds of self-fulfilling prophecy and the ghost quarter is behind us, the tension relaxes a little, and as we approach Paris Square I suddenly feel a need, an impulse, to go to the restaurant on the quay, and before I can examine my reasons I miss the entrance to Jacko's and I go on driving down Nathansohn Street to Jaffa Road. Jacko's is already far behind us but Naomi takes no notice, she's too dejected and abandoned to care where we eat, and only when we arrive at Bat Galim she wakes up and says, what are we doing here, I thought we were going to Jacko's, and I say, shit, I didn't notice, for some reason this place came into my head, I'll turn round at the next corner and go back to Jacko's. And since at this moment I really don't understand what I'm doing here I mean it too, and at the next corner I begin to turn round, but then she says, nonsense, let's go to the restaurant on the quay, and I don't know if she's saying it out of laziness or attraction, I don't know much, that, at least, I understand by now, and once more the ritual repeats itself: are you sure, whatever you want, whatever *you* want, and it turns out that we both apparently want the same thing, because suddenly we're both wide awake, and the picture of him sitting at the back table with his full head of yellow hair is so vivid that it seems perfectly possible to see him sitting there again, and we sit down automatically at the same table where we sat before, and order grilled bream, fried calamari, a glass of wine and a coke. We exchange a few obligatory remarks and gradually he begins to materialize on the empty chair in front of me, and I lose my appetite and order another two glasses of wine to wash the fish down my throat. I light a cigarette—my only salvation at the moment—and when Naomi goes to the toilet I order an urgent brandy to dull my anxiety, and when the waiter brings it I gulp it down and hand the glass back quickly so Naomi won't see, and at the same time a big guy enters the restaurant and sits down at the dead man's table, on his chair, and for some reason I'm mesmerized by him and his elaborate hair style—his hair is swept from one side to the other in a flat, jutting structure which sits on his head like a low fortress. Suddenly he freezes, transfixed by my stare, and I avert my eyes and call the waiter, but I can feel his look searing my face, and I look at him again. His face strains as if he's trying to remember something, I can see the wheels of his mind creaking, and I'm paralyzed by panic, I order another brandy, and suddenly he stands up and begins advancing towards me. My exhausted heart beats wildly, I no longer have any doubt that this is a witness of whose existence I knew nothing, and now he's standing in front of me, looking into my eyes, and saying, Ilan, right? Ilan Ben Navi? In a weak voice I say, Ben Nathan, and he says in a tone of rebuke, not Ben Nathan, Ben . . . Ben . . . something that sounds like Ben Nathan, are you sure it isn't Ben Navi? Ben Nathan, I say almost violently. Okay, if you say so, you should know, Ilan Ben Nathan, as large as life, what do you know? And he hangs on my shoulder and says, well, Ben Nathan, wake up the few brain cells remaining to us at our age and try to remember who I am. We haven't seen each other for thirty years, but I never forget a

face, and you've aged but you haven't changed, there's a difference you know, and I breathe a sigh of relief—whoever this
bizarre creature is he obviously poses no danger to me. I have
no idea who you are, I say. Tzetze, he says and laughs hoarsely,
Tzetze Goldwin from the bed-wetters summer camp! At this
moment Naomi returns and he says, your daughter, eh?
Congratulations, she looks like you, and now he transfers his
attention to her. Your father must have told you about the bed-
wetters camp, he says, and he pulls up a chair from the next
table and sits down without waiting for an invitation and begins
telling her in a coarse, jarring voice about the house in Rakevet
Street which served in the summer as an improvised therapeu-
tic camp for teenage bed-wetters. We weren't five years old you
know, he says, how old were we—he turns to me but I'm not
there—fourteen, maybe even fifteen. You father and I were in
the same room, you didn't tell her, did you? You were ashamed,
what's there to be ashamed about? My kids are crazy about the
story, their big daddy did peepee in his bed until the age of fifteen and survived to tell the tale! I shut myself off and think this
is it, my punishment has begun. Listen to this, he yells, the own-
ers of the place, they must have been forty, fifty, our age today,
they looked ancient to us then, were religious, and the man,
what was his name, Moruk, or Morduch, something like that,
beginning with Mor. His name was Pincus Rothenstein, I say,
and he stares at me, right, Morduk was the guy with the board-
ing-house in Jerusalem, never mind, and he turns back to
Naomi. To cut a long story short, this Rothenstein had developed a primitive, but as they say, effective, method to solve the
problem of chronic bed-wetting. And now this weird creature,
who for some reason has come hurtling into my life, takes a
paper napkin, removes a pen from his pocket, and begins drawing the structure of the bed for her. See, there was a mattress, on
top of it an oilcloth, on top of that a sheet, on top of the sheet a
wire net connected to a battery, on top of that another sheet

with another wire net on top of it, and the whole caboodle was connected to a bell, and the minute we began to pee it created an electric current and the bell rang and woke us up and we went to the lavatory. He put his hand on hers and collapsed in laughter. And your father, you hear, his bell would ring and ring and nothing happened, he went on sleeping in his pee, and there was plenty of it, believe me. In the evening they would make us drink oceans of raspberry cordial to fill up our bladders. Drink, dearie, drink, the woman would say, she had a number on her arm, remember, what was her name? Never mind, the names go first. And there was that girl in the room with us, Tali, Tali something from Pardes Hannah, remember? She was about thirteen, when she got undressed she would turn her back to us so we wouldn't see her little strawberries, only there was a mirror in front of her, you hear, maybe she did it on purpose, eh, Ben Nathan? She did it on purpose, the little whore! And I look at the coarse creature sitting opposite me and wallowing at my expense in nostalgia that brings a happy glow to his face. You remember the vegetable salad his wife used to make for us, he worked for the post office I think, she used to cut the vegetables in little pieces and pour yogurt on top of them, remember those yogurt jars that came in at the middle like Coca-Cola bottles? And again he paws Naomi's hand, the memories are sucking him in and I haven't got the strength to put a stop to it. Your father was a serious pisser, the first to arrive and the last to leave. You remember how your mother once came to take you to Nahariya and she let me come along, we rode in a carriage and she bought us white hats, she was a real bitch, your mother, is she dead yet? Way of all flesh, eh? Suddenly I call the waiter, he tries to continue but I cut him short, pay the bill, and we get out of there. On the way home Naomi strokes my hand and asks me why I never told her, and I say there are a lot of things I haven't told her yet. Darling Ilan, she says, poor baby, and I don't like her patronizing tone but there's nothing I can do about it at the moment, I haven't got the energy for self-irony either, I feel tired and heavy, and she suggests that we drop in to visit my mother, because I don't see enough of her. We arrive there just in time for the news, and she opens the door and confronts us with her haggard body. Do you have to come in the middle of the news, she grumbles and returns to the television set while Naomi goes to the kitchen to make coffee. Mother, I whisper in a pathetic voice. Not now, she says curtly, stop thinking about yourself for a minute and think of the world instead, it won't last long if people go on treating it the way they do, you're not the center of the universe you know, and in the meantime Naomi comes in with the coffee. Coffee in the evening, she grumbles again, and dismisses the tray, and Naomi asks patiently if she wants tea instead, and my mother thaws a little and says, no, thank you, and at the end of the news I signal to Naomi and we stand up. Naomi goes over to my mother and kisses her dry cheek—the first time she kissed her my mother was astounded, and now too she isn't exactly over-joyed, and she sends me a brief, penetrating look, and with a feeling of relief I get into the car and we drive home, where Naomi goes to bed immediately and pretends to be asleep.

21

I've lived long enough to appreciate the healing properties of time, time is my hope, and I give myself up to its rhythm. The day passes in relative cleanliness, but the garbage collects at night—Anton's mother used to say that tears are the dustbin of the body and dreams are the dustbin of the soul— and therefore in the mornings I walk around half-fainting, I see Naomi dissolving in front of me, her sadness is moderate and steady, the first longings have turned into something which I can't yet put my finger on, and little by little, at first in secret, like those transparent threads which sometimes hang in the air, perhaps actually there, perhaps an illusion of the light, I feel that I'm beginning to remember something. I don't know what it is, but I know that it's connected to the dead man, it sticks to me all the time, it lives in my consciousness and sleeps underneath it, and I try to grasp the thread but it eludes me, and now, when I finish drinking my coffee and staring at the newspaper, I think that it's related to something he said to me when I waxed academic to him about X-ray bursts, and it almost becomes clear, but the phone rings and shatters the little I managed to grasp, and I pick it up and there's no voice, only uneven breathing, and again I say hello, and the breathing is a little louder, and the third hello comes out nervous and jerky, and I slam the receiver down in a panic, and Naomi, who, ever since the disappearance of her lover, jumps to answer every ring, asks in a tense voice, who was that, and I say, I don't know, they didn't say anything. The cup of coffee in her hand trembles and the coffee spills, but she immediately pulls herself together and composes herself. It must have been a wrong number, I say in a controlled voice, and I kiss her and drive to the *Technion*—I'm not teaching today but I have things to do—and I arrive right in the middle of a commotion caused by Givon, it has come to his notice that Davis, behind his back, failed to recommend him as the next dean, and now he and Aviva are sitting in the office with grim expressions and waiting for a meeting with him, and as soon as I take in the situation I try to escape—I'm sick of putting out the fires lit by his grievances—but she grabs hold of me and says, Ilan, I'm asking you to involve yourself in this scandal, this appointment was promised to my husband more than once, and just because he's too noble to demand what's coming to him doesn't mean he should be taken advantage of. Givon lowers his eyes modestly, bowed under the weight of the injustice, and this coquetry gets on my nerves, and I feel like telling him that Davis didn't recommend him not because of some sinister plot, but because he lacks the administrative ability to run a grocery store, but instead I smile at his wife and say, what do you need this headache for, all the dean's job boils down to is sucking up to superiors and quarreling with inferiors, is that what you want to waste his talents on, and when she begins to answer me, the memory I tried to grasp this morning suddenly becomes clear: Golden Miracle, the Golden Miracle Old Age home. He told me his father was hospitalized in the nursing wing of the Golden Miracle Old Age home on the French Carmel, and the idea of visiting this father turns in a second into an urgent necessity, giving rise to tension and above all anxiety, it's clear to me that I have to visit this bereaved father, his only son has disappeared, after all, perhaps he hasn't got anyone else, and now, while Givon's wife harangues me feverishly, I'm only sorry that all these days have gone by without my visiting the old man, and I wait for her to

finish her sentence, and the minute she stops for breath I put
my hand on her arm and say, sorry, I have to run, I've just
remembered something. I add the futile phrase, it'll be all
right, and hurry out to my car, but next to it the female student
with the aggrieved face is waiting for me, and she steps up to
me and says in an urgent tone, excuse me, Professor Ben
Nathan, I have to consult you about something, and last week
at the reception hour you weren't there, they said you were
sick, so I wanted to ask you when I could talk to you. She stares
at me with eyes dripping distress, and I ask myself what is it
with all these frantic people who've been latching on to me
recently, and I suddenly realize that although until this minute
I haven't spared her a thought, she has a thing for me. During
one of my reception hours we worked on her seminar paper
together, and I remember thinking that she was acting strangely, but I didn't file her away in my mind, mainly because most
of the things existing outside my immediate environment are
wiped out while they're still happening, and now, as she stands
before me with that strange urgency, she begins to exist again,
and I ask, is it something urgent because I'm really in a hurry,
and she blinks and says, it's not urgent, it's just . . . I take
advantage of her petrifaction to say gently, why don't you come
and see me at my next reception hour, I'll give you as much
time as you need, and I get into the Volvo, but she goes on
standing there and staring at me with a look bursting with misery, and I feel an annoying discomfort and also indignation,
but I am incapable of driving off and leaving her like this, and
so I open the window and ask her if there's something the matter. Can I ride down to Neve Sha'anan with you, she asks, and
I reluctantly open the door, and as soon as she gets into the car
Givon and his wife emerge with grim steps from the building,
and I hope to get away in time, but they see me and begin rac-
ing towards me like two rivers of lava. What happened, I ask
unwillingly. Shoshie informed me that Davis is too busy to talk

to me, even though the meeting was arranged in advance, and I don't think I should have to put up with this insult as well, he says, panting from rage and running, why did you run away like that, why didn't you say anything? I feel like punching him on the jaw, but I only say, oh come on, you're exaggerating. I'm not exaggerating, Ilan, I'm not exaggerating at all, maybe I'm emotional, but I'm not exaggerating, he says and takes in the student, who has already entrenched herself in the car, and judging by his look I see that everything is coming together in his mind, I'm betraying Naomi and him, especially him, and at his expense, with this master's student, instead of taking care of his affairs I'm having a good time, and I say, it'll be all right, Givon, calm down, I have to run now, and in a tone which is the essence of insult he says, I understand, and his wife, who has just got her breath back, says, it's a scandal, it's simply a scandal, he gives his blood to this department, but Givon drags her away and I brush them out of my mind and drive off. My student, Nava Snir I remember she's called, huddles up in her seat, her silence creating an embarrassing intimacy. So what did you want to talk to me about, I ask, hoping to get rid of her in the reception hour, and she says, next semester I want to take your course on the astrophysics of high energies, and they told me in the department that there isn't any room, but it's very important to me, I need that course, so I wanted to ask you if you would agree to take me, she says all this in a desperate, imploring tone as if she's asking me to donate her a kidney, the triviality of her request is completely out of proportion with the emotional intensity behind it, I can't understand what's going on and I haven't got the time to go into it, all I want is to get rid of her gently. I don't think there'll be a problem, I say, where should I drop you off? Where are you going, she asks. To the French Carmel, I say, and for a second her look neutralizes me and I forget what I'm going there for. If you don't mind I'll go there with you, she says, and I don't

know what to say, so I go on driving, her strangeness turns her
into a kind of oppressive and enigmatic omen, I feel uncomfortable to an unbearable degree, and at the traffic lights of
Tchernikovsky and Jabotinsky streets I tell her that she'll have
to get out here because I'm not going any further, my tone is
polite but firm, and she sends me one last look, which I also
fail to interpret, and gets out. There's something going on here,
but I don't know what, and suddenly the thought flashes
through my mind, she knows something, she wanted to talk
but she didn't have the courage, but in that case why didn't she
go to the police, maybe she intends blackmailing me, she
behaved exactly like a frightened blackmailer, and I tense and
examine the possibility that she saw me that night, but come to
the conclusion that the chances are nil, and I relax, and Nava
Snir fades until she disappears into the sea of details drowning
in the general stream, and at the junction I see a pole with a
map of the city, and I get out to look for the old age home,
which turns out to be in the next street. When I park the car it
occurs to me that visiting him is the height of indiscretion on
my part, and I should drop this self-righteous idea immediately, but I also know that it's a lost cause, because the need to see
him is categorical and urgent, so I put on my mother's red
woolly hat which she left in the car that night, and my sun-
glasses, I take a black felt-tipped pen out of my briefcase and
give myself a big and rather prominent mole on the bottom of
my forehead, in spite of the sun I put on my long coat, and in
this idiotic disguise I enter the gate. An elderly nurse comes
hurrying up to me and I ask her where I can find Mr. Safra, and
she, too preoccupied to concentrate on me, points to an old
man in a wheelchair sitting at the far end of the garden next to
a mulberry tree, and without stopping she says, that's him over
there, he's not quite all there, and she disappears, and I go up
to the old man, who I immediately feel is at my disposal as he
sits there without teeth or lips, with a film over his eyes, his

gaze lost in the desolate spaces of his dwindling existence. I stand before him, Mr. Safra, I say, and he with difficulty abandons his stupefied staring into space, and turns towards me with a slow inclination of his head. In his flaccid face I immediately recognize his son, he is what's left over of his son. How are you, I ask mainly in order to say something, and he lifts up his eyes and fixes them on me, I find it hard to face the depths of confusion and fear reflected in them, and for a moment it seems to me that he knows. What's the matter, I ask, and he grabs my hand with a strength galvanized by fear, I'm hungry, he says, so very very hungry, something to eat please. Don't they give you food here, I ask. No they don't and I'm so hungry, he replies and I immediately beckon a very young nurse passing nearby, who comes up to us. Excuse me, I say in a reprimanding tone, Mr. Safra is complaining that he's hungry. Are you his son, she asks. No, I'm a neighbor, I answer her question, and she strokes his head, Shlomo, she says in a slow, sweet voice, why are you upsetting your visitors, they'll think we don't give you enough to eat here, and she turns to me and says, it's one of the symptoms of his disease, and suddenly he grabs hold of her gown and in a voice hoarse with pleading he says, I want you to be naked, I'll leave you money in my will, please, wait for me in the corner of my house naked. He speaks with elderly, ridiculous violence, the unadorned, essential end of a man deserted by his wits, and she smiles at him sweetly, with the youthfulness of her flesh, and says, I can't take off my clothes, Shlomo, my boyfriend won't let me. She says this naturally, as if it's only her boyfriend who's interfering with the passionate romance between them, and he grabs her hand, *meidele, meidele* he cries with the vestiges of life left him, sit on me, and he pulls her to him, and she smacks him lightly on the hand, that's enough Shlomo, you're behaving very badly, you have a visitor and it's not nice at all to see you like this. The old baby collapses back into himself, chastised and defeated, and

the nurse turns around and goes away and leaves us alone. Are
you cold, I ask him, and he seizes my hand and looks at me, the
sorrow pours out of his eyes, woman, wife, mother, he says—
his son doesn't exist in his disintegrating mind, that at least. I
go on standing next to him, he rests his head on me and sobs—
at a minute distance from the revealed reality exists a hidden,
parallel reality, which is not subject to the laws of the revealed
reality, and it is extreme and discreet, like the need of this old
man, in whom death is already dwelling, for a woman's body—
and as I stand over him, trying to absorb his sorrow, an idea
begins to take shape in my head. I'll come back soon, I say to
him, but he hangs onto me with the strength of a baby clinging
to a finger, I'll be right back, I say and prize his hand off mine,
and I run to the car, drive down Independence road, and within a few minutes arrive at the bar at the entrance to the harbor.
Because the task is specific I succeed in acting efficiently and
almost without embarrassment, I go in through the bead curtain and find the beefy prostitute sitting next to the bar drinking mineral water in a bottle through a straw, she looks at me
in my red woolly hat and says, can I help you, and I say simply
and clearly, I need a woman, maybe a bit of a cuddle, I don't
know, it's not for me, I add righteously, not far from here, in
the old-age home on the French Carmel, and she gets up, taller
than I remember, her heavy thighs and breasts bursting out of
her short dress. Do I fit the bill, honey, she asks mockingly.
Very much so, I say, and she flings a few instructions at the man
sitting in the entrance, and we get into the Volvo, she can't
manage the seat belt, forcing me to bend over into her enormous breasts, revulsion mixed with a queasy arousal turns my
stomach. Put on the radio, she says, in a coy, affected drawl,
and I turn on the radio and my eyes are unwillingly drawn to
the two massive lumps of flesh, put on the Voice of Music, I
love classical music, and thus, to the strains of the overture to
Fidelio, we head up to the French Carmel. Is it your father, she

asks. No no, I say, it's a person I owe a favor, to make him feel good, actually. Isn't that the same thing, she asks, and she flash-es me a smile full of bridges and fillings and crowns, her mouth is a network of iron constructions. You're right, I say, and she takes out a cigarette and offers me one too, I'll light it for you, honey, it's very dangerous to light a cigarette when you're driv-ing, they say it causes a lot of accidents, she says, and she lights two cigarettes and gives me one—there's no chance I'm about to put it in my mouth—and she sucks on her cigarette, spreads her thighs and lets her head fall back against the back of the seat and asks if we're going to him in the old-age home. Yes, he's sitting by himself in the garden in a wheelchair, I say. And is he capable of penetration, she says. Capable of what? I ask. Penetration, she repeats. I mean, can he get it up? she says, suddenly losing her patience. I have no idea, you're a profes-sional, you'll know what to do. Thirty years in the profession, she says without pride, what can you do, that's life, one big mistake, a human being lives by mistake and dies for real, what can you do, and I smile at her warmly and get rid of the ciga-rette. In Bucharest I studied for the opera, she says, but I had a problem with vibration, my whole body trembled when I gave a concert, like this, and she demonstrates to me, shaking her expanses of flesh, and the body's nothing compared to the voice, my high notes went to hell as soon as I opened my mouth, that's what happens when a person wants something too much. While we're waiting at the traffic lights she demon-strates a scale for me, and I'm surprised at the purity and pre-cision of the notes that emerge from her throat. Her voice is deep and warm and I say flatteringly, you've got a wonderful voice. That's now when I'm not excited, bring me an audience and it all goes to hell, she says, and when the lights change I take in the young couple in the van next to us, looking into the Volvo and laughing nastily. My whore who missed her vocation is insulted and stops talking, and when we arrive at the old-age home she says, let's go, honey, to work, and we go inside and make straight for him, he's still sitting in the same place, the garden is almost deserted, here and there old people go on sitting dotted about in the dying rays of the sun. That's him over there, I say, and she sways in front of me with her high heels and her huge bum which is also spreading out of the confines of her dress, and for a moment I feel a loathsome desire to drown myself to death in the vast expanses of her flesh. Hello Mr. Safra, I say to him, I want you to meet this lady. He looks at her and a shot of life is injected into his dead eyes, she bends over and kisses him on his dry cheeks. Hi honey, she says and he trembles and pants opposite her, and now she turns to me and says, we'll just move aside a little, under this mulberry tree, we had one just like it in our garden in the village where I come from, it makes a terrible mess, we'll go and see what we can do and you keep guard here so no one comes, we don't want any unpleasantness, he's a respectable man after all. She pushes the wheelchair in the direction of the tree while I stand there and supervise the operation, the young nurse chooses this precise moment to come out of the building accompanied by another nurse, she waves brightly at me and glances without interest at the old man and the blonde mountain next to him—as long as she isn't disturbed she doesn't ask any questions—and now she parts from her friend and goes back inside the building and my eyes are drawn to the tree, the feeling of excitement and queasiness increases, like the pleasurable squeezing of a painful pimple, and I draw closer to them, watching her masculine hand delving into his pants, where is our little man, where's he hiding, she says like a kindergarten teacher, and the old man, who doesn't have the faintest idea of what's going on, he's like a baby with a thrilling new toy, lifts his emaciated hand and lays it trembling on the mountainous cleavage while the other hand gropes over her fleshy expanses like an old puppy and confused animal moans escape from his mouth. Mama

Mama, he whimpers, and she shakes her bosoms in front of him, come to Mommy, she says, come to Mommy, and he buries his head between them while she sends me a wicked look. I can't take my eyes off this distilled and repulsive essence of human reduction, I can feel the punishment enveloping me in an ugly enjoyment, but suddenly something happens, because she pulls away from him abruptly. Come here, she says to me in alarm, and I run to them. I think he's dead, she says, I'd better go, I don't want any trouble. I go up closer to him, and bump straight into his open eyes which look sternly right through me, those are dead eyes, no doubt about it, and I realize immediately that I've killed his father too. You'd better go, I say to her, I'll fix things up here. You haven't paid me, she says in the tone of a tax inspector. My wallet's in the car, go and wait for me next to it, I'll be with you in a minute, I say and she hurries off, and I stand there for a minute, knowing that on no account can I run away from this death too, and after a minute I go inside to look for the young nurse, who's talking on the phone. From the doorway I make urgent signs to her, she puts the phone down and comes up to me. What's up, she asks cheerfully, I think Mr. Safra has passed away, I say, and we both hurry to him, he's slumped in his wheelchair, she takes his pulse. There's no pulse, I have to call a doctor, she says and at the same time waves to a nurse who's going off duty, he's dead, she says, and the remnants of the cheerfulness aimed at her colleague color the words in an optimistic shade. I'm sorry, I have to go, I say briskly, don't you want to wait for the doctor to certify death, she asks as if it's an experience it would be a pity to miss. I'm simply pressed for time, I have to go and pick up my daughter, I say, but since this sounds insulting I immediately continue, Mr. Safra wasn't a relative of mine, you understand, just a distant neighbor, and she, who couldn't actually care less about the whole affair, says, poor man, his son hasn't been to see him lately either, it's a pity that his son wasn't here to see him off at least, but never mind, she concludes on a fresh wave of optimism, I'll say goodbye then, and she goes off to make the arrangements—this death is part of her shift—and I remain standing next to him for a minute, and in a kind of routine begin to say *Kaddish, Yitgadal vayitkadash shmei raba, be'alma dibrakha reute uveyamlich malkhutei,* most of it I can't remember and so I improvise a bit, and when I'm finished I gently close his eyes and start walking in the direction of the gate. A moment before leaving I send one last look in the direction of my new dead man, almost invisible in the big chair under the mulberry tree, and I return to the Romanian waiting for me next to the Volvo and smoking a cigarette. This is a bad business, she says and I open the door for her, for you one hundred shekels, she says, and I pay her and add another fifty. Thanks honey, she blows a kiss at me, and we drive away, my left eye begins to jump and I rub it, there's no need to cry, a person lives and a person dies, that's the way it goes, and he was still lucky, dying in the middle of a blowjob, isn't it better to die that way if you have to die already? And she sighs, poor guy, his heart couldn't stand it, and by the way, if we're already on the subject, his prick couldn't either, excuse the expression, three centimeters maximum, and she turns on the radio and sighs, you should always remember that everyone was once a baby who somebody loved, and I say, right, and all I want is for her to get out of my life already. Where did I get the insane idea of bringing him a woman from in the first place, it just goes to show that good intentions really are lethal, and I only hope that this concludes his family, all I need now is for some uncle to show up and get himself killed by my good intentions. Here, turn right here, she says and rouses me from my fantasies of omnipotence, and I stop to let her off and take another fifty out of my wallet, let's keep this whole incident between the two of us, I say. Don't worry honey, I've forgotten it already, she says and spills out, leaving me with her heavy smell, and I drive off, deciding to go to my mother and unload on her a bit. I ring the doorbell, it seems to me that I hear faint footsteps but the door doesn't open, and for a moment I'm sure that she's looking at me through the peephole and she simply doesn't feel like letting me in. Mother, I say in a warning tone, and after a minute the door opens and she stands there in all her thinness. Are you sick, I ask. I'm not sick, stop nagging, do you want to eat, I'm just warming something up, and I follow her to the kitchen and sit down at the table. You don't look so good, I say. Why should I look so good at my age, and for a moment she fixes her gray gaze on me and asks, what happened, and I say, don't ask, and she says, well, what, and I say, a catastrophe, and she says, who else did you kill, and I say, his father, and immediately begin to pour out the whole story with the disguise and the whore, and she looks at me and begins to giggle, and the giggle expands into laughter which turns into bellowing and concludes in coughing and choking. That's fantastic, she wheezes, and in the end I too begin to see the comic side of the story, but after a moment this comic side depresses and mainly annoys me, I don't forget that I'm the chief clown in this comedy, and as I slap her on the back and bring her water I fall back into a gray and futile depression, and now she's not amused either, all she wants is air, and I lead her to her bed and sit down beside her, her coughing dies down and she takes in my dejection. I'm all right now, you'd better go, she says, we both know that at critical moments it's everyone for himself, and demonstrative identification with others repels us both. Go, I'm all right, she says again, and I cover her, turn off the light and go and sit in the living room, and only when I hear her angry breathing I go home to my reason for living who is staring at the television, she's certainly not watching it, that I can see the minute I open the door. Where have you been, she asks apathetically, and at that moment the phone rings, and since I'm next to it I pick it up, and again I hear the nervous breathing, and again Naomi tenses, and I slam the receiver down, and this time she doesn't ask who it was, only curls up like a hedgehog, and the rest of the evening passes in trivialities, do you want something to eat, no thank you, how was this and was that, neither of us has the energy to tackle a real subject, and at the end of the evening I get into bed with an old Raymond Carver, which succeeds to some extent in taking me somewhere else, and in the morning, when I emerge from the bedroom, I find Naomi in the living room putting a letter into an envelope, and even though I don't know if the letter is connected to the subject foremost in both our minds, I say that I can post it for her because I'm going to the post office anyway, and she says, no, it doesn't matter, and she puts it into her leather bag with the shoulder straps, and when she goes to the lavatory I quickly open the bag to see who the letter's addressed to, but she only went to get some toilet paper and she comes out again immediately, and I close the bag at once, all I managed to see on the envelope was the word "to", which isn't written in ordinary handwriting but drawn in print, which seems strange to me but there's no way I can check it now, and I say goodbye to her and go out to struggle with another day, which passes somehow, and on the way home I remember that I'm out of Valium and so I stop at the pharmacy on the corner. My old pharmacist isn't too keen on this arrangement of giving me Valium without a prescription, but I have managed to persuade him that I simply haven't got the time to keep going to the doctor for a few pills that can't really do me any harm, and now he asks me, aren't you overdoing it a bit lately, and I say, I'm under pressure at work, you know how it is, and he says, you shouldn't overdo it, and he only gives me one packet, and when I go outside I see a kind of beggar leaning against the door of my Volvo, looking at me as I advance towards him. Excuse me, I say to him politely, but he doesn't move, just goes on looking at me, will you please move, I want to go, I say less politely. Have you got a cigarette, he says, and suddenly it seems to me that I know his voice, and I look at him, trapped in his gaze. Give me a cigarette, he says again straight into my eyes, and when I take out my cigarettes a man comes round the corner dragging a small child who's screaming hysterically behind him. Shut up, the man says to him, shut up, you hear, and the child tries to say something, but his shrieks swallow the words, and he throws himself backwards, almost pulling his arm out of its socket, and the man stops, I see savage violence flooding his eyes and disconnecting him from the child and from his own self-control, and he brings his hand down with all his strength on the backside of the child, who flies forward and collapses onto the pavement. The man, not yet satisfied, picks him up savagely and drags him off, and the child goes on screaming in terror and rage and helplessness, and an old woman, brought out onto her balcony by the screams, says to the man, leave him alone, aren't you ashamed, and he says rudely, shut your trap. The beggar takes a cigarette from the packet in my hand and sticks it in his mouth, but he still doesn't move from the door, and I say to him, what do you want of me, tell me, and a horrible kind of smile settles on his face, and it suddenly occurs to me that this is the man who was sprawled on the steps the first time I went to look for Naomi in Wadi Salib, and now he's standing opposite me with a cigarette in his mouth. What do you want of me, I say, and my voice is trembling uncontrollably, a light, he says, and I put my hand in my pocket but I can't find the lighter, and in a ragged voice I say to him, I want to get into my car, and he says, give me a light, and I say, I haven't got one, and he says, so how do you light your cigarettes? Get out of my way, I say, and push him roughly from the door, and he grabs hold of my coat and doesn't let go, and I try to kick him off me, and at that moment the pharmacist comes running up to us, let him go, Leon, and the beggar lets go of me and says, a person needs pity too, and starts walking away. The pharmacist says, all kinds of characters have started showing up in this neighborhood lately, and I say, it doesn't matter, and I get into the car and swallow one yellow pill and go on sitting in the parking lot until the fear becomes clouded and the beggar goes back to being just another person who has shown up in our neighborhood lately.

22

Without my even noticing it, spring arrives, cool and clear with a polished sky. The days pass us by like a river sweeping everything along with it, no debris stands in its path, everything is swallowed up in its indifferent flow, my anxiety and Naomi's longings. One day, when I came home from the *Technion*, I happened to take the mail out of the mailbox before she got to it—ever since his disappearance she races to the mailbox before me—and when I came inside with a letter that had foreign stamps, she pounced on it almost uncontrollably. When I remarked pleasantly that it was the contract for my book from Bristol she smiled in embarrassment and said that she thought it was a journal about birds that she had ordered from New Zealand for her work. She pronounced the words "New Zealand" intimately, as if they were already part of her inventory but she didn't have to pounce—if a letter came for her I would give it to her without her having to snatch it from my hands—her desperation, and especially her hope, embarrass me. Time has not yet begun to heal us, neither her nor me, his face wakes up with me in the morning, in difficult moments it sharpens and lengthens, sometimes his father's shrunken face falls into his as in a kaleidoscope. Now I open the big window and go out onto the balcony, still dirty from the winter, the fresh air calms my nerves a little, Naomi follows me and we both stand silently leaning on the balustrade, feeling a certain expansion of spirit. Look how filthy the balcony is, she says and goes to fetch cleaning utensils, and we both begin to clean up. She sweeps and I wash the wrought-iron railing, and for the first time since that night we're partners again, even if only in cleaning the balcony, but in the desert of alienation we inhabit, even that's a modest oasis, and when we're done I bring her a cup of Nescafé with three sugars and we sit down to drink. The city lies beneath us in a Sabbath idleness, and in the clean light the terrors of the night grow vague and muffled, like the prickling of a mild burn, a persistent nagging rather than an actual pain, and again I think that perhaps things aren't as bad as they seem. We sit there side by side, sunk in optimistic silence, and suddenly Naomi turns to face me and says enthusiastically, let's take a trip to the Galilee, let's go for a long weekend, let's experience spring in the country, I'm sick of the city. I look at her radiant face and think to myself that she herself is the essence of spring, and I pull her towards me, chair and all, and she gets up and sits on my lap, throws her thin arms round my neck, and says, okay, then, we'll go? Wherever you like, I say, and she puts her perfect, heart-shaped lips to mine, and we kiss with a certain animation, and it's impossible not to feel a mild burst of renewal and hope. For the next two days we busy ourselves searching for the most suitable spot in the Galilee, she in order to compensate herself for her longings and me in order to escape the dead—not that I suffer from any illusions that they can't follow me to the Galilee, but at least the preparations provide an illusion of a sane life. Naomi runs through the options available, bed and breakfast, pension, hotel, *Safed* or a kibbutz guest house, and I tell her to surprise me and take me wherever she likes, and on Wednesday night while I mark some tests, she bustles round the house, full of the energy she's accumulated during the weeks of staring into space. I can hear her moving about, going up and down to the car—I can't understand why a weekend trip involves so much packing—and then the phone rings. I pick it up and my ear fills with nervous breathing, and suddenly I realize that it's Nava Snir—of course,

I should have known. Naomi drops everything and tenses, all our relative happiness is about to evaporate, I have to destroy her illusion that it's her lover from New Zealand. Nava, I whisper into the phone, talk to me, I know it's you, and instantly the breathing turns into a quiet whimper. Let's meet during my reception hour on Tuesday, okay? I say with all the gentleness I can muster, and she replies with a faint, miserable, "yes" and hangs up. I turn to Naomi, who's standing next to me disappointed and suspicious, and tell her about my weird student—she's in love with me, imagine—and Naomi's face clouds and she says, is there anything between you? This little display of jealousy, together with the strange love of the miserable Nava Snir, inject me with liveliness and strength and perhaps a little self-importance too, and I stand up, embrace her with a certain masterfulness, and say, there's nothing between us, she simply pursues me in the corridors. Do you swear, my beloved asks me. I swear, I say with a drop of irony, leaving a slender thread of mystery unraveled, and she resumes her preparations while I celebrate a double victory, over my fear of the unknown caller, and over Naomi's hope. My student's infatuation is a peculiar kind of bonus, and I get up and go to my desk, and when I note the meeting with Nava Snir in my diary, in red, so I won't forget, I feel Naomi's eyes on me. Maybe I'm suddenly not to be taken completely for granted, and indeed she comes up to me from behind and locks her arms around me and whispers, do you love me? No, I say, definitely not, and she kisses me slowly and languorously on my neck, and I close my eyes and abandon myself to the heavy sweetness and wish the world would stop right now and fuck the rest.

23

A t midday we're climbing in a broad, exposed, mountainous landscape, with only a few isolated houses dotted here and there in the sculpted, primal scene which lacks even electric cables, with wind turbines supplying energy directly to the houses. Naomi, who feels responsible for the production of this project, doesn't look out of the window but concentrates on the note with the directions, and guides me to a small, isolated stone house. You couldn't have made a better choice, I say, and she smiles a childish, gratified smile, and when I switch off the engine and get out of the car I can feel the ancient silence. I'm dying to sit out on the wooden porch with a cigarette and a beer but first I help her to empty the car of the supermarket of groceries she has crammed into it. I'm not moving from here, she says when I ask her why she brought so much stuff along, you go outside, I'll put everything away myself. I go outside, sit down on a long plastic lounger, and look at all this nature into which I am apparently supposed to merge in some modest way, and Naomi's bustling in the kitchen introduces something concrete into this quiet hole and somewhat neutralizes its power, and she comes out with beer and olives and goat's cheese and olive oil and sun-dried tomatoes, and I say, you couldn't have chosen a more appropriate meal either, and fall on the food and especially on the beer. In the meantime the light grows softer, and we're sucked into the silence, and as the sun begins to sink I bring out a bottle of iced vodka and pour us each a drink and the wind drops and the world stops. This is exactly the way everything was supposed to be, and the potential for perfection moves me and makes me sad, and now the sun is sinking fast behind the mountains, leaving a train of pale orange light behind it, and in the sadness produced by all this beauty Naomi's existence becomes less urgent. She falls asleep next to me and I light another cigarette and wrap myself in the rapidly gathering dusk. There are no lights in sight, everything's turning black, the silence grows oppressive and intrusive, and I rise heavily to my feet to bring Naomi a blanket, my bones are stiff with hours of lounging and with all the alcohol I've consumed, and I come back and cover her with the blanket. She seems serene, there's no sign of longing on her face, and I go out into the darkness and watch it swallowing up all the glorious nature which until a little while ago reigned here supreme, and a new, unidentified fear creeps up on me. I dull myself with a bit more vodka and little by little I submit to the unvanquished vastness around me and abandon myself, my insignificance, my singularity, and at some point or other the darkness swallows me too.

24

M y head's heavy and my mouth's dry and bitter, I've slept too much and moreover I've had too much to drink. It's already eleven o'clock, a smell of fried garlic wafts into the bedroom from the kitchen and makes me nauseous, and I go on lying in bed like a lump of concrete. Parts of last night have been wiped out, I only remember the muffled sense of fear, which had a different tinge to the one I'm used to, and as I try to drag myself out of bed I fight against the fragmentary pictures that assail me. Naomi comes in with a big, oily spoon in her hand and asks if I want coffee or something. Not yet, thanks, I say and go to take a shower. Under the strong jet of water my head drops, my muscles relax, the pictures fade away, and when I emerge from the bathroom, after two aspirins and one and a half Valium tablets, everything seems softer and duller. Naomi is fixing spaghetti and a spinach salad with yellow peppers and pine nuts, she kisses me without involving her hands which are busy stirring the tomatoes in the pan. You shouldn't drink today, yesterday you drank I don't know how much, she says. Of course not, I say and make myself a strong, bitter cup of coffee, take it out onto the porch and begin to accustom myself to the daylight. It's chilly outside, the air is fresh and crisp, gradually my head clears, the ache fades, thoughts float lightly in my head, none of them particularly painful. I'm not going to drink a drop of alcohol today, or tomorrow, and cigarettes are definitely out, even if I have turned into a murderer I can't afford to turn into a wreck, not yet, I have a young wife to think about, as my mother puts it, there are just two possibilities here; to be healthy or to die, anything in between isn't fair on Naomi, the least I can do for her is to try to be healthy, as far as it's possible to be healthy at my age, which is already a kind of disease in itself—I have to begin to exercise, I'll sign on at a gym as soon as we get back to town. This thought animates but also depresses me, and I look round aimlessly until my look turns to a blank, unfocussed stare, and at the same time I begin to sense a disturbance in the silence, which turns into a definite noise, growing more and more specific, and I try to rouse myself from my trance, and suddenly my eyes focus and I see a police car driving up the dirt track and making straight for me. In an instant I pull myself together: I'll deny everything, first of all I'll deny everything, all I have to worry about is the right mask, friendly but on the phlegmatic side, to give myself time to think. I decide not to get up until the car reaches the yard, and to be calm and matter-of-fact, calm and matter-of-fact, and the car drives up and I'm so busy thinking about my mask that at first I don't recognize Anton. He gets out of the Escort with a big smile and Naomi comes out of the kitchen and she smiles too, and they both chorus, Happy Birthday! That's all I need now, a birthday, and I smile glumly, trying to disguise my dejection as modesty, and Anton gives me a present wrapped up in black paper while Naomi brushes my lips with a glancing kiss. Have you forgotten that it's your birthday today? she says with arch rebuke, you're forty-eight years old today! Big deal, I mutter ungraciously, and she says, so I invited Anton for lunch, to give him a chance to relax in the countryside. Look how beautiful it is here, she turns to him, and he smiles at her and strokes her hair in a casual gesture, and in the meantime I open the present and it's a pipe, a beautiful Stanwell with the grain in the wood running impressively up the bowl in the approved manner, and I admire it and thank him but as I raise my eyes from the pipe I suddenly grasp the context and in a second I slide headlong into para-noia. The pipe burns in my hands, he's testing me, he didn't bring me a pipe for nothing, he knows and I'm lost. What's the matter, Ilan, Naomi asks, and I pull myself together and say expressionlessly, nothing, and Anton smiles at me and says, I hesitated between this Stanwell and a black Savinelli. An excel-lent choice I say and tell myself that it's all in my head, he does-n't have to buy me a pipe in order to arrest me, and this latest anxiety too fades and I calm down. Ilan, stop daydreaming, he says, standing opposite me with his impressive poise, and I wake up and say, it's a great present, I've just decided to stop smoking again, and we both sit down on the porch and Naomi brings him a beer. Ilan's on the wagon today, he drank enough yesterday for his birthday too, she says, I'll go and lay the table. Anton immediately offers to help her but she refuses his offer. It's a woman's job, she says with charming irony, and we sit on the porch and conduct a fitful conversation, which doesn't bother Anton, who sips his beer and smokes his cigarette, unselfconscious and at his ease, taking in the stunning view without making an issue out of it. I look at the fig tree coming into leaf opposite me, with my faded senses I try to grasp its beauty, but I feel that it's got nothing to do with me, and I tell myself that everything's going to get worse, and at the end of the mental suffering there's still the physical suffering waiting to descend and fill all the voids at one blow with its concrete reality. How's your mother, he asks, and I reply, she says she'll all right, and Naomi calls us to come and eat. I help her to serve, Anton opens a bottle of wine, Naomi says, you're not drinking, right, Ilan, and I shake my head vigorously and watch Anton pouring wine for himself and for her, and they raise their glasses to me while I sit there with a glass of soda water like someone suffering from a terminal illness, empty and bored. Even my dead have deserted me. Anton refills their glasses. Outstanding wine, Naomi says, as if she understands the first

thing about it, oh my goodness, the tomatoes with the moz-
zarella, how could I have forgotten? She jumps up and runs to
the kitchen and after a minute she returns with the tomatoes,
and we begin to eat, Anton praises her cooking in his authoritative voice and she giggles at him and drinks some more,
drops of wine dribble onto her white shirt. Does wine stain?
she asks Anton in agitation, and he picks up the saltcellar and
strews salt on the stain with deliberate movements, and a new
thought begins to trouble me. Something loathsome is going on
here behind my back—why did Naomi invite him, when did
she talk to him? Moral indignation takes root in my mind and
grows into self-righteous hostility. I have nothing in common
with these flushed people, I can't bear to see him here opposite
me, swelling in self-importance in front of her, my sobriety
sharpens with every glass they drink, and a feeling of sulky,
childish grievance begins to well up in me. Are you all right,
Naomi asks, I'm apparently transparent, and Anton gives me a
dark look. I'm perfectly all right, why shouldn't I be all right,
it's my birthday isn't it, I say in a neutral voice to which I add a
flavor of contempt. By the way, how's Suhil, I ask Anton, and
he says, he's fine, he's in the municipality, everything's okay
with him. Who's Suhil, asks Naomi. Anton's cousin, he works
in the municipality, I say, and then, for no obvious reason, I
begin to tell a story which has no connection to anything happening here except for my hidden wish to hurt Anton, to belit-
tle him. It happened a few years ago, I begin, leaning back in
my seat and taking care to disguise my malice. One day, when
I was visiting my mother, I saw Suhil through the window walking past the house. When he recognized my car he decided to
come in, but I didn't have the strength for him—with all due
respect to Anton's family Suhil can be a real pain in the neck—
so I told my mother to say I wasn't at home. The trouble was
that I didn't have time to slip into the bedroom because he
would have seen my from the window, so instead I shut myself

up in the lavatory. My mother didn't like it but she cooperated and told him I wasn't at home, and then he asked her if he could use the phone, and he came in and began with the phone call and my mother brought him something to drink and I realized that he was going to have to take a leak soon and I began trying to lock the door from the inside, but the key was rusty and it wouldn't turn. He finished making his phone call and got up to go, but then I heard him say, just a minute, I have to go to the lavatory, and my mother, who chose the right minute to teach me a lesson, said, *tfadal*, in her German accent, be my guest, and I heard his footsteps approaching. I leant against the door and he tried to push it, and I pushed from the inside, and we stood there pushing the door from either side until my mother decided that I'd learnt my lesson and she said that the door was broken and took him to the bathroom leading off her bedroom. He had to be an idiot not to realize that I was inside the toilet, but he never mentioned it to me afterwards. I conclude my stupid story, which mainly embarrassed Naomi, and achieved nothing, not even humor, and say into the embarrassed silence, I don't know what made me remember that, and Anton pours the last of the wine into their glasses. Their eyes meet and part and Anton says, I'll help you clear the table, and she says no, it's all right, I'll do it myself. She jumps up and breaks the embarrassment but he insists and begins taking the dishes off the table and stacking them in the sink, and she says, sweet of you, and joins him, and the two of them begin working harmoniously together. She washes and he dries and I go on sitting at the table, sober and useless, and Naomi arrives with a wet cloth and begins wiping the table without looking at me. Would you like some grappa, she asks him and he says, I'd love some, and she pours them each a grappa and they come out and join me, sitting down at the table with their grappa like two Tel Aviv yuppies, and I can feel the insult burning in my belly. A wind blows up and wreaks havoc with the newspapers and

Naomi gets up and runs after them. I have to pull myself together, what's going on here anyway, but something is going on here, you have to be an idiot not to see it, Naomi's in a tizzy, this sleepy man has woken her up, and she drinks more grappa and turns to me as if I'm a sulky child and says, why so sour, Ilan? Anton sends me a guiltless look and for a moment I cheer up, nothing's happened, she invited the only real friend I've got in honor of my birthday, it's not her fault that I haven't got any others. By now I'm convinced that there's no plot here and no grounds for my suspicions, and I say, I'm not sour, I simply haven't had anything to drink and this is my natural condition, and this matter-of-fact statement takes the wind out of their sails and puts an end to the conversation. We sit in silence, but the two of them are silent together, in the camaraderie of alcohol, and I'm silent on my own, in sobriety and emptiness. Why don't we go for a walk, Naomi suggests, we haven't been for a walk since we arrived. Good idea, says Anton and stands up. She stands up too and stumbles into him, and the contact between them is brief but electric, and a picture splits my mind: Naomi sitting on him naked with her white flesh, he's a dark version of her yellow-haired lover, they're both big and solid and paternal and mature. Come on, Ilan, let's go for a walk, she says—he doesn't even bother to invite me, he just begins walking—and I look at his bull's neck which leans forward as he lights himself a cigarette. Come on, Ilan, what are you waiting for, she says and begins walking after him without looking at me, and the insult brings an old memory rising to the surface. I was about four years old and one day when I was with my mother in the center of the Carmel I stopped to look into the window of a toy shop. I didn't want to budge and she began saying "Come on, Ilan, come on already," but I dug in my heels and she began walking away, and I knew that she would stop like she always did. But she didn't stop and she went on walking until she suddenly disappeared and I was left

alone in the middle of the big shopping center and I began to
cry in a terror I can still feel now, and all the time she was hiding in the entrance to a building and watching with satisfaction
as I learned my lesson. And now Naomi and Anton set off with
the glasses of grappa in their hands, and I wait for them to turn
round to see if I'm coming, and in fact they do stop and turn
round and wait for me to catch up with them, as if I'm their little brother, and in the meantime he tells her something and she
laughs, throwing back her head and stretching her white neck.
I catch up with them but they're so absorbed in each other that
they don't notice me and therefore they don't begin walking
again but go on standing there looking at each other. It turns
out that they're discovered a mutual friend I never knew existed, and this unites them completely, and I stand there like an
idiot in the middle of their excitement, hearing only the bitter
seething of my insult. Anton's lit up like a chandelier, I haven't
seen him so animated for years, when it's just the two of us he's
usually as dull as a dog, and gradually I begin to lag behind
them, at first they stop and wait for me, but I lag further and
further behind until they disappear into the darkness, and their
voices disappear too, and I imagine them standing in this
remote darkness, looking strange to each other. The darkness
shows a different face, they're not completely themselves, and
therefore the inner darkness is at liberty to show itself. I know
how darkness can be charged by a sense of sin, there's a loaded
silence between them, he doesn't give a fuck for me and with
her it's already routine. All around me it's as quiet as the grave,
not a murmur anywhere, and suddenly the silence is torn—
where are you Ilan? and they're next to me. I've never experienced such silence in my life, says Naomi in a soft voice, we
stood in the middle of this desert of darkness and it was like
magic. Anton lights a cigarette, in the flame of his lighter I
don't read anything in his face. It's amazing here, she says, simply amazing, isn't it Anton? Absolutely, he says and his tone

isn't lecherous but deep and hoarse, and we go back and sit on the porch, and on the spur of the moment I get up and fetch the vodka, why shouldn't I have a drink if I feel like it? I thought you weren't drinking today, she says, and Anton swallows a smile, and suddenly I'm positive that there's something between them and it didn't start today either, let's not forget that she's got a free space now. The whole thing is so clear to me now that I can't believe they don't know I know, what we have here is deliberate malice, with Naomi playing the part of a corrupt woman in a film noir. I take a long sip of vodka which cauterizes the insult like a burn. What now, am I going to have to start killing all her lovers? Maybe my mother knows about their affair too and that's why she said that disgusting sentence to me. Ever since that night I've become complacent about Naomi, I've stopped asking myself where she goes, I've allowed myself to relax—and all the time she's been consoling herself with Anton. I look at him and he looks to me like a stranger, the past is another country, our common memories don't count here. Naomi brings him coffee and as she bends over him to put the cup down her shirt brushes his face. I stretch my arm out to him in a sudden movement and he recoils. A cigarette, I say, I just wanted to take a cigarette out of your shirt pocket, you don't have to jump. He gives me a cigarette and Naomi sits down on the lounger between us, Naomi and her fathers, and the vodka dulls the insult but sharpens the recognition: he doesn't give a fuck for me, life's getting short and he wants my wife who wants all the father figures in Haifa—he doesn't know yet that he shouldn't mess with me. My self-perception now is clear and cruel, everything is disgusting and full of shame, I want to nullify myself, not listen to her asking him about his work like some silly little groupie, asking him to tell her about mysterious unsolved cases, while he, with annoying cynicism, says dismissively, what's there to tell, a murder here and a murder there. But she's dying to hear, come on, tell us a bit, it's awfully interesting, and he sits there with his cigarette, basking in the importance she showers on him, and at first I catch only waves of general flattery—there's no more effective method of trapping someone than getting him to talk about himself and especially to praise himself—and in the end Anton falls into her net. He tells her animatedly about his last murderer, how complicated the investigation was, how much cunning and understanding of the tortuousness of the human mind was needed in order to identify the dark and hidden motive for the murder, and it was only because of a hunch, an intuition on his part—intuition is the main weapon of the detective, he says in a pedagogical tone—that he insisted on concentrating on a certain unimportant suspect as opposed to all the other members of the team, who refused to believe that this ordinary, harmless person was the murderer. He goes on talking, carried away by his story, seeing himself through her eyes, swelling into the size of the suit she's sewn for him, and gradually my jealousy is tinged by anxiety and uneasiness, and I try to efface myself, even though I hardly exist anyway as far as they're concerned. She asks him if there are any borderline cases, cases that aren't investigated because there isn't enough evidence to justify an investigation, and the alarm bells don't go off yet, I'm still preoccupied by the last case. He asks her what she means and she says, nothing in particular, just in general, like oil in the ground, even if nobody discovers it it's still there, no? Surely there must be all kinds of things that happen that nobody knows about except the person who's responsible for them, of course, and she stretches, making the question sound casual, provoking him to make an effort on her behalf. I don't understand what she's getting at, but it's obvious that she's getting at something, and Anton, completely enthralled by her enthusiastic interest in him, asks if she means undetected murders, and she says, yes, for example, and he says, if there's no corpse there's no murder, and she says, always? He says, as a rule, and she asks what the exceptions to the rule are, and I shrink, and he, relaxed and pleased with himself—he feels no suspicion, only gratified vanity—says that actually a few days ago he had received an anonymous letter from a woman who wrote that her lover, who lived in Wadi Salib, had disappeared and she suspected foul play. I turn to stone in my chair, my heart stops, but Naomi's expression doesn't change, all she says is, "really," in a curious but impersonal tone. So that was the letter whose printed "to" I saw in her bag! What else did the letter say, I ask with the last of my strength, and Anton remembers my existence and turns to me rather guiltily, she said that the disappearance of this man seemed strange to her because he left his money with her, so it didn't seem logical to her that he would go off to New Zealand without his money, which is where he said he was going in the unsigned letter he left for her. And she also wrote that she'd been in touch with the British Consulate, which is responsible for visas to New Zealand, where they informed her that no visa had been issued in his name. Interesting, says Naomi tonelessly, and Anton says, not particularly, and gets up. Are you going? she cries in alarm, almost abandoning her poise, afraid he's abandoning her in the middle of the investigation. I'm just going to take a leak, he reassures her, gratified by her disappointment, and all my silly jealousy vanishing in the face of the new danger posed by this letter. That's why she invited him, it's not him she's interested in, she put the whole show on to goad him into action, my cunning spider wove her web around him coldly and soberly, and he galloped right into it, neighing like a horse. Now he's taking a complacent leak, gratified by what he's sure is her admiration, and for a moment a vindictive pleasure blunts the panic which begins to overcome me as we sit alone and wait for him to come back from the bathroom. I never took a development like this into account, and in a single moment the whole thing becomes too big for me, I can't begin to comprehend the immensity of what I've done, it's clear to me that more and more problems are going to come up in all kinds of contexts, the nightmare will only get worse. What was I thinking of when I went to confront him in Wadi Salib? I wasn't thinking, that's what happened, I numbed my brain, for more or less the only time in my life I didn't think, I didn't plan, I wasn't in control. Interesting, isn't it? Naomi says, and in a second I focus my thoughts, yawn to demonstrate indifference, and say, yes, very interesting, and she shuts up and waits for Anton, she's not interested in discussing the subject with me, and when he returns, even before he sits down, she asks him what he intends doing about it. About what? he asks. About the letter, she says, and he says, I don't know, I haven't really had a chance to think about it yet. He's really not interested in talking about work, he wants her the way she was before, bending over him in her T-shirt, but she elegantly leads the conversation back to the letter and announces that she finds the story about the woman and her lover fascinating, she'd really like to know what happens, because there's no question in her mind that the police should open an investigation into it, no woman would write a letter like that just for the heck of it, nobody would write a letter like that without a motive, and motive was the name of the game, wasn't it? And she fixes him with her most appealing look, he obviously hasn't got a clue about what's going on, and she keeps on chattering nonchalantly in this vein, fixing him with her looks, until Anton, who realizes that a pretty woman isn't just a toy to play with but also wants to be taken seriously, says that there could be dozens of reasons for the lover's disappearance, he really hasn't got the strength to go into them. But she hones in on him immediately. What, for example, she says, and he conceals a yawn and says, maybe her husband hid him. I immediately go on high alert in preparation for her look, which indeed comes flying in my direction, and judging by the startled surprise which raises her eyebrows I realize that up to this moment it hasn't entered her head that the husband might be involved. I smile at her and stretch myself with an expression of mild boredom, and she relaxes immediately, no chance of anything like that, she must be saying to herself, not with her delicate husband. And Anton goes on, or maybe he just got tired of her, some people don't know how to break up, so they run away instead. Naomi clouds over, evidently considering the possibility, and Anton takes advantage of her silence to get up—to talk about work he doesn't have to drag himself all the way to the Galilee—and we accompany him to his car. Keep in touch, she says, standing on tiptoe to give him a glancing kiss on the mouth, and tell me how the story turns out. Anton is confused by her kiss and he stands there for a moment exposed and childish—ever since I began inhabiting this parallel reality on a regular basis people have been revealing a disconcerting many-sidedness to me. Drive carefully, she says as he gets into the Escort, and he says, thanks for everything, and drives off, sending a last look at the real Naomi before she turns into a wild fantasy—for I have no doubt that she'll be visiting his bed tonight—and now, as the Escort disappears from view, I say to myself that he probably won't have the patience to wait till he gets home, he's probably lifting her T-shirt right this minute, maybe I should start killing off the fantasizers too. I go on tormenting myself a bit longer, and when we get into bed she asks me in the same tone of a sweet interrogator what do I think, who could have been responsible for the disappearance of that lover, and I say there are a number of possibilities, and she rolls over to me and sits on top of me and looks at me and says, what, for example? Junkies, gangsters, I say and without intending to I add, the husband, and she stares into my eyes, disguising her probing as seduction, but she doesn't come up with anything, my look is perfectly innocent, and so she bends down and kisses me with her velvet lips. I feel that I really need her to look at me now, just the two of us together without anybody else, but she closes her eyes and I can't help thinking that maybe she's busy fantasizing about Anton now, just as he's fantasizing about her, maybe a little Bacchanalia is being conducted here at my expense, but now she begins rocking on me with long, sensual movements and all thought swoons away, until only physical pleasure remains.

25

The days pass in tension and suspicion. I don't know what's going on behind my back, I have no idea if Anton's taking the letter seriously, or if Naomi's spoken to him again. The knowledge which was once mine alone is beginning to spread to others and I'm no longer in control of the situation. I sit in my office waiting for Nava Snir, who comes in with her usual defeated expression, and I don't see how I can be expected to deal with her troubles in my present state. Hi Nava, I say, sit down, and I take out her test, hoping that something concrete and practical will divert her attention from the infatuation which I need like a hole in the head. I praise her work, explain in detail why I deducted five points for her first answer, and she sits cowering in her chair, listening with damp eyes. Her submissiveness enrages me, a murky wave wells up inside me, if she doesn't get out of here soon it will flood us both, and I avert my eyes from her doggy look and swallow the lump of loathing choking my throat. When I hand her the test paper I look up and meet her eyes, only to see two fat tears rolling down her cheeks. Her fleshy lips begin to tremble and she whispers, what have I done? Just tell me if I've done something wrong! Her voice is urgent and demanding. What are you talking about? I ask. About everything that happened between us at the beginning of the semester when you used to look at me like that and then in November when you told me to wait after the lecture and you asked me to bring you the summaries of the course and you invited me to the cafeteria, but lately you've been so cold, and I just want to know if I did something wrong or if I made you angry, because I don't want to spoil what there was between us. Perhaps I shouldn't be saying all this but you ignore me as if there was nothing between us and I haven't got anybody to talk to about it. Suddenly the outpouring stops, she looks at me sorrowfully, and in her eyes I see reflected the imaginary edifice she constructed out of the crumbs I threw her without paying any attention. It's incredible how desperation rehabilitates itself with the help of the imagination—while I was scarcely aware of her existence at all she was playing out a passionate drama in her head—and for a second I look deep into her eyes, into the heart of the tempest, and pity, and especially wonder, dissipate the loathing, and I ask myself how far the pain of others touches us at all, beyond the theoretical concept. Not the pain of the others we love, where self-forgetfulness enables us to take a real interest, but insignificant others like Nava Snir, who it transpires is a person in her own right, with all the fullness and importance of a human being in her own eyes, and whose world I undermined without meaning to and without even giving it a thought. A sweet, sentimental compassion begins to uplift me, I consider my response to her confession carefully, I don't want to shatter her illusion rudely, only to dissolve it gently—but at that moment there's a knock at the door and Givon comes in. The charged atmosphere in the room immediately enflames his nerves and he begins backing out saying, sorry, sorry, as if he'd found me with my fly open. I'll see you when I'm finished here, I say to him, but Nava Snir jumps up like a spring and says, excuse me, I just remembered something, I have to go, and she runs out of the room. Givon's eyes leap after her, and I say immediately, so, what's up with you, as if nothing special had happened here, but since in any case he's only interested in himself, especially in these fateful days of the election of the new dean, he dismisses Nava Snir from his mind and begins to tell me about the complicated negotiations he's conducting with the faculty council. He speaks seriously and sternly, without a drop of irony, the centrality of the subject is unequivocal—if he isn't dean there's no point to the world—and when he finishes I say, don't worry, Givon, it will be all right, compensating for the cliché with an authoritative tone. He sinks into himself, taking comfort in the thought that it is apparently his destiny to bear a cross on his back, and only when I inquire about Aviva he resurfaces, I can see his ego expanding to make room for her as well. Aviva has been very hurt by the whole affair, he says with a pained expression, it's very, very hard on her, for Aviva it's an open wound, and when he says Aviva he relishes the word, as if its taste is always fresh in his mouth, and suddenly I'm sick of the sight of him and I can't wait for him to go so that I can be alone and fall with my heavy load into the pit of despair and loathing and guilt, which is the only place where I feel at home.

26

A heavy silence pervades the house, the silence before the storm. Exactly where it will break out is hard to tell. The melancholy induced by Naomi's longings has given way to a kind of brooding, her thoughts are tense, to me she behaves with reserve. I make no demands of her, but all the time I'm on the alert for hidden currents. At night I sleep the three or four hours afforded me by the pills, but most of the time I lie and absorb the reality which in the stillness of the night is revealed in all its many layers. Under every layer there is another layer with sub-layers, behind which there are more and more layers, and if every law of physics has its spiritual equivalent, presumably the dark inner layers are as infinite as the outer systems. The revelation of this endless proliferation increases my anxiety and impotence, and in the mornings I wander around in a daze. Last night I dreamt that I woke up from a dream of killing someone by accident, someone I didn't recognize, and the waking in the dream was very real, I felt all the relief of waking from a nightmare, and then, in the middle of the relief I woke from the dream awakening into the nightmare of reality. That's the way it goes, and now I lie buried in the blanket, unable to calm my agitation, and time crawls by, and little by little the clamor of death contracts into a single conclusion—I have to put an end to it, there's no other way, I have the Hypnodorm in my bathroom cupboard, despair will give me courage, thirty pills and it will all be over, but then fear rises up and swallows the despair. Not yet, not now, only when it's really necessary, there's no hurry to do something that can only be done once, the option cheers me up and at the end of the morning I manage to drag myself out of bed. Under the stream of hot and cold water I detach myself from the view in depth, the layers dissolve and I calm down and succeed in getting to my class on time, and conducting it as usual, and when I arrive home at about three I see Naomi's yellow Beetle charging out of Hannah Senesh Street. She hasn't seen me, mainly because she's so intent on reaching her destination, which is still unknown to me. I wait a few seconds and begin to follow her, taking care to keep at least one car between us, and when she climbs Zionism Avenue I realize instantly that she's on her way to the French Carmel to look for his father. Next to the city map she stops to check, concentrated and unsuspicious, and with her head thrust forward resolutely she drives to the old-age home. I park at a short distance, she gets out of the Beetle and vanishes behind the gate and I hide behind a bougainvillea bush and wait. After a while she comes out again with the very young nurse, who is telling her something vivaciously, waving her young arms in the air, and pointing with her finger to a spot on her forehead. I understand that she is telling her about the man with the red woolly hat and the black mole at the bottom of his forehead who came to visit the old man with a big, blonde woman, and I hurry back to wait in the car, hiding deep in the seat. After a few minutes she comes out with a distracted expression and walks to the Beetle with an absent-minded air. For a moment it seems to me that she recognizes my car in the mirror, but that's impossible, my old Volvo is too ordinary to stand out, and she's too far away to see the license plate. She sits there for a minute or two before starting the engine and taking off, and with me at a safe distance behind her she drives down Hasan Shoukri to Wadi Salib. I understand that she is conducting a private investigation into the disappearance of her lover, parallel to the official investigation which she has initiated, and I say to myself that not Anton but my wife will solve the case, my reason for living will be the death of me, and so be it. This fatalism relaxes me and I don't climb the steps after her, but remain sunk in the car seat, waiting for her to return, In the meantime I light a Gitane—lately I've been consoling myself with lethal cigarettes—and when I inhale the bitter smoke it occurs to me that Anton might choose this precise moment to turn up here in order to investigate the anonymous letter, who knows how much Naomi's been nagging him since she first brought it up. My fatalism melts away, an uneasy tension takes its place, I glance into the mirror, looking for his Escort, imagining to myself how he'll arrive and climb the steps and find Naomi there, and she'll confess to him and he'll understand everything in a flash and summon me to an interrogation and get a confession out of me without any difficulty. My nerves are fraying, I ask myself how much more of this I can endure, and only when I see her appearing at the top of the stairs do I stop to wonder what she was looking for there and what she found. She gets into the Beetle, makes a full turn back into Hasan Shoukri, and drives up it in the direction of the district court, passes the junction and slows down next to the bistro, looking through the window for Anton. But Anton isn't there and she continues in the direction of Prophets Street, and the uncertainty is killing me and after a brief interval I follow her into the house and ask her in a friendly, neutral voice how her day was. I open the mail and kiss her casually as if everything's normal and she says, fine, with the same absentmindedness I noticed in her before. I cut up vegetables for a salad and in order to clear the air I tell her about Givon who has declared a third world war against the department. The story soon falls flat, because it's impossible not to see that she's straining to try to tell me something. What is it, Naomi, I say in a benevolent, avuncular voice, tell me what's bothering you. Nothing, it's not important, she says, and from the tone of her voice I conclude that we're not talking about any dramatic discoveries here. I open my arms and say, come here, Naomi, and she immediately surrenders herself. Tell me what's happening to you, I whisper into her hair, and slowly she extricates herself from my arms, sits down on the arm of the chair, sneezes, and goes to get a tissue, sits down again, sneezes again, rubs her eyes, gets up and comes over to me. I don't move, whatever I do now won't change anything anyway, I just try to be as relaxed and matter-of-fact as possible. Ilan, she whispers in a kind of hopelessness, where were you on that night? For a minute I say nothing, mainly in order to think one move ahead, and then I give her a warm, loving and, especially, innocent look and ask, what night? That night when you woke up the next morning with pneumonia, she says. I look down at the carpet and take a lot of time, and then I say in a dry, thin voice, I'm sorry. She says, what about, and I say, I don't understand how it happened, how I did such a thing, how I let myself get into such a situation. What situation, she asks, opening her eyes wide, and I look at her with genuine sorrow and say, being unfaithful to you, and fall silent. I'm fully aware of the satanic situation I'm creating, but I haven't got another choice. With your student? she says, and I say, yes, it doesn't mean anything, I'm sorry. She gets up and walks around a bit, goes into the bedroom, the bathroom, the kitchen while I stand still and wait for her to come back to me, and when she returns I see that the darkest clouds are gone. She has dismissed the possibility that I murdered her lover, and in relation to that infidelity is small change. Even though I don't believe that the jealousy of the cheated partner is relieved by his own cheating, I'm sure that she won't permit herself to make a scene now, and I go on standing in front of her in all my shame. I love you so much, Naomi, I say, and I feel that this is the only reality I'm capable of truly experiencing. Something of this apparently rubs off on her, because she looks at me with gentle sorrow, and now a long silence brings us together and my heart goes out to her in her sorrow—

it seems that a person can be a murderer and nevertheless love
with all his heart—and I lift her chin with my finger and tell her
that my one-time unfaithfulness with my student was necessary
to me as a kind of escape from my too-great love for her, and
that nothing like that will ever happen again. She looks at me
with transparent pearls glittering in her eyes, overcome perhaps
with her own guilt, and murmurs that she's tired, all she wants
is to sleep, and she turns away and goes to the bedroom, saving
us from the situation which weighs heavily on us both. I go out
to the balcony with a brandy and a cigarette, where I sit and
stare at the sea spread out below like a carpet, and everything is
calm and solid, and again the thin shell isolating me from the
heavy weight of reality cracks, and in one charged moment the
whole picture is screened in my mind: the discovery, the investigation, the arrest, the trial, the verdict, the sentence, the end
of my life, all illuminated by poisonous flashes of the clear
understanding that I'm lost, whatever happens I'm lost, and
because of me Naomi's lost too, and there's no way out, and
nevertheless I go on sitting on the balcony in all my unjustified
existence, breathing the clear evening air.

27

A ring at the door startles me from the computer and I get up and go to peek through the peephole. The woman from across the landing is standing there and waiting apathetically. I consider not opening the door but right then I see her leaning forward to look through the peephole, which is blocked by my eye. I immediately move away, but since I think that she may have seen me anyway, I reluctantly open the door. She says hello and smiles, and I smile back mechanically and wait for her to tell me what she's short of, which is usually one of the basic commodities, but she goes on standing there smiling, and since I don't like asking her what she wants, I move aside to make way for her and she enters and walks straight into the living room, limping slightly. I leave the door open, to make it clear that the visit is strictly on a temporary basis, and she stands opposite the big window, looks outside and says, very nice, my apartment faces the street. Yes, I say, and she says, you could say that I live with my back to the sea, still without looking at me, and I think that perhaps she came in to enjoy the sea view, but then she turns round and stares at me, and I sense that she wants to say something but she can't get the words out. I begin to feel uncomfortable and I say, is there something you wanted to say? She smiles a crooked smile and says, there are so many things I'd like to say that I wouldn't even know where to begin, and I don't understand what she wants so I say, what? And she says, you can imagine that there are things I could say, no? In order to evade her eyes I light a cigarette, and in the meantime I decide not to let my paranoia take over and to stick strictly to the facts, which are basically rational and can therefore be relied on. I breathe out the smoke and also the superfluous air trapped in my lungs and say, what do you mean? and she keeps her eyes fixed on me and says, what do you think I mean? I haven't got a clue, I say almost rudely and she asks, you're looking for the reason why I came in here, aren't you? That's natural, isn't it, I say, and she takes her eyes off me and says, yes, it's natural, and begins walking to the door. I'm sure she's going to close it and start talking, but she says, I really don't want to bother you, and walks out, and I go on standing there, rapidly going over what she said in my mind, and paranoia sends me rushing to her door. I ring the bell but she doesn't answer. Tova, I say loudly—I've never used her name before, but I read it every day on her door—and after a minute she opens the door and I rush in immediately, what did you want to tell me? My voice must be transparent, because she says, are you really interested, and I think I can hear a note of hidden mockery in her question. Otherwise why would I ask, I answer, and she begins to turn round and asks, what will you have to drink? Nothing, I say and in a flash I remember that she works as a stage manager in the Haifa Theater, which has a branch in Wadi Salib too—that's what this is all about, she must have seen me there and followed me. I sit down so as not to have to worry about my control over my body and say, I don't understand what you want, and she stands over me and says, just to talk a little, that's all. What about? I ask, and she says, I decided not to use the excuse of a cup of sugar, I just wanted to drop in to talk a little, but it doesn't matter now, because *The Young and the Restless* is about to begin so I'm fixed up for the next hour. In my relief I shower her with cheap sympathy, and after listening to the story of her life, which it transpires was dictated by her slight limp more than anything else, and giving her a few pieces of authoritative advice, I say

I'm sorry but I have to fly to the *Technion*. On the way I ask myself the meaning of these frequent encounters I've been having lately with people whose loneliness is so savage, why are they suddenly showing up in my life, and the whole bunch parade through my head, the skinny Arab girl, and the soldier, and the Russian woman from the rubbish dump, and now the neighbor from across the landing, and although I remind myself that none of them are connected to what I did, their crowded appearance in my life, and above all the riddle of their existence, troubles me now no less than the deed itself. I go into the office, where Shoshie informs me that Givon has finally succeeded in wearing Davis down and getting him to back his candidacy, and after a stormy meeting of the faculty council he was chosen as the next dean. And now Givon himself, proud and happy, buttonholes me in the corridor and announces with the magnanimity of a victor that Davis is actually a remarkable man, he and Aviva were simply mistaken about him and slandered him unjustly, and accordingly they intend inviting us all to a dinner which they themselves will cook, and in the meantime they're trying to make up their minds between vegetarian and fish—he and Aviva are vegetarians who eat fish—and first of all he wants to know if Naomi and I eat fish, because if not they'll go for vegetarian. I feel my aggression rising at his hysteria, but I only say, fish is fine, and go into the class which is already waiting for me. Nava Snir is standing next to the overhead projector, the first transparency is already screened on the wall—since the reception hour I've managed to elude her, even though she lay in wait for me twice in the office, but I only smiled at her sympathetically and told her tactfully that I was busy, and now she's standing in front of me with her papers, waiting for me to signal her to begin her lecture. Go ahead, Nava, I say, and she takes a breath, tries to control her trembling hands and voice, and begins: Most astrophysicists today think that the number of binary systems is greater than those we are able to see. We know that the dominant characteristic of binary systems is the dynamic interaction between the components of the system, with the dynamic behavior of each component being influenced by the presence of its companion. When the mass of one star is significantly larger than its companion's, the system's binarity is hard to detect, although the partner with low mass does have a significant influence on the system. In the first part of my lecture I'm going to talk about the physics of binary systems, and afterwards I'll talk about close binary systems, in other words, when the two components of a binary system are too close to each other. Here she sends me a look hungry for approval, and gets it, and continues: The basic physics of the system stems from the gravitational interaction between the components of the system. Two objects which attract each other gravitationally, and execute a periodic circular motion, will continue that movement only if the centrifugal force created by the rotation balances the gravitational force. The two components of a binary system revolve with the same frequency around their common center of mass, and the distance of each component from the center of mass is in inverse relation to the mass of that component. If we use a coordinate system centered in the center of mass, we get this formula—she turns to the transparency on which the formula is written, and I stop listening and look at her. All of a sudden I realize that she can save me, she can provide me with an alibi for that night both for Naomi and for the police, and while she analyses the formula I plan how I'll present it to her, how I'll invite her to my office and direct the conversation to the place where I want it to go, she's like putty in my hands, I'll make her believe in my secret love for her and ask her for her help. When she concludes her lecture I praise her enthusiastically, calling her a model student, and she looks at me with moved eyes and burning cheeks, and when the class is over and she folds up the projector, I ask her to come to my office, I want to talk to her. I hardly have time to get there myself and she's already walking through the door and sitting down opposite me. Nava, I say to her, and she says, yes, and leans forward, yielding herself up to me, and I look at her stubby little nose and suddenly I'm appalled at myself and the idea of exploiting her so meanly, how could I have contemplated such a thing, how much lower am I going to sink? I quickly pull myself together and say with all the tact and delicacy I can muster that she's a young and exceptionally gifted girl, with a good chance of going far in the field of astrophysics, and I'm sorry if I misled her into thinking that there was anything between us, I wouldn't have dared to contemplate it even though she's a very attractive girl, of course. My sympathy for her grows as the sadness in her eyes deepens, and I go on to say that sometimes students fall in love with a teacher's image and not necessarily with the man himself, especially when he's not such a great bargain to begin with. She smiles faintly, and I smile back warmly, and she says, can I come and talk to you sometimes? Whenever you like, I say, and I feel genuinely sorry for her. How could I have contemplated doing something so despicable? How quickly a man can become brutalized at the expense of others in order to save himself, I think to myself and she leaves and I go on sitting there trying to decipher the sign. She is a kind of mirror in which I am supposed to find myself, apparently with regard to the meaning of excessive love—but to some extent the whole story could also be the music of chance, and accordingly I abandon my efforts at finding a deeper meaning and begin surfing the Internet. For almost two hours I succeed in resting from myself, and towards noon I meet Davis and the two of us get into a discussion about the Givon affair. The problem with Givon, says Davis with mild Anglo-Saxon irony, is that he has no idea of who he is. He's at sixes and sevens between all his different identities, and in any case, he goes on, all these identities together tormented me for two weeks, day in day out, so in the end I gave in. He and Aviva will be the next dean and all we can do is hope for the best. Never mind, I say, let's not forget that he's the only really brilliant scientist in the faculty, and Davis says, you won't be able to get out of being dean forever, Ilan, you know that. There are some people who can't do it, but you can and you will. I say, absolutely, and we part with silly pats on the shoulder and I drive home, but on second thoughts I climb the Carmel to have a beer in the bar opposite the park where I used to sit before Naomi, who said that she didn't get the idea of the place and didn't enjoy being there, the combination of roughnecks and yuppies got on her nerves, and apparently she isn't the only one, because when I get there the place is empty. I sit on a stool at the bar and order a large beer, and after few sips I light a cigarette which I enjoy very much, and while I'm sitting there a tall girl with a child comes into the bar. The girl is wearing extravagant, brightly colored rags, but when she approaches the bar I realize that it's a young boy with exaggerated make-up on his face, and he sits next to me and says to the little girl, go and make a peepee now, Saraleh, or else it'll come out in the street. His voice is deep in spite of his effeminate manner of speaking. Give me a 777 and an orange juice, he says to the barman, who extricates himself from his newspaper and says, so what happened with the dame from Tira, and the boy says, forget about it, I saw her lying on the steps of the Cinematheque. There is a kind of authority in his speech, which is in striking contrast to his appearance, and now he turns to me and I can feel him staring at me from the side and I turn to face him and he looks me up and down with eyes that look like two black holes in the painted mask of his face. I take out my wallet and ask for the bill, intent on getting out of there before this apparition swells with all the meanings I force down its throat, and without waiting for my change I start for the door, but he says, excuse me, and I stop and say, yes? I read faces, he says, if you're interested it'll cost you twenty shekels, and I say, what, and he says, it's called physiognomy, and the barman says, he's good at it, you won't believe the things he sees, his mother was a witch in Tira, people came to see her all the way from Tel Aviv. The boy says, my name is Avner Turgeman, maybe you've heard of me, there was an article about me in the paper. I say, no thank you, but he puts a ring-adorned hand on my arm and says, ten shekels, I'll tell you everything, and I say, no, really, thank you, I have to go. In the meantime the little girl comes back and the barman says, that's his sister, she's already got all kinds of powers too, it's in their genes, it's worth your while, believe me, I wouldn't let him make a nuisance of himself to my customers if it wasn't something special, he told me all about myself. I have to go, I say again, and walk out, but before I reach my car I turn round and go back into the bar. The boy is sitting with his back to the bar as if he's waiting for me and I go straight up to him and ask, is there enough light here for it, and he says I'm not a skin specialist, and I sit opposite him and empty my mind of thoughts. He looks at me intently, his little sister sits on the floor and sucks her orange juice noisily through a straw, and he says to her, without taking his eye off me, shut it, Saraleh, and goes on fixing me with his eyes with their fringe of artificial eyelashes. A kind of reckless desire for something to happen begins to make my flesh tingle, I summon up the image of the dead lover and transmit it to him, my heart thumps in awful excitement, and the little girl says, tell him, and I turn to her and ask, tell me what? Suddenly the boy stands up and says twice, forget about it, forget about it, and begins walking out with the little girl behind him. I get up and run after them, wait a minute, I call, and he stops for a minute and says, leave all that shit alone, and gives his hand to the little girl, who gives me an unpleasant, grown-up look. I return to my car and begin to drive and I know that wherever I go these messengers will be waiting for me, and without thinking I drive down to Hadar again.

Something unclear is beginning to grow inside me, as if I'm ripening for something, and when I find myself going down Bialik Street and turning into Hasan Shoukri, I realize that I've come to look for Anton. I don't know exactly what I want from him, and while I'm waiting I ask myself if I've come to him to obtain information or to pour it out, because what's so urgent about seeing him, and since the reason isn't clear I assume that it grew from one of the sub-strata which I have no direct communication with, and I decide to flow with myself and leave things to sort themselves out. I see him sitting there, the Ben Nathan family detective, with his beer and his cigarette and his dark glasses, and he says, Hi, Ilan, and pulls up a chair for me. I order a beer and a vodka and as the waitress, who is fading away before our eyes, bangs the drinks down on the table, I think that perhaps I've simply come to turn myself in. This thought alarms but also arouses me, because at least I'm doing something, and after we exchange a few perfunctory remarks he opens the paper at the mourning notices and says, look here, Shimi Lerer's dead. The name Shimi Lerer throws me back abruptly into another time—Shimi Lerer, his father had a bakery, he was our age, I say with the instinctive dread that clutches at us when we hear that someone of our own age has died. So we're beginning to die, he says in my mother's brusque tone, and I think a little about Shimi Lerer, who used to wear short pants without underpants so that he could scratch his enormous balls at his ease, and he would sit scratching himself for hours on end like a zombie. So Shimi Lerer's dead and the sky hasn't fallen, I say in philosophical sadness, and Anton says, it doesn't fall so quickly. I look at the notice in order to take my leave of Shimi Lerer and see that his funeral is taking place at half past three today at the Sde Yehoshua cemetery. All at once I decipher the sign: it wasn't for nothing that I came here to see Anton an hour before the funeral of Shimi Lerer who is about to be buried next to our kindergarten teacher and my dead man, it's clear to me now that I have to go there with Anton, I have to follow the signs not because they're certain but because I have no other direction in the hopeless chaos engulfing me. I read the bit about the funeral aloud and Anton says, well, what about it, and I say nonchalantly, why don't we go, but he doesn't understand what I want of his life and he says, why on earth should we go to Shimi Lerer's funeral? When was the last time we remembered he was alive at all? Come on, let's go, it's the least we can do for him, I persist, but Anton says again, what for? I haven't even thought of him for thirty years, why should I go to his funeral now? Come on, we really should go, I say firmly, like someone who knows exactly what he's doing, and he gives in and says, all right, let's go, maybe God will give us credit for it, and as we're about to get into his Escort which is parked on the pavement, Naomi's yellow Beetle appears in Bialik Street. She's looking for Anton again, and he says enthusiastically, here's Naomi, and waves to her and she stops next to us, putting on a poor show of surprise, and says distractedly, what are you doing here Ilan? Having a beer with Anton, I say and put my hand on her shoulder, but what are *you* doing here? I dropped into the Mashbir to do some shopping, she says, and indeed there's a plastic carrier bag from the Mashbir lying on the seat next to her. We're going to a childhood friend's funeral, I'll be home late, I say in a friendly voice and give the Beetle a symbolic push to signal her that it's time to leave. What funeral, Anton suddenly wakes up, I've got work to do, I haven't got the time for this nonsense, I'm going back to the office, and he says goodbye to Naomi, who's already looking for a way of remaining alone with him, and starts getting into his car. But I know that it's out of the question for him to go now, he has to come with me, and I say almost violently, damn it Anton, screw work for a minute, Shimi Lerer isn't going to die again, let's pay him a bit of the respect we never gave him when we were children, and I get into his car, ignoring his protests, and say, let's go, if we don't leave now we'll miss the whole thing, we're already late as it is. Naomi, who has gotten out of the Beetle in the meantime, gives me a strange look, and I realize that I may have gone too far in my insistence, and I say, more mildly this time, let's go to the funeral. By now I'm ready to give in but suddenly Naomi says, let's all go, I like strangers' funerals, they give me an opportunity to cry a little, and she adds mockingly, let's pay some respect to Shimi Lerer and to Ilan too. Anton gives in and while she parks her car and he makes some phone calls to his office I say to myself that if Naomi has arrived now, for reasons of her own, she too is part of the sign, and it's all preordained—the three of us will go to this funeral next to her dead lover's grave and whatever happens will happen exactly as it's meant to happen. We set out, I sit on the back seat with the natural inferiority of the person sitting in the back and taking no part in the consultations about the journey because there's no point in raising my voice for every little thing, especially since Naomi switches on the radio and I can't hear anything anyway, and only when we stop in the traffic jam at the Carmel Beach junction I realize that they're talking about the anonymous woman's letter. I lean forward, preparing myself for Anton's answer, but he only curses the traffic jam, and Naomi asks again, conveying infantile curiosity, and he says that they made a few inquiries, the lover has no family, because his old father just died, so there isn't really anyone left to question, except perhaps in Wadi Salib, where they spoke to a few spaced-out junkies who didn't have a clue. Naomi says, there's no such thing as a person with no family at all, there must be some uncles or aunts or cousins or something, and Anton, who isn't really interested and who's busy concentrating on the traffic jam, says that there's some old aunt who hasn't heard from him in years, and he sent someone to talk to her. This old aunt wakes me up completely, but I immediately tell myself to keep calm and not go rushing in, I'll confine myself to finding out discreetly if the old lady needs anything. Naomi says, so are you telling me that there's nothing more to be done, but Anton is now concerned exclusively with the traffic jam—traffic jams drive him crazy, all his composure crumbles in a traffic jam—and after a few minutes he takes out the "Kojak," slaps it onto the roof, turns on the siren, and we begin driving rapidly along the verge of the road, ignoring the traffic jam. And so it happens that I'm driven straight to the scene of the crime in a police car with its blue light flashing and its sirens wailing, and the situation is so satanic and so drastic that I can't step to the side and simply observe it, and I sit there paralyzed with terror. But in the midst of the panic is a kind of calm that comes from a strange sense of security, as if I'm in the place where I'm meant to be and therefore I'm protected, just as a sick man feels in hospital, where side by side with his anxiety he also feels safe. We arrive at the cemetery where we park the car at the entrance. Anton and Naomi walk in front of me, Naomi is explaining something to him and he's listening without turning to look at her, while I bring up the rear, dragging my feet in the gravel. Opposite me I see Nahal Siah and the house with the inner courtyard, and when we enter the gates we look round for the funeral. There they are, says Naomi, pointing to the grave containing my kindergarten teacher and her lover, and indeed, not far from there a very poorly attended funeral service is being conducted for Shimi Lerer. A handful of old people are standing next to the open grave with shocked expressions, no doubt worried mainly about themselves and their own health, and we go over and join them. I stare at the earthly remains of Shimi Lerer wrapped in his shroud, and for some reason his death suddenly seems self-evident and no big deal, so Shimi Lerer's dead, it already sounds like a cliché, and now the rabbi turns to Shimi Lerer's wife, I imagine she's his wife because she has a ritual rip in her blouse, and asks her who's going to say *Kaddish*, and she's confused and she doesn't understand the question, and the old woman sitting next to her on a little folding chair—I recognize her immediately, she's our kindergarten teacher's sister, they lived across the road from Shimi Lerer—says that there's no son, only a daughter in Canada who couldn't make it to the funeral. I push myself forward, avoiding Naomi and Anton's eyes, and say, I'll say *Kaddish*. The rabbi asks me who I am and I say, a childhood neighbor, and he says that I'll be doing a *mitzva*, and hands me the prayer book. I begin to read, *Yitgadal vayitkadash shmei rabba be'alma dibrakhe ure utei veyamlikh malkhutei behaiyekhon uveyameikhon ubehayei dekhol beit Yisrael ba'agal ubizman kariv ve'imru amen*, and this time, since it's an official funeral and not a grotesque stolen moment like that night, I take my time and read slowly, trying to feel intent and ignoring Naomi's questioning look. When I'm finished and the ceremony is over I go up to Shimi Lerer's purblind wife, introduce myself, squeeze her thick arms and say, may you know no more sorrow—from the day I learnt to say this sentence confidently I like using it, it doesn't make any sense but it moves the person who says it—and while she murmurs, thank you, my eye falls on the kindergarten teacher's sister, who's still sitting on her folding chair and looking at the grave. All those years they lived together, sometimes she would come to help out in the kindergarten, the Schwester sisters people called them in the neighborhood, my mother said they were lesbians and it took me years to understand what she meant. And now, because this little old lady is connected to the circle of my dead, I read her too as a sign which may be on the point of revealing its secret to me, and even though I remind myself that she used to live opposite Shimi Lerer and therefore her being here doesn't constitute a sign, I go up to her with a certain excitement. She's busy folding up her stool and converting it into a walking stick—she's as small and hunched as a little devil but full of energy—and I greet her warmly and introduce myself, I'm

Erna Ben Nathan's son, your sister used to be my kindergarten teacher. She examines me for a minute and says briskly, yes, yes, of course, you're a big boy now I see, my sister, may she rest in peace, used to say you were a sensitive child, and she looks at me with old, defeated eyes, and I can't understand how I dared to desecrate the memory of her beloved sister like that, as if she had no other reason for dying, and like a lethal poison, coming to replace the previous one which isn't strong enough any more, a new strain of shame and self-loathing fills me, and in order not to abandon myself to it I call Naomi and Anton and introduce them to her. She presses Naomi's hand and examines her with a trembling head. Yes, my sister may she rest in peace told me that you married a young girl, it must be refreshing, she says, and I can't hear any mockery in her voice, only a statement of fact, and I take in Anton's satisfaction as he lights two cigarettes and give me one. You remember Anton Karam, I say and turn her towards him with exaggerated gentleness, she's so small and crumpled I'm afraid she may fall to pieces in my hands. Yes of course, the Arab child whose mother knew a lot of languages, she says with concentration, it's important to her to shine and prove that she's still a human being who deserves a place in the world, and she asks, is your mother alive? She's alive, he says gently, she was at your sister's funeral. I don't remember anything about my sister's funeral, she says and her face closes, and Anton says, I'm sorry, I didn't intend to remind you, but she waves her hand and says in a curt, dry, Germanic tone, we lived together for eighty-three years, how can I forget, and now if you young people will excuse me I'll pay her a visit. She begins walking towards the grave which is starting to burn inside me and which I feel impelled to visit too, but I go on standing where I am, because at the same time I know that I should get away from here as quickly as possible. I look at Naomi and Anton who have started walking in the direction of the gate, and I decide to visit the grave, but fear paralyses me,

I'm not sure I can make it on my own, and when they stop and Naomi says, come on, Ilan, I know that I need them with me at the grave, something like going for a fateful medical test with a person close to you, so you can collapse on his shoulder if necessary and from whom you can expect nothing but sympathy and compassion. I hurry after them, nervously lighting another cigarette even though I'm short of breath, and call in an urgent voice, we have to go and put a stone on Henzi Bauer's grave, we didn't go to the funeral, it's the least we can do, and they exchange glances like a married couple, and Anton says, okay, we'll go and put a stone on Henzi Bauer's grave, but what are you getting so excited about? I realize that from their point of view I'm making a fuss about nothing, they've got no problem with putting a stone on the grave, I've forgotten that it's only my brain being crushed in this avalanche of thoughts, and I immediately put a brake on my hysteria, and since I'm still quite far from them, I make a sign to say "I can't hear," as if the urgent tone they detected in my voice was only a question of volume. They come up to me and we all walk over to the grave together, like a team, and the first thing I see is that they haven't put up a gravestone, it's all just as I left it, and before I can stop myself the words come out of my mouth, why isn't there a gravestone? The old sister, interpreting my words as a criticism of the family's burial practices, says, with us it's customary to put up the gravestone on the anniversary of the death, everyone does as they see fit. She says the last words angrily, and I say placatingly, of course, you're quite right, and Anton and Naomi put a stone on the grave, which is what they came for, and I stand there staring at the pathetic little mound of earth, which I now see I made a sloppy job of, and I feel like tidying it up, to make it a bit more dignified, but I don't move. In the meantime Naomi stands over the grave in silence, with her head bowed, easily connecting to the sadness and loss basic to her personality, which apparently led her, among other things, to choose me and my age, and Anton, polite and bored, with the old lady sitting directly opposite him, begins to read the names and dates on the graves on either side, which are also mounds of earth without gravestones. I see that he'd like to move on but politeness forbids it, and so he looks from one to the other, pouring over the letters as if he's reading an article in newspaper, pausing from time to time on my grave too to read the sign on it, and gradually I begin to realize that he isn't doing it out of boredom, he's discovered something that intrigues him and rivets his attention, and now he bends down over the grave on the left, pulls a stalk of grass out of the mound and feels it with his fingers, then he does the same with the middle grave, pulling a piece of grass out of the mound and examining it. I still have no idea of what he's up to but my heart begins to run amok, and after he's finished with the grass he stands still and sinks into thought, and the silence is driving me crazy, he's onto something, that's clear, but I don't dare say anything, hoping against hope that it's all happening in my sick mind. This isn't what I wanted to happen, all I wanted was to commune a little with the place of my fall from grace, Anton's silence hangs over me threateningly and only when Naomi has exhausted her sadness and says to the old lady—she says it simply and unselfconsciously—may you know no more sorrow, I hear Anton say, mainly to himself, strange, and only my heart skips a beat, Naomi and the sister are somewhere else, and I say noncommittally, what's strange? Somebody's disturbed this grave, he says, and Naomi, who heard him this time, wakes up and says, what do you mean, somebody's disturbed the grave, and I suddenly feel myself thrown outside the reality of the situation, my exhausted mind retires and leaves me impermeable and uninvolved, as if a few key nerves have been disconnected from the system, and Anton says again, someone's tampered with this grave, there's no other explanation. No other explanation for what, says Naomi, and now the sister too straightens up and asks, what are you talking about? Anton pauses, perhaps to impress Naomi, and the sister demands to be told what's going on, and Naomi says, Anton claims that someone's tampered with the grave. Which grave, the old lady asks in alarm, and Naomi says gently, your sister's grave, and by now the old lady is so upset that she can't understand anything. What, what, what, she pleads, and Anton says gently, nothing, I didn't say anything, Miss Bauer, everything's fine, after which he turns to us and says in an undertone, there are three graves here that were dug on the same day, but only two of them have long grass growing on them. On this one, and he points to Henzi's grave, the grass is sparse and short. In other words, the ground was turned over a week or two after the burial, and since then no significant growth has taken place because at about that time it stopped raining. In short, someone, for a reason which I can't imagine at the moment, has tampered with this grave. He falls silent, and then I hear him say that someone's dug up the grave, and Naomi asks, but why should anyone dig up this grave, and the old sister wrings her hands and says, what does it mean, what does it mean, and Anton puts his hand on her tiny shoulder and says, everything's all right, there's nothing to worry about, nothing's happened, and Naomi helps her to fold up her stool, and the two of them begin walking slowly to the gate, with Anton and me behind them. It's really strange, he says to himself and to me, and I say, what's so strange about it, all I know is that I have to make light of his discovery, a passing dog or cat must have done it—this stroke of brilliance comes to me in a flash—what's there to get so excited about? And I suppose the cat or the dog tidied it up afterwards too so as not to hurt the family's feelings? he asks, and I realize that he's going to open the grave—he'll get permission to dig up the grave and he'll find the lover from Wadi Salib and in the end it'll lead him to Naomi, who knows how many people there are in Haifa who saw them together? I have to put the idea out of his head, but

I know that fear will make my voice tremble and so I keep quiet, and in the meantime I try to pull myself together, and when he stoops over to light a cigarette in the wind I manage a yawn and say, the whole thing's nonsense, who'd want to disturb Henzi Bauer's grave, and he takes a drag on his cigarette and says, I haven't got a clue, all I know is that everything has a reason, anyway let's leave it now. But I don't want to leave it and I say, the reasons are usually so trivial that nobody bothers to think of them, and he doesn't react, but I go on anyway, ninety nine percent of the things that might happen don't happen, and he says without stopping, and what about the last one percent, that exists just as much as the others, you're the one who always says so. Naomi joins us and we say goodbye to the old lady who gets into a taxi, and walk to the Escort, and the subject remains up in the air, and as we drive back to town I realize that I'm going to get out of the car without knowing what's going to happen, and there's nothing I can do about it, the situation has slipped out of my control long ago, and impotence makes me withdraw into a stupor again and I lean back and close my eyes, abandoning myself to a future shrouded in a fog of uncertainty. Ilan, what are your plans? Naomi turns her head to look at me and sees nothing, are you coming home or going back to the *Technion*? I look at the back of Anton's neck and his bristly hair and I say, I think I'll drop in to see my mother, an idea which pops into my head the moment I utter the words. Do you want me to come with you? she asks and I say almost inaudibly, no, there's no need, and she says, what? and I say haltingly, it's all right, go home, and she turns right round and says, why don't you want me to come with you to your mother's? Why shouldn't I want you to come to my mother's with me, I say, and in order not to sink into a stupor again I start to talk, collecting a few words first and waiting for them to compose themselves into a subject, and they look at me— Anton looks through the mirror—and they can't understand what I'm getting at, but I ignore them and go on babbling about nothing, and as I do so, I sense that I'm suddenly experiencing difficulties in pronouncing the sibilants, s, z, sh, and so on. In fact, ever since the operation on my gums a few months ago I've had a problem with these letters, and this is what I tell them too: ever since the operation on my gums I've had a problem with sibilants, like s and sh and z, I hope they haven't been screwed up for good, haven't you noticed that I've got a problem with them? Naomi turns around to look at me and says, Ilan, are you all right? I immediately drop the subject and yawn as if the only thing wrong with me is tiredness, and I smile at Naomi and say, so I think we can sum up today by saying that Shimi Lerer is dead, and Anton says, may he rest in peace, and stops next to my Volvo. I can't see his face, but for some reason it seems to me that he's suddenly in a hurry to get rid of us, he doesn't even try to keep Naomi with him, I'm sure he's going to run straight to the authorities to get permission to dig up the grave, he doesn't even want to wait till tomorrow morning, he wants to go right now and find out why that grave was tampered with. But when he turns to me to say goodbye I see that he isn't in a hurry at all, he's simply impatient, he's already wasted too much time on my caprice, there's a whole world out there that's not connected to me and my grave. He says a friendly goodbye to Naomi, my head clears a little and I accompany her to her Beetle. So we'll meet at your mother's, she says, and I rumple her hair and say, why don't you go home and make spaghetti, I'll be here in half an hour, I haven't eaten a thing since breakfast, and she says, you can't wait to be rid of me, and she smiles sweetly, blows me a kiss and drives off. A feeling of loss stabs me, this is the way it could have been if I hadn't done what I did, Naomi and me without the dead man between us, and the feeling of loss chokes me, it could so easily not have happened, I could so easily not have done what I did, the whole thing is so outlandish, so out of character that for a moment it seems possible, theoretically at least, that it actually didn't happen at all, and I abandon myself to bitter-sweet feelings of regret for what might have been, but the finality of the situation quickly extinguishes this consolation and leaves me sitting in the car like a cold lump and driving toward my mother's to pour my heart out. How will I get through the days, how will I get through the years, how will I survive, and I say out loud, I murdered a man. I roll the word round in my mouth to empty it of its meaning, and as I drive up Ben Gurion Avenue I say honestly to myself that what I did was the kind of thing that happens by force of inertia, without being planned in advance, that is, this fact explains only the how but not the thing itself, and I try to grasp the moment as it occurred in space not in time, and as I approach my mother's house I slow down and for the first time I dare to reconstruct myself, with him, not as a memory but as the thing itself. The pictures race through my head as I try to get inside them, I see him sitting there with my pipe and asking for a light, and I try to get inside my emotional state at the time, but succeed in experiencing only blindness, like being blinded by a strong light, I approach him with the lighter in a round, stooping movement, after that a moment of violent confusion, like a street brawl suddenly erupting in the middle of a tense silence, my hand pushes the pipe into his mouth, surprise floods his eyes, and now I squeeze myself into the blurred sensation of that blinding moment, the moment between before and after, and I try to charge the words and penetrate their meaning. The senses may abdicate for a while, but what comes to take their place if not other, hidden, dormant senses that awake from their dark slumbers and begin to operate in an anarchic stream of their own, resulting in an inevitable conflagration when they come into contact with the external circumstances, exactly like a chemical reaction, and this thought affords a little clarity and an imaginary feeling of control. Like my mother says, anyone capable of seeing reality crystal clear can in some way master it, in some very pale way, and I drive into the parking space but go on sitting in the car, until my mother, who has heard the car, comes out of the house and walks up to me. What now, she asks, and I say, I'll tell you in a minute, and go into the house and sit down on the sofa. She sits down next to me with an expression of despair on her face, it's obvious she can't take any more dramas, and I tell her the facts without interpretation, how I dragged Anton and Naomi to Shimi Lerer's funeral, and how I insisted on visiting Henzi's grave with them, and she doesn't say why did you bring it on yourself? She only leans back and looks at her parchment yellow palm as if she's discovered something there, and I abandon myself to silence, waiting without involving myself, just like I used to do my arithmetic homework with my father. I would read him the problem and wander off to other realms, waiting for him to find the solution, and now, when her silence lengthens and she goes on staring at her hand with peculiar concentration, I begin to think that she's lost it altogether and she's no longer with me, I've exhausted her to the point of total collapse. But then she takes her eyes off her hand and says in a voice free of judgment, what are you going to do? and I realize that I haven't thought about what I'm going to do, only about what I've done, and I've come here to pass the buck to her, as usual, and I lower my eyes to the carpet, ashamed but unrepentant. Well, what are you going to do now, she repeats, and I say, what do you think I should do, and she says, you'll have to wait for dark and take him out of there, or what's left of him, and bury him somewhere else. You can't take a chance, tomorrow morning Anton might go to the people living near the cemetery and ask them if they saw anything that night, and who knows what kind of people wander round there at night and see things—all kinds of perverts who lie on graves, God knows what, and we were walking round there with the luggage trolley at two o'clock in the morning,

that's not something you see every day. You can't let him find
the body because if he finds the body he'll find you too. She
falls silent and I understand that this time I'm on my own, I
can't expect her to come with me on this round too, I'm alone
in this and it's right that I should be alone, after all I was alone
when it happened and nevertheless I succeeded in doing what
I did. She gets up and says, I'm going to lie down, I've got a
touch of the flu, and I go on sitting in the same position, and
she says, go, Ilan, you haven't got a choice, and I say, it's not
dark yet, I'll wait till it gets dark, and she says, fine. I say to
myself, so there actually comes a stage when the mother business is over, there's a limit to what my mother can do, she can't
perform miracles, for example, and I go on sitting on the sofa,
where I close my eyes and slowly sink into a kind of stupor. Her
lover stands before me with his yellow hair, and I realize that
he's been standing here for a long time already, I just didn't
notice him, and I immediately wake up and apologize to him
for my tiredness. He says in a pleasant voice, I haven't got any
strength left, I have to rest now, and his hand pats my face, the
dry hand of a dead man, and suddenly I open my eyes and see
my mother patting my cheek with her hand. Don't fall asleep
now, she says, you've got a lot of work to do, and I look outside
at the gathering dusk, and the telephone rings and I hear her
say, hello Naomi, how are you? Yes, Ilan's here, if you don't
mind I'd like him to stay with me for while, I don't feel so well.
No, it's nothing serious, a touch of the flu, and after a few more
general remarks she hangs up. I stand up and say, okay, I'll get
moving, and she leads me outside and says, you have to find the
strength, you haven't got any choice, and I kiss her shriveled
cheek and she brings me the spade and the trolley, and I drive
away, feeling as if I'm in the sequel to a movie. As I crawl down
Ben Gurion Avenue I try to reconstruct the dream I had before,
but it's already disintegrated, he said something to me as he
stood there alive in front of me, but on no account can I

remember the words, only the tone, which was soft and appealing, and I give up the attempt and try to concentrate on the monstrous task awaiting me. When I reach the Carmel Beach junction and turn left, in the direction of the cemetery, I know that there isn't a hope in hell that I'm going to dig up that grave again, I won't even be able to enter the cemetery gates, and I park at the side of the road, without even switching off the engine, all I want is to close my eyes and rest a while, and without as yet defining the plan vaguely taking shape in my mind I abandon myself to the relief of not having to dig up the grave again. On the way home it dawns on me, slowly but clearly, that the journey is over, tomorrow morning I'm going to turn myself in, and I imagine myself phoning Anton and telling him that there's something I have to talk to him about. For some reason I hesitate on the formulation, I can't find the right words, and therefore I decide not to phone but simply to turn up at his office, fall into the chair and give myself up. To Naomi I won't say a word, maybe later on I'll write her a letter, even though there's nothing to say. What can I say? That I loved her too much? Literary and self-indulgent. All there is to say is that with my own hands I ruined her life, and as I park outside the house a new thought begins to gnaw at my mind, and I dismiss it but it won't go away, and in the end I give in to it and I understand that this is the only way I can achieve a relatively right repose and even preserve a scrap of dignity and honor. The thirty Hypnodorm tablets have been waiting for a moment more or less like this—even though this wasn't exactly what I had in mind in the pharmacy—and I concentrate on the physical effort of swallowing the pills, but fear claws at my heart and I lean my head back and wait for the wave of anxiety to break—I know the rules of an anxiety attack, you have to be calm and matter-of-fact and not let yourself be sucked in—and after a few minutes the attack passes, leaving only a bit of dirty scum in its wake, and I know that I can't do it yet. Tomorrow morning I'll get up, pack a small bag, and go to Anton, this thought calms me and I pull myself together and go inside, where I find Naomi asleep in front of the television. I pick her up gently and for a moment I stand like that, she curls herself round me without waking up, and I lay her on the bed, cover her, kiss her, swallow two sleeping pills and wait for them to take effect.

28

I wake up straight into yesterday's decision and go over yesterday's events in my mind, careful to avoid any thoughts which may deter me from the course of action which even in the light of day seems the only possible one. I go on lying in bed, saying goodbye in my mind to its comfort and waiting for Naomi to vacate the bathroom. I'll behave as usual, as if I'm going to the *Technion*, and leave it to Anton to tell her this evening, asking only that he tells her in person, not on the phone, she shouldn't be alone when she hears the news. I'll ask him to go to her and stay with her as long as necessary, I can already see him sitting opposite her and telling her everything in a kind, fatherly voice, I can see her eyes widening in comprehension, in horror, and most of all I can see his big hand comforting her, she clings to him helplessly and he smells the delicate fragrance of her soap, she cries into his shirt and his heart goes out to her, he offers to stay the night so she won't be alone. I can't take any more and I jump out of bed and shout to Naomi to hurry up because I'm late, and after a moment the bathroom door opens and she comes out, holding a pink cardboard box in her hand. She seems withdrawn into herself, she hardly sees me, she walks to the kitchen with a distracted air, leans against the doorpost and buries her head in her hands. Naomi, I say, are you all right? I can't understand what's happening here. Her back trembles slightly and suddenly she hurries over to the rubbish bin under the sink and pushes the cardboard box into it. Then she turns to me and says, I'm fine, I've just got a bit of a migraine, and I understand that there's something significant in that cardboard box. Go and lie down, I'll bring you a cup of tea, I say, intending to fish it out of the bin, even though I also say to myself that it might just be an empty box of tampons, and the storm I imagine seeing in her may be raging in me. But she says, look at the mess here, I'll clean up a bit first, and she opens the bin and removes the blue plastic bag with the cardboard box, which I now know is not just some innocent packaging, and before I can stop her she's already out of the door. A cold panic surges through me, there's definitely something incriminating in that box, I'll have to wait for her to return and then find some excuse to go down and rummage in the garbage, nothing new to me, and I begin to count the minutes, but she's back in a jiffy, and without looking at me she says, I'll go and lie down for a bit, and buries herself in the quilt. I get up quietly, open the door, lifting it so it won't creak, and run to the garbage bins, four overflowing bins standing in a row. There's no blue bag in the first one, and I open the lid of the second, when a clear, bell-like voice says, why are you looking in the garbage? A little boy on a bicycle is standing next to me, looking at me with round eyes, next to him is a very small girl, almost a baby, I sometimes see them in the neighborhood, always together. What's your name, the little girl asks. Ilan, I say, because what else can I say, and the little boy asks again, in exactly the same tone as before, why are you looking in the garbage? and now the baby girl chimes in, in a perfect imitation of her brother, why are you looking in the garbage? They stand there with solemn faces, fixing me with their pure gaze, and I say, I lost something, and begin rummaging in the second bin, which contains a blue plastic bin-liner, but no pink box. What did you lose? they ask in a chorus. A little pink cardboard box in a blue bin-liner, I reply in a business-like way, as if they're my collaborators in this enterprise, and the little boy opens the lid of the third bin and begins to rummage inside it. Pick me up, says the baby, I can't reach, and he picks her up clumsily, she almost drowns in the bin, and he says, there's a blue bag here, and I see the pink box peeping out of it. Thank you, that's what I was looking for, I say in a tone of dismissal, but they go on standing there in concentration, waiting to see what will happen next. "Clear Blue" it says on the box, "home pregnancy-test," and I open it and find a white plastic stick that looks like a thermometer, but I have no idea how you see if a pregnancy exists or not, and so I take out the instructions, where I read, in big red letters "Test Results" but the rest of the print is too small for me to read without my reading glasses. Do you know how to read? I ask the little boy urgently—I have no idea if he's four years old or eight years old—and his sister says, yes he does, and lifts her tiny nose to me. I hold the instructions at arm's length, trying to get the print into focus, I have to succeed in reading it, I have no intention of relying on a couple of babies, and I succeed in identifying two illustrations of windows with something drawn or written on them that I can't make out. I'm in grade one, says the little boy in a practical tone. So read what it says here to me, I say, thrusting the instructions under his nose, and he pores over them effortfully—he has his sister's expectations to contend with—and begins scrambling the letters in a halting voice. Just tell me the names of the letters, I say, forcing myself to be patient, and after exhausting efforts I understand what I already know—Naomi's pregnant. What's inside the box, the little boy asks, and I say, something for grown-ups, with my blood in a turmoil, and the baby girl asks, what's inside the box? Something you don't understand, her brother says, and she says, I do too understand, and her face crumples. The picture of a big, blonde baby with a mane of yellow hair stabs my heart, and I tell myself that this baby is a sign which has come to me at the very last minute, and even if the timing is accidental I can't ignore it, a coincidence like this can't be insignificant, and the significance is clear—I'll have to change my plans. My new mission is to be a devoted father to this baby, which I'm certain isn't mine, and perhaps this is nature's remedy—his baby will continue the line which I cut off, and I've been let off lightly. I stand there holding the kit, breathing deeply and trying to compose myself, with my two little partners tugging at my trouser leg. What's in the box? the little boy asks again, and his sister chimes in, what's in the box? I take out the white plastic stick and announce, my wife's pregnant, and the little boy says, oh, and the baby girl says, what, and her brother explains, his wife 's got a baby in her stomach, and a feeling of an unfamiliar hue swells my chest, and my eyes fill with tears. Don't cry, says the baby and her face crumples and she herself bursts into frightened tears, and I pick her up, embrace her with the warmth that suddenly fills me, and tell her not to cry, but her brother tugs at my shirt and says, put her down, we have to go home. I return his sister to him and he drags her away—no doubt remembering his parents' warnings about strangers—and I remain standing among the garbage bins. The knowledge that I'm going to be a father is real and clear and stirring—I'm going to be the father of my beloved's baby, I say to myself as I go upstairs, and I sit down on the bed next to Naomi, and without any introduction I say, I want this baby, but she doesn't react, and I say again, I want this baby. The turmoil inside me is so great I haven't even noticed that she's asleep—Naomi, I whisper and shake her gently by the shoulders, and without giving her a chance to wake up properly and orient herself I say, I want this baby. She wakes up instantly and gives me a startled look, I want us to have this baby, I say again and fall silent, and even though the silence is charged and heavy with obscurity I fix her with a long, responsible look, and she stares into my eyes without embarrassment, with a kind of concentrated inquiry, trying to read me but not saying anything. I decide to wait and let her break the silence, and after a long pause she says in a sad, sure voice, I want it too,

I want it very, very much, and I say, then we'll have it, and I kiss her hair and get up immediately—it's impossible to continue the conversation now, we both realize that. I have to go, I say, I have a class in twenty minutes, and when I'm already at the door she runs into my arms and buries her head in my neck. What is it, Naomi, I whisper, and she raises her face to me, and suddenly she isn't beautiful, her eyes are bleary and her nose is red and wrinkled, there's something quite ordinary and dreary about the way she looks, and I feel a twinge of disappointment, which I could never have imagined feeling in connection to her before. But as I drive down to the *Technion* this tear-stained look captures my heart, and I can't understand how that shadow could have fallen across my feelings, the human soul is so perverse, it would take a lifetime to understand it. The day passes in intensive activity and in the evening, on my way home, I remember Anton, all day long I've managed to ignore him and now I say to myself that everything depends on him, if he decides to open the grave I'm lost, and since I've decided to return to life I have to know where I stand, and I turn the Volvo round in the direction of the bistro. Anton isn't there, but the need to see him is now so imperative that I park the car anyway and sit down with a bottle of beer to wait for him. Anton hasn't been here today, says the old owner of the bistro, and while he bemoans the disappearance of the irritable waitress who ran off with three cartons of Parliament cigarettes, I say to myself that Anton has been busy digging up the grave all day, and my enthusiasm about my dubious paternity now seems idiotic and embarrassing. What did I have to celebrate, I ask myself, and suddenly I see Anton entering the bistro, so sunk in thought that he doesn't even see me. Should I get you a beer, I ask, and he wakes up and orders a beer and meatballs, but I can't read his expression, and I ask, what's new, and light a cigarette, the main thing is to keep busy. He says, nothing, and I calm down a little and think to myself that it may be suspicious not to ask him about the disturbed grave after he made such a fuss about it in front of me—either I'm too egocentric to take an interest, or I'm the one who tampered with it—but I'm afraid my words will give me away, so I say nothing and wait. The old man brings me another beer and I drink it and feel a little more relaxed, the urgency fades, and even though I now feel capable of asking with innocent curiosity, by the way, what happened about that grave, I see no reason to provoke fate, and as he sits opposite me with a neutral expression on his face I relax completely. My former elation returns, I have no doubt that my grave has not been dug up, the whole thing has slipped his mind, he isn't about to dig up trouble for himself from under the ground, his ambition faded a long time ago, he has no need to impress anyone with unnecessary initiatives—ever since he wasn't promoted to Chief Superintendent last year, mainly because of his flaunted individualism, he's lost interest—and in order to celebrate the temporary respite I order a brandy. What's happening to you lately, Ilan? he says suddenly and stares into my eyes, catching me unprepared. What do you mean? I stammer. There's something going on with you lately, I've known you too long not to notice, who're you going to talk to if not to me? he says and lowers his eyes to his beer, realizing that he's caught me off guard and giving me a chance to recover. Why do you think there's something going on with me, I say noncommittally, leaving the way open to retire from the conversation. Who're you going to talk to if not to me, he says again, in the same matter-of-fact tone. What do you think is going on with me, I ask and immediately regret it as too provocative, and suddenly he asks me in a colorless tone, is Naomi cheating on you? The first thing I feel is resentment and indignation, as if he's gloating over her infidelity to me, and the ancient archetype of our relationship is immediately revived, with his superiority as the calm, authentic one. All I want now is to get away, and I say, I have to go, as if I haven't heard his question, and he says, bye, as if he hasn't asked it either. On the way home I try to concentrate on the main thing, the brandy helps me to eliminate parasitic thoughts, and I clarify what the bottom line of the situation is, experience has taught me that in states of emergency this is the only thing worth thinking about, and the bottom line here is clear and sharp: the baby, that's the main thing—my job is to keep it and save it, and if I save myself too in the process that's pure profit—and Anton fades out of the picture, together with my anger, which now seems groundless, but at least it charged me with energy, and I open the door and walk into the apartment full of animation. Naomi greets me as if this morning never happened, the pregnancy isn't mentioned, and she says, I got out a video of *Pulp Fiction*, you remember you didn't want to go and see it when it was on, and I feel like seeing it with you, you'll be crazy about it, and I also made a real pizza with yeast dough, Noam gave me his mother's recipe, so we'll watch the movie and eat home made pizza, how does that grab you? She says all this in an uninterrupted stream, the tension makes itself felt only when she comes to the end of a sentence, and I gather that she doesn't want to talk, only to carry on as usual, which suits me fine. I too have no desire at the moment to translate what's happening into words, and I look at her as she brings in the professional-looking pizza, and say to myself that it seems as if a hidden code is coming into being between us, and even if its origins are still obscure, it nevertheless exists more in the area of an intimate alliance than the area of cold alienation. My appetite is aroused, the pizza is authentic and impressive, I praise her in the kind of detail she likes, and she seems gratified and puts on the video, which grabs me from the first scene with the infantile couple in the restaurant. Perhaps because of my preoccupation with deciphering signs I immediately identify with the absurd naturalism of the movie, with the murder, the five-dollar milkshake, and the discussion—on the way to the murder—of European interpretations of the American hamburger. There is no significant and insignificant here, everything fills the void with an indiscriminate stream of random and grotesque events, just like my dead man, and his father's whore, and the garbage tip, and as the film proceeds my life too takes on a dimension of existential absurdity, a kind of imitation of reality where everything is both insane and possible, human limits are flexible and therefore capable of stretching to include deviations from the norm, such as Naomi and me and the dead man, and the baby fathered by one of us, everything's important and not important, and the potential of life as a comic book calms my nerves, and I don't know what tomorrow will bring, but at the end of the movie I feel a kind of calm joviality, and when Naomi asks me what I thought of it I say, I think it presages the New Order. She doesn't understand exactly what I mean, and so she says, I enjoyed it even more the second time, and later we make love in a different way, the result of the secrecy and the ambiguity, tense and silent sex which excites us both, and after she falls asleep I begin speculating about how much she knows. She knows something, the question is what. For example, that I only know that she had a lover, or that I also know the baby's paternity is uncertain, or perhaps she thinks that I don't know anything, or that my knowledge is only partial, and so on and so forth. She may, of course, know everything, but since doubt can save one's life—even while making it miserable—she's decided not to open it up, but on the other hand perhaps she doesn't know anything, she's only a child after all, how much can she already know, and I sum up to myself that the price of silence is uncertainty, and I'll have to live with this too, and since I have almost no doubt that a secret code now exists between us, I decide to go along with it, to go with the flow— there's a certain maturity in being a cork floating on the water, if a storm blows up I'll fight it or I'll sink with it, in any case I've already understood that what will be will be. But in the meantime she's sleeping here next to me, so near and yet so far, with the baby growing inside her, and I'm grateful and at the same time aware of the hubris in my position, and so the days go by, with a few words and a lot of consideration, and a sense of renewal as after a crisis. Anton isn't mentioned and he doesn't get in touch—as far as the level of his knowledge is concerned I haven't got a clue about that either, I assume that it's low, almost two months have passed since that night and the more time passes the better it is for me, and gradually we begin to rehabilitate ourselves, both of us begin to let go of her lover and to concentrate on each other—I adapt myself to her rhythm and let her take the lead, and in the meantime I begin to invest a bit in my work too and initiate together with Givon an international conference on the subject of the theory of degenerate matter. He's full of enthusiasm and the wish to please, ever since conquering the commanding heights of the faculty his gratitude has known no bounds, and I invite him and Aviva to come and have dinner with us on Saturday night at Naomi's suggestion. She's never held a proper dinner party yet and now she decides that it's high time she did so, and since an intimate evening with Givon and his wife is out of the question, I also invite Ra'ed and Michal, whose authenticity is capable of drawing even neuroses the size of the Givons' like a magnet, and on third thoughts I invite Davis and his wife too—at the vegetarian fish dinner Givon had apologized to him elaborately—and in the meantime, on Thursday evening, after the baby hasn't been mentioned between us since I first discovered its existence a week before, Naomi suddenly says, let's go and tell your mother the news. I can't understand why it's so urgent to inform my mother of the existence of this dubious grandchild, but Naomi insists, and I understand that this is her way of making it a normal, family matter. My mother receives us in her dressing gown, a little grumpy but quite friendly—she may not like the idea of Naomi but she loves Naomi herself, to the extent that she's capable of it—and we sit with her and drink lousy brandy which puts Naomi in a merry mood, and after a second glass she holds my mother's hand and says, what a sweet son you have, and how lucky I was to meet him. I don't know about sweet, says my mother and I smile at her, at peace with her, at least she and I have knowledge in common, which is a relief, but we still haven't told her about the baby. I'm leaving it to Naomi, who in the meantime goes on talking about me. At first I'm embarrassed and amused, but gradually I begin to understand that a signal is being transmitted to me, and I have to concentrate, this is the way she's chosen to speak to me about our situation, by way of these praises. He's clever and wise and funny and handsome and generous and not at all petty, she says to my mother, as if she's a teacher writing an evaluation of my character on a report card, and he's got the virtue of not prying into other people's souls, he knows how to respect privacy and he's even prepared to pay a price for it. My mother, also put on the alert by the transmission, glances at me briefly and says, what price, what do you mean? And Naomi answers lightly, I don't mean anything specific, just that he's a mature person who understands that you pay a price for things, in general, I mean, and she blows me a kiss, her face is bright and open and her expression is predominantly innocent, and after my mother serves ancient *burekas* which Naomi praises extravagantly, she says: Erna, we've come to tell you that you're going to be a grandmother, and my mother's face, always ready for surprises and reversals, collapses in self-exposure. She immediately grasps the dubious provenance of this grandchild, but she recovers at once, and since with her comprehension and decision are simultaneous, she opens her arms and engulfs Naomi in her shriveled body, while sending me a keen look from her sober old eyes, and for a moment we are united in the profound irony of the situation, which for some reason makes us both feel better. When Naomi goes outside to pick some

mint from the garden she asks, what's going on, and I say, nothing, I didn't return to the grave, I couldn't face it, and she says,
that's what I thought, and we retire into an unoppressive and
only slightly embarrassed silence. I begin to tell her about the
conference I'm organizing with Givon, but the weight lying at
the bottom of the casual conversation drags the words down
and dries them up, and it seems better to keep quiet. Naomi
comes back with the tea and the conversation revives. She asks
my mother to tell her about me when I was a child, what kind
of a child was he, she asks and strokes my hair. It wasn't easy
for him with all the men I used to bring here, my mother says,
once upon a time I liked men, how absurd, and she bursts into
her cracked laugh, and Naomi blushes in embarrassment. You
were a young widow, you were entitled, she says uncomfortably,
and my mother says, that's one way of looking at it, in a tone
that puts an end to the conversation, and I'm not sure that
there isn't some sort of signal here too, this time from my
mother. What's she trying to tell Naomi—that I'm used to seeing the women in my life with strange men and therefore I'm
congenitally tolerant of adulterous women? Or maybe she was
taking the opportunity to apologize to me for her wild nights,
when I was such a nuisance, standing outside her locked bedroom door and whining mommy, mommy, mommy, over and
over like a stuck record, and she would shout, go to bed, and I
would go on until she came out wrapped in a sheet, tall and
alarming, with a pagan fire in her eyes, her hair wild and whorish, sweetish smells would sometimes waft out of her room,
and she would drag me to my room and push me into bed.
Daytime belongs to children and nighttime belongs to children's mothers she would say sharply, kisses or hugs didn't
come into it. The Ben Nathans don't kiss, I heard her once say
to Anton's mother, who saw human oddity as a part—albeit
flawed—of life and always related to my mother matter-of-fact-
ly and according to the circumstances, and my mother, who

had been used to facing criticism all her eccentric life, relaxed in the naturally nonjudgmental attitude of Anton's mother—which is what she always called her because she couldn't pronounce her name. I would stay with them every summer, a permanent arrangement which began when I was about eight and my mother went off to Italy to cheer herself up, a few months before my father died. He and I remained in the house alone, she went for two weeks which turned into two months, and every week she would send a postcard saying that she was sick of Italy and promising to return next week, and every week my father and I would go to the harbor to meet her, I remember him with fag ends of dead cigarettes dangling from his mouth, we did this three or four times in a row, it seemed quite natural to both of us, and after the fourth week he was tired of looking after me and gave me to Anton's mother, who told me that my mother was a special woman, not every child had the luck to have a special woman for a mother. I believed her, even though it had no practical effects on my social status with peers, which improved mainly because Anton, who was a natural leader, was instructed by his mother to take me under his wing, and Anton always did what his mother, who was the head of the clan, told him to. And now I look at my disintegrating mother, who says, okay, so I'm going to be a grandmother, I suppose I'll manage, and Naomi hugs her warmly—incredible how much this orphan needs a mother and father—and my mother says, Granny Erna, that really sounds silly. It sounds wonderful, Naomi says, and when the news begins, my mother, who in recent years has begun to interest herself in politics and become a militant right-winger, tells us to leave or shut up and watch the news. On the way home Naomi says, your mother's amazing, and I say, yes, as long as you're not her son, and I put my free arm around her shoulders, and she picks up her knees and nestles up to me and says, let's drive down to the sea for a bit, there's a full moon tonight. We get out of the car into the dewy air of the beginning of summer, Naomi and I and our baby, but the silence is charged with the crookedness of the existence I have brought upon us, and I know that we'll have to wait patiently until the routine of everyday life straightens this crookedness out, and in the meantime we stroll along the beach in silence, and I have no idea where she is, and the thought that I'll never really know what's going on in the back yard of her mind brings back the sense of hopelessness and despair. The uncertainty in which I previously found hope now appalls me, how am I going to get through hours and days and years in the dark, and it isn't only me, I don't have the right to think of myself now, I have to think of her, this is the only life she'll ever have and she deserves to live it in the light. The decent thing to do would be to break this cowardly silence, to confess to everything, and to pay the price, and I stop and say, Naomi, but before I can continue she says, how do you find the North Star? I've never understood how you find it, there must be a simple way to find it, please explain it to me so that I'll be able to find it for once, and she leans against me and looks up at the sky. She doesn't need my confessions, that's what she's telling me and she couldn't make it any clearer, but now too I can't be sure that this isn't simply innocence, maybe she really doesn't know anything, maybe this sudden interest in the North Star isn't a way of changing the subject but only of demonstrating childish curiosity and paying respect to my professional superiority—as if astrophysicists spend their time gazing up at the sky and looking for the North Star. I try to read her expression, but it's open or hidden, however I choose to see it, and I draw her face close to me and pass my fingertips over it and say very quietly, Naomi, and she doesn't respond, only looks at me intently. What exactly do you want me to tell you, I say in a flat voice, and she says, equally flatly, how to find the North Star. I say, fine, and she stands in front of me, leaning against me, her hair tickling my neck, and I take her hand and point to the sky and say, you see that group of stars opposite your hand, you see that they make the shape of the letter W, that's Cassiopeia. Now draw a line to connect the two stars at the extreme points of the W, and from it draw a vertical line one and half times the length of the first line and you'll find the North Star at the end of the line, right there—see it? And what's so special about the North Star that everybody wants to find it, she asks. People can rely on it, because it doesn't change its place during the course of the night like other stars do, I say. Why? she asks and turns to look at me with shining eyes. Because it sits precisely on the axis of rotation of the earth, I say, and she says, there's so much I don't know, and I say, me too.

29

On Saturday morning we sit on the balcony drinking coffee and Naomi describes the menu of the dinner party to me. I have no opinion on the matter one way or the other, my job is to provide emotional and practical support. Yesterday I went with her to the supermarket and pushed the trolley while she bustled about importantly like a busy housewife, and when I saw her wrinkling her brow as she hesitated between the various wines on offer I thought again that perhaps she knew nothing, and she was just a young woman excited about giving her first proper dinner party, an event which preoccupied her to such an extent that we didn't even have time to read the weekend papers. Even though I'm not a big expert on dinner parties myself, my experience in the field is a lot wider than Naomi's, thanks to Gillian, a physicist from Bristol I met on a sabbatical and with whom I spent an entire year of academic dinner parties. Gillian was a rather charming, sarcastic Englishwoman, who conducted her social life with the right mixture of naturalness and hypocrisy, and who was repelled by the vociferous conviviality she found on her visits to Israel—a fact which immediately endeared her to my mother. Gillian's main virtue in my mother's eyes, among others, like age, for example—she was more or less the same age as me—was the fact that she was a gentile. A *shiksa* is good, a Dutch *shiksa* is perfect, she would say when I was a child—in her eyes gentile Dutch women were the complete opposite of herself, and someone like her was the last thing she wanted for me, but she also understood that my relationship with Gillian lacked the fire capable of keeping us warm during out long separations. In the first year after my return from my sabbatical we flew to visit each other a few times, but the meetings weren't a great success, and thus, in spite of the unique symmetry in the relations between us, the affair was soon over, but now as I stand working in the kitchen with Naomi—I keep a low profile, peeling and crushing a vast amount of garlic—I find myself thinking of Gillian again, and for some reason one memory in particular stands out. We were driving to a conference in Plymouth, and when we entered the town on the way to the hotel I got into the wrong lane by mistake and held up the traffic. The driver behind me stopped and started yelling angrily, I immediately apologized with all the obsequiousness of an Israeli abroad, I'm a foreigner, I'm not used to driving on the left side of the road, I'm sorry, please forgive me—and then, all of a sudden, his whole expression changed, the anger was replaced by emotion, in an eager tone he asked where we were going, and when I told him the name of the hotel he told us to drive after him, even though he was going in the opposite direction. He brought us to the hotel and then he got out of the car, came up to me red in the face, and before I could thank him for taking so much trouble, he began apologizing in a tone full of remorse for his anger, he actually laid his hand on his heart and asked us to forgive him. Gillian and I were dumbfounded by the man's extraordinary behavior which we could make no sense of, he hadn't even insulted us, he had simply expressed completely natural and justified anger at my holding up the traffic, and the affair continued to perplex me all evening. I remember saying to Gillian that this man apparently lived with a very heavy sense of sin, perhaps he had even murdered somebody, and Gillian said something like, you don't murder someone so quickly, and as I mix the crushed garlic with ketchup and soy sauce and honey according to Naomi's instructions, I try to penetrate the sense of guilt of that English driver, with whom I now feel a kind of pact, but the penetration lacks reality, the memory is almost dead, and what good will it do me to reinvent it? You don't have to stir so hard, it isn't a pudding, Naomi says and brings me back to her. What should I do now, I ask. Pour the sauce over the chicken pieces in the pan, but try to pour it evenly, use your hands if you have to, so it penetrates properly, and when you've finished wash the lettuce, leaf by leaf, so there's no grit left. She's preoccupied and intent on what she's doing, and I too work seriously, without cutting any corners, seeing how important the dinner is to her. Only use the nicest leaves of the lettuce, don't be miserly, she says with sweet bossiness, as if I could give a damn about the bloody lettuce, and when I'm finished washing the leaves one by one I roast the shelled sunflower seeds. Lower the heat and stir them all the time, if you burn them the whole salad will be bitter, she says and in the meantime she lays the table. Do you think you can do two things at once? she asks and I say in a responsible tone, I think so. Then while you're watching that the sunflower seeds don't burn fold the whipped cream gently into the melted chocolate, but really gently. Okay, I say, and now that I have two tasks to perform I succeed in emptying my mind of thoughts and throwing myself wholly into the concrete tasks that I have been assigned, moving judiciously between the whipped cream and the sunflower seeds. Nice work, she says to me, and again I think that this is exactly how things should be, and when everything's ready and I emerge from the shower I find her bent over the newspaper which is spread over the table, and the rigidity of her body roots me to the spot, and even before she raises her face from the newspaper and I see her expression of horror and fear, I know what's written there. My feet refuse to move and she gets up slowly, her hands fumbling distractedly until they fall to the sides of her body, and comes slowly towards me. I wait for something to happen, but she walks straight past me without looking in my direction and goes into the bathroom. She doesn't slam the door, but closes it in a menacing silence, and I go up to the newspaper, put on my glasses, and read that the body of Oded Safra, a nature photographer living in Wadi Salib, has been discovered, the investigation is being headed by Chief Superintendent Anton Karam, and arrests are anticipated soon. I take off my glasses and clean them in order to give myself something concrete to do at this moment when I know that the heavens have fallen even though you can't see it yet, they're still spread outside, blue and steady, and here the table is laid and the guests will arrive soon and Naomi's locked up in the bathroom. While I'm trying to gather my thoughts I hear a kind of murmur coming from the kitchen and I go to see what it is and find a furiously boiling pot and I don't know whether to turn down the flame—I haven't got the heart to go and ask Naomi now—and so I put on my glasses again and open the lid to see what's inside and decide myself, and the steam erupts with a violence which loosens my glasses and they fall into the pot which is full of rice and a jet of boiling water splashes onto my face, but partly because I vaguely remember a rule about never opening the lid of a pot in the middle of cooking rice, and mainly because of my general confusion, I put the lid back on with a distracted movement which almost knocks the pot over. I steady the pot with my bare hands, and still I feel nothing, my only thought now is that I have to get my glasses out of the boiling rice, and again I open the lid quickly and thrust my hand in and fish them out, and only when the task is accomplished I begin to feel the burns on my face and hands. The physical pain swallows everything, there's no murder, no guilt, only pain, and I run to the tap and pour cold water over myself, which immediately brings relief, but before the fire soaks up the water and begins to burn again the door-bell rings, I open the door and Givon and his wife come in with a bottle of wine and a gift-wrapped parcel. In the confusion of their entrance they don't notice the state of my scalded face, and before I can shut the door Ra'ed and Michal arrive. What happened to your face, Michal asks as soon as she comes in, and I say, I got a bit of a burn, and the Givons rush up hysterically, full of guilt and self-reproach, Ilan, forgive us, we didn't know, how could we not have noticed such a thing, and so on and so forth, until Ra'ed says, okay, okay, nobody's blaming you, and Givon collects himself and says, of course not, what does it matter whether we noticed or not, we're not the important thing here, the important thing is Ilan's burn, we have to consider what to do about it. Calm down, I'm fine, I say, but in his need to appease his guilt he showers me with superfluous and hysterical attentions, and in the middle of the uproar Davis arrives—without his wife, who's on a trip to China—and Givon reports to him on the state of my health in the tone of a general in a war room and the advice begins to fly from all directions, to anoint it with herb tea, with toothpaste, with urine, with everyone defending his remedy possessively. There's no need of all that, it's just a little burn, I say, but Givon refuses to allow me to make light of my injury and begins to describe his own personal burns, and the suffering he endured because of them, and his feeling of identification with me now as a result of these sufferings. I go to the kitchen to take two aspirins and as I swallow them I ask myself how I'm going to get through this evening, with Naomi shut up in the bathroom and the newspaper open on the coffee table, and my burning hands and face, and suddenly it occurs to me that Ra'ed may have already heard the whole story from Anton, who gave him instructions to behave normally, and I send him a quick glance but can't read anything, and even as the mills in my mind go on grinding I know that I'm not going to ask them to leave, even though I've got a real excuse to do so. I don't know how to do things like that, even in extreme circumstances social embarrassment defeats me, and so I just display pain and suffering and hope that they'll suggest it themselves, but it doesn't even occur to them to do so—the suffering of others is theoretical, it can always be endured. Listen to me, says Michal, go into the lavatory, pee into a paper cup, and smear the pee on your face and neck, it works, don't be ashamed and do what I'm telling you—out of the corner of my eye I see Givon looking as if he's going to vomit, and all of a sudden the embarrassment evaporates and I'm on the point of telling them bluntly that I think they should go, but at that moment Naomi sails into the room, beautiful and radiant as if nothing has happened. In a moment she's got them all eating out of her hand, she opens a bottle of wine, pours them all a glass, chatters airily, goes into the kitchen, opens and closes saucepan lids, and only when Michal says, Ilan go to the lavatory and do what I told you, she turns to me and my scalded face. What happened Ilan, she asks in alarm, and because I have no desire to open a new discussion of my burn, but mainly because of the signal I have received from her to carry on with the evening as if the newspaper item doesn't exist, I say warmly but decisively, thank you very much for your concern, but it really doesn't hurt, it must look much worse than it actually is, everything's fine and we can change the subject now. They all breathe a sigh of relief, the burn reverts to being my personal problem, and while Naomi skillfully plays the hostess—her acting is improving by leaps and bounds—I give in to the pain searing my face, close my eyes and wait for the pills to take effect. All I want now is for it not to hurt, everything else can wait. Naomi announces that dinner is served and refuses my offers of help, whether because of my burn or because she doesn't want me next to her, and the evening proceeds with Givon singing the praises of the food even before he tastes it, and everyone joining in like a Greek chorus. Gradually the pain fades and I'm capable of thinking clearly and seeing things as they are, and I know that everything is lost and it's only a matter of time, and when I float up from myself for a moment into the dinner party going on around me as if nothing has happened, I hear that the subject under discussion is *Pulp Fiction*, for and against. Givon and Aviva are categorically against. Reality is a little more than a sack full of attractive images, pronounces Givon, ready for battle, and an in-depth treatment of emptiness is a pretentious contradiction which the movie fails to make good on, because its shallow treatment not only flattens reality even more, but also flattens the emotions of the characters, with the result that it treats emptiness by means of another emptiness, which is no less empty than the first. His voice rises as he says, there are no real feelings in the movie, and not even post-modernism can survive without real feelings, and Aviva says, exactly. You're talking nonsense, says Ra'ed, and Givon immediately contracts in insult, this is a movie which gives us a different, much more realistic, perspective on reality, it doesn't judge reality or prosecute or defend it, the shit and the strawberries and cream come together, just as they do in life, and since there's no humbug in the movie, people like you are shocked. Davis takes no part in the discussion, he doesn't concern himself with this kind of movie, as far as he's concerned anything less than *Doctor Faustus* is a waste of time, and although he's learnt to disguise his snobbery and doesn't flaunt it, Givon, with his excessive, self-focused sensitivity, is aware of the man's passive disdain, and at the margins of my superficial interest in the conversation I see how vital it is to him to win the argument. What's the matter with you, Michal says to him, it's a great movie, Ra'ed and I wet ourselves laughing, and Givon, red and agitated, his eyes popping, says, you think it's funny, what's funny about human suffering? The fact that it can't be helped, Michal says and crams a chicken wing into her mouth, and Ra'ed adds, its absurdity is funny, what can you do about it, it's funny. What's that supposed to mean, it doesn't mean anything, says Givon in an aggressive tone, and since Michal is busy struggling with her chicken and Ra'ed doesn't really care one way or the other, Givon takes the opportunity for an additional assault on the way to the victory he's determined to win, even at the cost of insulting an Arab, which as a closet racist is a no-no for him—he's the only person in the room who's bothered by the fact that Ra'ed is an Arab, with all the stomach-churning fear and obsequiousness that this fact arouses in him. Your arguments are frivolous and superficial, he says, this film not only doesn't lead to catharsis, it leaves you with a feeling of emptiness and futility, and Naomi who has been functioning to perfection all this time, serving and clearing away and dishing up and refilling plates and glasses, says, actually there is a catharsis at the end of the movie, but it comes mainly as a result of the admiration you feel for its originality and structure—by the way, did anybody notice that there was a mistake in the time scheme of the movie? I don't know if it's deliberate or not, and I can't get over the naturalness and sincerity of her behavior, as if the sky hasn't fallen—now that she's read the item in the paper there can't be any doubt about what she knows, she must have put two and two together by now, and nevertheless she's chosen to play this peculiar game, and I don't know just how diabolical it is. It seems that I've lived with her for two years without encountering entire areas of her personality, and now I watch her maneuvering with a skill far superior to anything I could produce, occasionally throwing me a look which contains something I can't identify, and I prepare myself for the moment when we're alone and for the conversation that will have to take place, and I can't even imagine this moment, I only know with sharpness and clarity that my life is over. For some reason the knowledge doesn't frighten me in spite of its clarity, and suddenly, without planning to do so in advance, I get up, excuse myself, and go to the bathroom, where I open my cupboard and take out the three packets of Hypnodorm. I'm not thinking about anything, only how to do it as cleanly as possible, and I decide to swallow the tablets, say I've left my car lights on, go downstairs and drive to Wadi Salib. I'll fall asleep there and they'll find me tomorrow. I have to swallow the tablets now that my fear has somewhat dulled, there's no point in putting it off until a new wave comes along and sweeps away my courage, or my lack of fear, and I look at the first box and start to open it, but my eyes fall on the date and I see that it expired more than two years ago. I have no idea how significant this is, taking into account the possibility that the manufacturers set these dates for commercial motives as well, like with milk products, but I'm afraid to take the risk, how do I know what spoilt pills can do to you, the last thing I need is to be half-dead, and in the meantime the inner debate flares up again and undermines my resolution. I know that I've missed the opportunity, and I put the pills back in the cupboard and return to our guests, where I find everything as I left it, with Naomi saying, not to mention John Travolta, who's reason enough in himself to die for the movie. John Travolta, John Travolta, a coarse, greasy male with a stupid face, shrieks Givon, beginning to smell defeat now that Naomi is against him too. Come, come, children, it's only a movie, says Davis placatingly. You can say that about any work of art, says Givon and all of a sudden the fight goes out of him. Let's sum up the discussion, says Davis, hiding a yawn, by saying that this movie is an excellent illustration of the generation gap, and if the younger generation chooses to see it as their idea of modern art they have every right to do so. So are you saying that my view of art is outmoded? Givon flares up again. Not outmoded, says Davis, old and good, and I ask myself if I should go to Anton tomorrow morning or wait for him to come to me, but at the moment I'm incapable of deciding anything because the effect of the aspirins is wearing off and my face is beginning to burn again. It's got nothing to do with the generation gap, says Naomi, Ilan's your generation, and he loves the movie, right Ilan? Everybody turns to me and my face must be in really bad shape because they all start talking about my burn again. Naomi, I think you should take him to the emergency room, Davis says, it looks very bad, and I get up and go to look in the hall mirror. My face is a fiery red, and the horrid sight only increases the pain, which is now really unbearable. You have to take him to the hospital, Givon is almost crying, how could we let him sit here all evening without seeing that it was getting so much worse, when we arrived it wasn't nearly so bad, was it Aviva? Naomi immediately collects herself, takes her bag and keys, brings the evening to a close, and within moments we're on our way to the Rambam hospital. During the drive I experience the most oppressive silence of my life, I can say that without any hesitation, and as we pass the Central bus station, for all the talent we both possess to function in parallel realities, it's impossible not to feel the black cloud about to burst over our heads. Naomi drives with concentration, her face sealed, and I can't stand it for another second, I have to drain the terrible heaviness. Naomi, I say in despair, and she gives me a mature, serious look and says, the first fire we have to put out is the fire on your face. She says this with simple concern, and I can only love her with all my unworthy heart and soul, and when we walk into the Emergency Room the doctor yawns in my face and says, first of all you have to have a tetanus shot, and as the nurse gives me the shot and dresses the burn I feel like a man condemned to death getting a tooth filled on the eve of his execution. Why didn't you come at once, the nurse asks Naomi with an exclamation mark rather than a question mark, the answer doesn't interest her, she's got the rest of the night's shift ahead of her. I didn't think it was so serious, I say apologetical-ly—she's got an ugly mole on her upper lip and I can't under-stand why she doesn't have it removed with all her connections in the hospital. What's the treatment at home, Naomi asks, and the nurse says, it will be written down, and with that she concludes her business with us, and when we get into the Beetle I say, how superfluous all this is now, what did I have to go and open that damned pot for, and she says, there's no point crying over split milk, and for a moment she sends me a serious look and adds, and that goes for the other things too. We resume the silence which she dictates, and when we get home she says, go to bed, Ilan, I'll clean up here, and I lie in bed tense and wakeful, listening to her movements in the kitchen. After a while I hear her going into the bathroom and she comes out wearing the yellow T-shirt she uses to sleep in, I don't move or breathe, and she lies down in the bed on her back, I'm almost sure that her eyes are open, the silence pounds in my ears and now my knee begins to itch too, but I don't dare scratch it. I lie there petrified in a kind of conscious faint, waiting for what will happen, because it's clear that at some point something will happen, but nothing happens, except for the tense silence, and when I'm beginning to think that maybe she's fallen asleep I suddenly feel her hand creeping towards me and I close my eyes and wait, maybe it's some sort of hallucination, but I feel her slowly lacing her fingers in mine, her touch is light but sure, and I close my fingers around hers until there's no space between our hands, and I feel as if our whole existence is draining into that gentle touch, which is full of strength and fellow-feeling, and after a long time the words succeed in freeing themselves. Tomorrow morning I'll go to Anton, I say, and ask him to help me arrange for our divorce at the same time as the legal proceedings. Naturally you'll get all my property, and I promise you that I'll do all I can to see that you suffer from the situation as little as possible, that's it, Naomi, it seems that love really kills. I stop talking and scratch my knee and begin to breathe normally, and she listens quietly without moving, and after a while I say, say something, Naomi. It isn't always necessary to say something, she says, and I say, you think so? and she says, I'm sure of it, and little by little her grip tightens, her fingers stiffen in what might be despair, or violence, or sorrow, and after a little while she lets go of my hand and I think that she's going to turn on her side and bring the evening to a close, and I accept it, of course, but instead she sits up and brings her face to mine until our lips are touching. At first they touch lightly and glancingly, and then she closes her eyes and we abandon ourselves to long, slow kiss, the most intoxicating kiss possible, and the world stops, and only much later she says in a clean voice, I don't know what will happen tomorrow, or next week, or in five years time, but now I don't want to leave you but to be with you in this, that's the most honest thing I can say to you. I don't dare look at her, or talk to her, or in any way disturb this delicate and luminous moment, which I must not abandon myself to, I know that, I am only permitted to hoard it, deep down, for the days of darkness to come.

LAST CHAPTER

I haven't got all day, Ilan, and it's not so important either, Naomi says to me. She's standing in a big room with folding walls, dressed only in a tee-shirt, impatient and angry even though I'm trying my best. Behind her stand Anton, Givon, the lover, his father in his wheelchair, and somebody else I don't recognize even though she looks familiar. They stand silently and wait for me to make up my mind as I face them with my father's antique Leica, trying to find the correct pose. I feel that I have to freshen up the cliché about the young girl and the old men, but since I only have one shot at it I try out various possibilities first. The men are lifeless, they cooperate apathetically, only Naomi spreads nervous energies through the room. Please let me do it properly, I say, and because it's important to me my tone too is aggressive, and now I remember who the unidentified woman is, it's Shimi Lerer's sister, Rina Lerer, or Raya Lerer—childhood names always come back to you attached to their surnames—and I don't understand what she's doing here, she's supposed to be in Canada, that's why she wasn't at the funeral. Now I understand that she's the one holding up the shot, she's simply superfluous, and however embarrassing it is I have to get rid of her, the photograph has no chance of speaking the truth if I put Raya Lerer in it merely out of politeness and a reluctance to hurt her feelings. She must have realized what's happening because now she's looking at me with liquid eyes, and I'm incapable of telling her to leave— she had a religious friend called Guta, and on Saturdays we used to throw paper half-piastres at them and sing, Guta, Raya, liar, liar, and now she's looking at me with the same pathetic look as then, and I try to think of a way of saying it without insulting her, and all the time Naomi's demonstrating impatience. Suddenly the phone rings, but first of all I have to get rid of Raya Lerer, the thought of her spoiling my picture with her doggy look arouses my worst instincts, I have to control myself, I can't drag her away by force, and the ringing is driving me crazy, and Raya Lerer lies down on her back and waves her hands in the air like a dog, and Naomi says, that's exactly how my mother lay down on the ground on the day of the funeral when we couldn't find the key, I can't bear to look at her. She begins walking away and I run after her, the camera falls out of my hands and I know that it's all up with me, my father warned me not to touch his Leica, which was of great sentimental value apart from its financial value, and Naomi turns to me with fires blazing in her eyes and screams, answer the telephone Ilan, just answer the telephone, and I know that everything's lost and I can forget about the photograph, and I answer the phone and hear Anton's voice, I can't understand how he can be on the phone if he's here in the room, and only when Naomi comes in dressed in her bath robe I wake up. I'm on my way to your place, Anton says, we have to talk, and I wake up completely and say, I'll be waiting, and hang up, and Naomi asks, was that Anton? He's on his way here, I say, and she sits down on the edge of the bed next to me. I feel calm and relaxed, the commotion is over—there's nothing so soothing as the resolution of doubts, and I get out of bed and announce that I'm going to take a shower and pack a few things, and when I'm at the door she says, let's hug a bit and steps into my arms. The love and the warmth dispel the reality of the situation a little, and now we exist only in this continuing moment, which I succeed in experiencing almost totally, and when I come out of the shower she's waiting for me on the balcony with coffee and toast. I've packed a bag for you, she says, get dressed and we'll wait for him on the balcony, and I say, you'll be late for work, and she says, I called to say that I wouldn't be in today, and I get dressed and join her on the balcony. Should I make you fresh coffee, she asks, this coffee's cold. No, no, I say, just sit here with me, and she moves her chair next to mine and laces her fingers in mine, like last night, and I ask, how long have you known? Ever since I wanted to know, she says, before that you don't know, sometimes even when it's staring you in the face if you don't want to know you don't know, and she loosens her fingers and says, you should call your mother, she's known all along, hasn't she? I get up immediately, I've forgotten all about her, for some reason I haven't given her a thought for the past two days, and I dial her number, now at least I'll have the relief of being able to talk to her openly, but there's no answer, and I say to Naomi, I'll call her from the . . . But I can't bring myself to say the word, and when we see Anton's Escort driving into the parking lot Naomi turns to me and says, listen to me Ilan, it's not at all certain that he's coming with a warrant for your arrest, maybe he only suspects something and he's trying to fish. Don't say anything to him without a lawyer, and her practical tone brings the whole thing down on me like a ton of bricks—up to now there was some kind of ambiguity, and I know that before Anton arrives I have to free her from me. I look at her responsibly and say resolutely, look here Naomi, it'll be much easier for me if you leave me. If you stay I won't be able to cope with it all, and she says, we already discussed it yesterday, and the bell rings, and I insist, I have to face this alone, and she waits for a second and says, we don't have to decide anything on the spot, and goes to open the door. I remain sitting on the balcony, more or less prepared and quite calm, and when Anton walks in I stand up and say apologetically, you didn't really have to come here, we could have made an appointment to meet at your office, but he takes a seat and says, sit down, Ilan, there's something I have to tell you. I prefer to talk in your office, I say, I don't want to talk here. He turns his chair to face me, looks me in the eye and says, why? I say, because . . . and dry up. He goes on looking at me in a way I can't understand and asks, is there something you wanted to tell me, and I can't stand it any more so I say, spit it out, Anton, say what you came to say. He takes his time but keeps his eyes fixed on me, and in the end he says quietly, your mother's dead, Ilan, she took pills, and for a minute I don't understand what he's saying and what pills he's talking about, and I say, what do you mean? And Naomi, who's standing behind me, puts her hand on my shoulder and says to Anton, when did it happen, and he says, the maid found her at six o'clock this morning, she apparently took the pills yesterday afternoon or evening, we haven't got the pathologist's report yet. His eyes are still fixed on mine, and before the meaning of my mother's death sinks in, I realize that this is all some kind of macabre farce. He hasn't come to arrest me, he's come to condole with me, but the coincidence is too much for me to swallow, and so I say, did you only come to tell me that my mother's dead? Isn't that enough, he asks, and before I can answer Naomi puts her arms around my shoulders and hugs me like an orphan and says, we'd better start making arrangements for the funeral, but Anton says, just a minute, and we look at him and I know that now it's coming. He lights two cigarettes, gives me one, and says, I didn't come just to tell you she was dead, and I feel Naomi's fingers digging into my shoulder, and he takes a drag on his cigarette and says, I also came to bring you the letter she left, it's addressed to me, but I don't think she meant you not to read it. He doesn't take his eyes off me for a second, his eyes bore into mine, and I open the letter and immediately recognize my mother's wildly erratic handwriting: Dear Anton, I'm addressing this letter to you because from the practical point of view it concerns you. As you know I never succeeded in being a real mother to Ilan. I confess that at the time when it counted it never even occurred to me that I should make any efforts in that direction. And so he grew up mainly thanks to your mother's help and yours, and he survived, which is the important thing. I won't go into the details of an old mother's guilt here, because I believe that people should endure their misery without disturbing the peace and quiet of their neighbors. I'll only tell you that I couldn't stand seeing him suffer the torments of jealousy. I remember myself how much they hurt. It seems that for the first time in my career as a mother I succeeded in feeling real identification with my son, if you can imagine such a thing. So I hired a professional to kill Oded Safra in Wadi Salib in March this year. This was my idea of compensation, each according to the dictates of his own nature. The killer left the country the morning after the murder with a fee of twenty thousand dollars. Naturally the idea of burying the body on top of Henzi Bauer, may she forgive me, was mine. I imagine that the witnesses, who apparently saw us that rainy night and led you to dig up the grave, told you about an old woman in a red woolly hat. The problem arose when Ilan began to suspect. I had no option but to tell him, otherwise he might have incriminated himself. I don't need to describe his reaction to you. That's the reason why he dragged you to the grave on the day of Shimi Lerer's funeral. He couldn't live with the secret, he's a good boy. On the other hand, you can't expect a son to inform on his mother, you wouldn't do it either. So I'm glad that I can free him of this burden too, the more I can help him the better. I'm taking the pills without any fear. Everything's over for me anyway, and in any case I have no intention of wasting my time on treatments whose sole benefit is the advancement of science. I haven't reached that level of public-spiritedness yet. So I rely on you to close the case and let them get on with their lives. You can consult your mother if you're not sure. Yours, Erna Ben Nathan. P.S. I don't know if you know that Naomi's pregnant. You'll agree with me that it would be a shame for this baby too to grow up without a father. I'm the living proof that a biological parent isn't always an advantage. I go on staring at my mother's erratic handwriting and I remember how she once told me that she was the kind of mother whose children begin to appreciate them when it's too late, and I said that she shouldn't count on it, but we hardly ever had conversations of that kind, mainly because of the basic indifference characteristic of our relationship, underneath the unhappiness and anger that faded with the years. Now her head floats opposite me, detached from her body, I see only her sharp face, the sharpness softened but not effaced by age, and I feel something shifting inside me and opening a lid which has been closed for years, and an unfamiliar feeling is released, which is more powerful than gratitude or admiration for her cunning nobility, which is apparently the thing itself, and I am aware of the lyrical absurdity of the situation but I don't resist it, what happened happened, exactly as I knew it would, and I catch the warm, triumphant look which Naomi sends me, but I don't allow myself to celebrate yet. You can keep that letter, says Anton, it's only a copy, the original's in the file. Silence falls and suddenly I'm not at all sure that he isn't going to arrest me, he still hasn't said a word concerning me, maybe all this silence now is only in honor of my mother's memory, and the moment of truth is about to arrive. I have no doubt that he hasn't swallowed a word of this letter, the whole thing lacks credibility, where was my mother supposed to find a hired killer, for example? But then I remember the Greeks who lived next to the swamp, Anton knows about the connections she had with them, how she kept in touch with them all these years, and if he wants to he can think that they organized the hit for her, he knows very well that she never had any moral inhibitions. I glance quickly at Naomi and see that her expression has changed, she's worried too, but we both keep quiet and wait for Anton, who leans on the balcony railing and looks at the sea with the same expression of deep concentration with which he looked at the grass on the three graves. The old panic comes back—oh my God, what has he discovered now in the sea?—but I don't move and I wait again for whatever will happen to happen, and after a while he turns to me and says, I once read an article that said that people who live next to the sea stop hearing the sound of the waves, is that true? I can't understand what he wants, and I only say, I never thought about it, but I imagine that if you listen you hear it, and he says, yes, I imagine so. Suddenly it occurs to me that he himself hasn't yet decided what to do with me, and that's why he's hesitating. The suspense is becoming unbearable, and therefore Naomi says, so what now, and he turns to her and asks, what do you think? I think the case is closed, don't you? she says, and Anton puts on his dark glasses and says in a colorless tone, yes, I suppose so, and begins walking to the door. I want to go after him and say something to him, but nothing comes into my mind except for thanks, which I say in a lackluster tone, failing to breathe life into the banal word. He stops for a moment and says, what a pair of women you got, eh, Ilan, and I don't give a damn if I'm being sentimental and I say, and what a friend, and he doesn't react, but only says, take care, Ilan, and walks out of the door. I feel that my last sentence was out of place, full of a solemn and superfluous pathos which embarrassed him—I only hope he identified the sincerity at least—and Naomi returns to the balcony and says, we have to start making the arrangements, the funeral will have to be tomorrow. I know, I say, I'll take care of it in a minute, and I light a cigarette in order to gain another few second, and then I go on, I think you should go to work, I'll organize the funeral arrangements myself, I'm good at it—the last words I don't say aloud, and she says, why don't you want me to stay with you? I gather her into my arms and say into her hair, because the best thing we can do now is carry on as usual, and she frees herself from my embrace and says, do you think so? I'm sure, I say, if you leave now you'll hardly be late, and she kisses me gently on my burnt cheek, which I've completely forgotten—only the kiss brings back the pain—and leaves. I immediately throw myself into practical arrangements, make a series of efficient phone calls, do everything that has to be done, hesitate as to whether to put an announcement in the paper—I don't need the whole physics faculty at the funeral and I decide against it—and when I'm done I go out onto the balcony to smoke a last cigarette, but I go on sitting there long after I've finished smoking it. Time passes and I don't move, I only look at the sun coming closer towards me, it's getting hot, the burn's bothering me, I should get up and move the chair into the shade, but I go on sitting there, turning to stone in the heat like a Bedouin in the desert, staring at the unshocked world existing opposite me and absorbing everything, like a gigantic rubbish dump, and I know that a new day will dawn in the morning and sink in the evening, indifferent to my sorrow and my insignificance, neither for me nor against me, and I'll go on sitting and waiting patiently for the end of days. Who taketh away the sins of the world have mercy on us.

About the Author

Edna Mazya was born in Tel Aviv in 1949. She is one of Israel's most lauded and popular playwrights. In 1997, she received the Margalit Prize for her play *Family Story*. Her performed plays include *Wien by the Sea, The Uncle from Capetown, Games in the Backyard* and *Herod*. *Love Burns*, published in Israel in 1997, is her first novel. She currently teaches dramatic writing at Tel Aviv University.